Advance Praise for *A Hundred Years of Happiness*

"This beautifully written, imaginative story of love and redemption is the must-read book of the year. The ending is so surprising and powerful that it will linger long after the last page is turned."

—CASSANDRA KING, author of *The Sunday Wife*

"*A Hundred Years of Happiness* is a fast-paced, intriguing story that will draw you in quickly and leave you full of hope."

—KATIE CROUCH, author of *Girls in Trucks*

"*A Hundred Years of Happiness* is a poignant glance at the tender bonds of family and the power the past holds over us all . . . [Nicole's] careful eye and warm prose help the reader to embrace a lost hero, and perhaps accept an imperfect past."

—KAREN WHITE, author of *The Memory of Water*

"Nicole Seitz takes the loose threads of her characters' lives and ties them together in a vibrant pattern of love, forgiveness and truth. In words that resonate with emotion, Seitz writes of things that are only understood with the heart."

—PATTI CALLAHAN HENRY, author of *The Art of Keeping Secrets*

"*A Hundred Years of Happiness* is a courageous novel that explores the pain and repercussions of the Vietnam War on two families today. Nicole Seitz writes with keen insight and compassion as the past collides with the present, and her characters must face the choices they made nearly a lifetime ago."

—MARYANN MCFADDEN, author of *The Richest Season*

"With lyrical writing, Nicole Seitz weaves a story of love, loss and redemption in *A Hundred Years of Happiness* . . . fans of this Lowcountry writer are guaranteed another great reading experience."

—MICHAEL MORRIS, author of *A Place Called Wiregrass*

"A Hundred Years of Happiness takes readers on a journey through the color of the low-country, to the unspoken pains of war, to the unique way each heart heals. A novel that will remind each reader of the power of our own stories and how the past so often determines the future."

—DENISE HILDRETH, author of *Savannah from Savannah*
and *Flies on the Butter*

A HUNDRED YEARS OF HAPPINESS

a Fable of Life after War

NICOLE SEITZ

THOMAS NELSON
Since 1798

NASHVILLE   DALLAS   MEXICO CITY   RIO DE JANEIRO   BEIJING

Other Books by Nicole Seitz

Trouble the Water
The Spirit of Sweetgrass

Published in Nashville, Tennessee, by Thomas Nelson. Thomas Nelson is a registered trademark of Thomas Nelson, Inc.

Thomas Nelson, Inc., titles may be purchased in bulk for educational, business, fund-raising, or sales promotional use. For information, please e-mail SpecialMarkets@ThomasNelson.com.

Publisher's Note: This novel is a work of fiction. Names, characters, places, and incidents are either products of the author's imagination or used fictitiously. All characters are fictional, and any similarity to people living or dead is purely coincidental.

Library of Congress Cataloging-in-Publication Data

Seitz, Nicole A.
  A hundred years of happiness : a fable of life after war / by Nicole Seitz.
     p. cm.
  ISBN 978-1-59554-502-2 (softcover : alk. paper)
1. Vietnam War, 1961–1975—Veterans—Fiction. 2. Vietnam War, 1961–1975—Psychological aspects—Fiction. 3. Fathers and daughters—Fiction. 4. Racially mixed women—Fiction. 5. Charleston (S.C.)—Fiction. 6. Psychological fiction. I. Title.
  PS3619.E426H86 2009
  813'.6—dc22

2008044447

Printed in the United States of America

09 10 11 12 RRD 6 5 4 3 2 1

For Hollis, my American hero

The mistress of War is Silence.
She feeds on fear and shame and regret.
She lies, she waits, masking herself in valor and humility,
All the while breeding confusion and loathing and distance.

Distance from loved ones. Distance from God.

The mistress of War is patient and long-lived.
Silence sweeps the dust from her lover and coddles him,
Keeping him fed and ready to rise again.

— N. S.

THE CAST

JOHN

A Vietnam veteran who is now a wealthy builder in Charleston, SC. *John Porter* is husband to *Betty Jo Porter* and father to *Katherine Ann Porter Banks*.

KATHERINE ANN

A former malpractice lawyer turned stay-at-home mom. *Katherine Ann Porter Banks* is wife to *RC Banks* and mother to *Tradd* and *Cooper*.

THE WATER LILIES

A group of friends who meet at the Porter house every morning for water aerobics and the planning of the Annual Water Lilies Synchronized Swimming event. Group members are *Betty Jo Porter* and her daughter *Katherine Ann (Katie-bug)*, along with eighty-five year-old widow *Tillie Archer*, her live-in nurse *Connie Monroe*, and *Hilda Gossweiler*, a German divorcee.

ERNEST

John Porter's Army buddy whose spirit still lingers in Vietnam.

LISA

A Vietnamese-American fry cook and restaurant owner in Georgetown, SC. She is daughter to *Doan Vien Le*.

DOAN VIEN

A Vietnamese immigrant who lost everything in the war. She lives with her daughter, *Lisa Le*, and has gone mute since her brother *Uncle* died.

PROLOGUE

The Ghost

I am not a ghost. Some may say I am no longer living, but one could argue with that. One might argue that before I left the earth, I was not actually living, but swimming, going through the motions, clueless as to how the universe works. I am much more real now than ever before—more real than the country boy from Georgia, more real than the soldier in Vietnam. In fact, one might argue that you, friend, are the ghost. Earthly lives are often veiled and wispy—just as you imagine me to be now.

After I took my last breath and entered heaven, I was able to see the whole picture—the mazes, the intricate workings, the coming together for a common good. For this knowledge, for the Truth, I will always be grateful. Know this: Life does not simply end when we die. There is something after. I promise there is. What *it* is just depends on us.

I am in a much better place, so don't worry for me. I am happy now. At peace. I'm going to tell you my story so you can see for yourself how it all works, how it all comes together. Seeing that no life is solitary, but we are all tangled up, strings of souls here and there, some more twisted together than others—this story is not just about me. It's about us, we who bump and tussle, pull apart and go our own ways.

It's about you.

Some characters in this story I knew very well. Others, I only learned of after my passing. Upon reading, you will find your own place in this story.

Know that I still pray for her and for many in these pages. Never underestimate the power of prayer. Even when you think it's too late for it. You're about to see how it saved a lost soul like me.

This story may not be like any you've ever heard. Be prepared to open your mind to possibilities. The mind is such a powerful thing. May all who hear this tale be blessed by it, you, children of sacrifice, and you, fathers and mothers of battle. And to my fellow soldiers, my brothers in arms who fought valiantly and are still fighting to this day, I say this:

Take comfort. Your battle is not in vain. Know that one day soon, your war, too, will come to an end.

PART ONE

WATER

Đời cha ăn mặn, đời con khát nước.

When the father's generation eats salt,
the child's generation thirsts for water.

—Vietnamese proverb

CHAPTER ONE

~~~~~~~~~~~~~~~~~~~

THE BEACH
Charleston, South Carolina, May 2008

Katherine Ann

He's wrestling with the folding chairs and losing. His finger gets pinched, and he spouts a four-letter word. "Why'd we have to come to the beach when I got a perfectly good river in my backyard? Shoot, no ugly people in bathing suits at my house. Well, except for a couple of you Water Lilies."

"That is just rude." I turn and watch my boys somersaulting in the sand.

"I wasn't talking about *you* . . ." Daddy says.

"But those are my friends."

"Well, I wouldn't have had to haul all this crap halfway across town if we'd stayed home. Here. Make yourself useful and help me with this." I grab a tent pole and hold it steady for him while he jabs the others into the ground.

My father would like to own the world. If it's not his—his river or his boat or his kayak—why the heck would we want it? Like the beach, for instance. We live so close, but we never go. It's a sin, really. Well, we're here. With Mama's help, I finally twisted Daddy's arm and talked him into leaving behind his fortress along the Cooper River. It's like any other day, the sparkling ocean spread out before me, warm sand blowing across my feet, and my father—making me wish I'd stayed at home.

"This is not about you, Daddy. It's about the boys. They love it here. Look at them. They need a place to run wild."

Mama and RC, my husband, are walking now along the water's edge with Tradd and Cooper in tow. They look so tiny, so vulnerable there. It's all I can do to resist the urge to join them, but I know this expanse of space and quiet will help me recharge as a mother, as a wife. This is good for us all.

Daddy finishes putting the tent up, grunting and cursing, and I move toward the sandy dunes, digging my toes in the soft heat. I watch everybody I love from a calm distance. Every now and again, the boys stop to pick something up and throw it into the water. They run squealing from the waves, and RC scoops one and then the other up high over his head. He's such a good daddy. What did I ever do to deserve him? Mama pulls her beach hat over her ears again and stares up into the clouds, checking for rain.

With the boys taken care of, I walk and breathe and ponder until I find myself bored with solitude. At this time in my life, my family is what defines me, and apart from them I am a single balloon drifting in the sky. Long gone are the days when I wore a suit, carried a briefcase, practiced law. I was defined by the work I did then and proud of it. But I want to be there for my kids like my mother was for me. I never had to struggle for her attention. She was just there when I needed her, usually at the kitchen sink. No, I rarely miss the old me, my life before family.

I see my father sitting alone in our encampment, his once-trim belly hanging over a crisp blue bathing suit. He holds a bottle of water in his hand, and his ankles and feet are perched in front of him, blue-white from never taking his shoes off. He looks so alone.

I drag my feet. Daddy and I don't talk one-on-one very often. Or ever. So, what will I say? My shoulders itch, sandpaper just under the skin. If this was Mama sitting there, I'd be by her side in a heartbeat. Wouldn't give it a second thought. Sitting and chatting with Mama is as natural as breathing. But Daddy?

"Hey," I say, walking to the beach blanket and leaning down under the mammoth man-made shade Daddy bought from a wholesale store. The whole beach setup, from chairs to towels to picnic basket, is new and still has the tags on, Minnie Pearl–style.

"Have a seat." Daddy stirs and pulls a chair closer, beckoning for me.

I sit and melt into it. "Nice chairs," I say.

"Thirty-eight dollars at Price-co. Can't beat that."

"No, you can't." I look around and watch a fiddler crab emerging from a hole. He ducks back in again. "Sure is beautiful out here."

"Mm hmm." Daddy keeps his stare on the boys and Mama. Or is it the horizon? I can't tell behind his sunglasses. A container ship cruises far off in the distance at a snail's pace. I watch it go by.

"RC get a raise yet?" Daddy asks, jarring me.

"No. And please don't ask him about it again."

"I won't! I'm just talking. Can't a man talk?" He takes a swig of his water and screws the cap back on. "How 'bout you? Making any money these days?"

"Daddy . . ." I grab the armrests, sitting up, and he shakes his head.

"You could help out too, that's all I'm saying."

"You know I'm watching the boys. It's a full-time job." My chest tightens and my throat attempts to close. I cough and sputter.

"Well, your mother worries about you and those boys all the time. That's all I hear. Just you and those boys. It's gonna kill her one of these days." I'm reaching for the open bag of pretzels when he looks over at my stomach rolls.

"What—are you pregnant again?"

"No! I'm not!"

"Well, you gotta start taking better care of yourself."

"Look who's talking!" I squeal.

"Your husband's a personal trainer, right? Why don't you get him to whip you in shape?"

I drop the bag and cover my belly with my arms. I have the sudden urge to dig a hole in the sand and hide like that fiddler crab. I'd get up and walk away except for the fact that he'll be staring at my plump legs and rear when I leave. I don't want to give Daddy the satisfaction of being right.

I grow silent and Daddy does too. Why in the world did I come over here? To relax? After a few minutes, I'm done. I suck in my stomach and count down in my head. Three, two . . .

"I don't know," he mutters, as if we've been carrying on a conversation. Which we have not been.

"Don't know about what?"

"Oh, you and RC, your mother, everything." He says the words as if they're heavy bricks on his tongue.

"What? We're fine."

"Yeah, but you *could* stand to make some more money, Katie-bug. Know what I mean? Private school's expensive. Don't come looking to me to help out."

"Could you please stop talking about money? Truly. And the boys are going to public school. We've already told y'all that."

"Oh, no. No, you can't do that. Your mother won't be able to stand it. She'll drive me crazy." He turns to me. "Why couldn't you marry a man with money? Another lawyer. A doctor. What's his problem anyway? When's he gonna get a real job?"

"That's enough." I stand and face my father, hands on hips, the urge to bless him out working its way up to my tongue.

"You're just like your mother, you know that?" he snips. "She can't stand me either." He turns away from me, staring down the beach.

I stop, surprised. Still standing, I realize my hindquarters are exposed, but something in the tone of his voice made me think he was sincere for once. He sounded so sad. Wounded.

"Oh, come on now," I say. "You're not that bad. I can stand you just fine. I'm sure Mama can too."

"I'm serious. Your mother's gonna leave me one of these days. She's getting very testy in her old age. Doesn't put up with much anymore."

"She's not gonna leave you. Why do you think she's stayed with you for thirty-seven years?" I sit down again. I think of telling Daddy about hormones and what menopause does and how he should never, ever, mention *old age* around Mama, but I can't seem to get the words to come out right.

"I don't know," he says finally, defeated. He seems to be talking, not to me, but to himself. Or maybe to the warm breeze. "Maybe God's punishing me or something."

"Really? What'd you do?" I ask, half joking to lighten the mood.

"Hell if I know. I guess it was something pretty bad."

"Well, I hope you figure it out soon before we're all in real trouble. Right? Before we all go down in flames."

I laugh, but Daddy doesn't say anything else. He just sits there morose, dark sunglasses aimed at flying seagulls. My blood chills with his sudden change in persona. And when I get up to join Mama, RC, and the boys near the waterline, Daddy doesn't even turn his head to acknowledge I was ever there by his side.

CHAPTER TWO

The Water Lilies

Katherine Ann

The one time we let Daddy get in the water, he'd been drinking too much and had just come in off the boat with RC. "How's the water feel?" he yelled. "Got room for two more old farts?" Then he cannonballed his way into the pool and splashed Mama's hair all wet. "John!" she wailed. She hates to get her hairdo wet. I watched in horror as my father grabbed one of our big yellow flotation noodles and flaunted it as an extension of his manhood, even sticking it down in his madras shorts and everything.

Mama didn't think it was funny one bit, and she fussed at him like a mockingbird with black mascara running down her face. I was mortified at Daddy's behavior, though not surprised. Somehow Tillie was aroused by it all—as excited as an eighty-five-year-old woman can get, anyway. She clapped her hands and grinned from ear to ear, egging him on and yelling, "Take it off! Take it off, John!"

Well, soon as we got him out and on dry land, all five of us put our hands up—one in the air, the other over our hearts—

and *doubledy-dare-swore* not to let another man set foot in our pool when the Water Lilies were in session. Even Tillie knew it was for the best.

We've been meeting like this, man free, for the past four years now—five if you don't count Daddy's wet noodle incident. Oh, the men can watch when we want them to—at our annual synchronized swimming event or pool parties and such—but that's on *our* terms. If there's one thing you need to know about the Water Lilies, it's this: Our meetings are sacred, private. And they're all about power, real or perceived—power over our bodies, over our families, over our lives. Whether it's real control or not doesn't seem to be the issue. It's about the exercising of it, about going through the motions, about making real-live ripples we can see and feel and touch.

"Katie-bug, be a dear and bring me my towel, would you?" I hear a voice call from the water. They call me Katie-bug, all of them do, like I'm twelve years old still. At thirty-six, I am the youngest of the Water Lilies—not by design, but by default. My mother, Betty Jo Porter, started this group with Hilda Gossweiler after escaping the tyrannical ruler of Jazzercise class. Then Mama's cross-the-street neighbor, Tillie, came in, towing Connie with her. I sort of had no choice after just having had Tradd and needing some way to get my pre-pregnancy figure back.

It was easy enough in the beginning. We had this cute little polka-dot umbrella set up over the playpen, and Tradd would coo and watch us splash. When he started running around though, I considered quitting the Water Lilies. By that time I was pregnant again, and RC knew what it meant to me to have "adult time" in my day, so he shifted his work hours to afternoons. Not every man would do that, I tell you. Well, now the boys are in preschool so things are pretty much worked out. I soak up sun and sanity here, and by the time I pick up the boys from school I am ready to focus on them 100 percent.

"Katie-bug, did you forget my towel?"

"Sorry, Connie. Be there in a minute." I sit on the bench and turn my head upside down between my legs, wrapping a towel turban-style around my wet hair and letting the blood rush to my head.

Our history together begins around the time Daddy put a sunporch on the back of his house—his magnificent house with its faux-finished walls and three-story elevator, and landscaping to just die for. The swimming pool sits flanked with rose bushes out in the lawn between the rolling river and the still, protective pool house.

Daddy built this pool house for Mama and Hilda when they first started swimming on a regular basis. It was right after the sunporch went up and Daddy was tired of the headaches of building on his own home. Mama's fussing about the dust and noise was one of those headaches. Daddy fumed for days, complaining he wouldn't be able to see the view from his new porch, but Mama convinced him otherwise.

"Absolutely, you can see the marsh from here," she said. "See? But we need this. This is my house and I will not have water tracked throughout. We are grown women, and we need a proper pool house for us to change in. Not to mention it will give you a place to put your paddles and lifejackets and boat whatnot."

Mama thinks it was the bribing of the boat whatnot that did it, but I don't think so. I think Daddy loves Mama more than life itself. She might fuss at him and he might fuss at her, but the way he looks at her, he'd do anything for that woman—anything to keep her happy.

Once he got to building the pool house he started whistling, and when that thing was done, boy, you should have seen the look on his face. He was beaming. Had everybody over for a great big shindig, Charleston-style, and that pool house became our home away from home.

Ah, the pool house. This old place could tell a story or two—it's been privy to some of the most scandalous, nonproductive talk to ever come out of greater Charleston, South Carolina, I assure you. If the pool house could speak, it would tell of lavish conspiracies, shameless indiscretions, not to mention the three Ms, our favorite topics of conversation: Medication, Men, and Menopause. I've had enough *men* and *medication* to last me a lifetime, though I have yet to reach the latter, *menopause*, and simply listen on in horror.

If it had emotion, the pool house would shudder with memories of the naked female bodies—in all shapes and sizes—it's held within, sheltering them from the elements and from the leering menfolk we love so much. And it would swell with pride and wonder at the sheer strength of the Water Lilies at the times when life has been most severe.

My parents' pool house is sacred to me with its driftwood-looking walls and bleached-out starfish dotting eyelevel all the way around. I helped Mama decorate it, so it is in this place where my fascination with the Water Lilies began. I used to think it was strange, my desire to be around women so much my senior. I wondered what was wrong with me. Now I'm thankful for it. At the time, I swear I had no idea how becoming a Lily would open my eyes—to myself and to a world I'd mostly slept through up till then.

Not to mention what it would do for my thighs. Thank heavens for small miracles.

I grab Connie's green towel off her hook and slip my flip-flops on. Then I move slowly to the water, feeling the sun on my shoulders, and watch the women I love tread water.

Yes, we Lilies have been treading water for eons now, but there are side effects to swimming so much. Our fingertips are wrinkled like prunes and our faces are showing our love for the sun, some more than others. But you know that feeling you get when you've been in the water too long? The way your lungs hurt from sitting up so high in your chest and you just can't seem to get enough air in them? Can't breathe deep enough? Well, that's the way I've been feeling lately, now that some strange things with my father have started bubbling up to the surface. Look at Mama there, rubbing more sunscreen on her face, desperate to keep that youthful glow that defines her. Whether Daddy, Mama, or any of us will be able to keep our heads above water and survive all this madness—well, that is yet to be seen.

CHAPTER THREE

~~~~~~~~~~~~~~~~~

The Enemy

John

John Porter treads carefully on the newly laid grass as if trying to avoid trip wires or land mines. It doesn't make sense, he knows, what with the suburban homes and white picket fences surrounding him, but still. It's something he carries with him always—that feeling as if the ground may ignite when he least expects it.

He's wearing a button-down shirt and khakis, brown shoes— standard uniform for a rich man in the sweltering Lowcountry of South Carolina. John loves this place. He loves building houses for folks to live in, houses that dot the earth with his name, his signature, saying, *Look at me, I was here*. Building's like breathing to him now; he's been doing it for nearly forty years. He can build in his sleep. He runs a tight schedule and keeps everything on track, on budget, barking orders with the vigor of a drill sergeant. John Porter is a good builder, but it doesn't fill his soul anymore— it's the air he breathes now, nothing more, nothing less.

At one time, though, killing was like breathing to him.

Killing.

They were *killing machines*. That's what they made them, called them that too. Young men so full of testosterone they couldn't see straight. Boys who felt invincible, who'd rather take a bullet in the gut for real than just play war games. They'd played them for eighteen long months in Germany. Thick German beer and women filled their nights; war games filled their days. Only games. It was near torture. By the time they saw the green-leafed hell of Vietnam, they were so pumped and primed to see real action they didn't know what hit them.

That's exactly how John feels on this day, nearly forty years later, when he sees the man standing before him.

He's been inspecting a house that's just gone under contract in a wealthy neighborhood east of the Cooper River. His blood is pumping—*ta-dump, ta-dump*—like it always does with the smell of fresh lumber, paint, and pinestraw settling down to the earth. Smells like money to him. The man in front of him has a rake and stares at the ground as he scrapes the brown straw into neat heaps.

Scraaape . . . scraaape . . .

The sound of the scraping gets under John's skin and he turns to watch him. That's when it happens. His past comes back and wraps around him like a snake, constricting, squeezing.

Scraaaaaaape . . .

He nearly chokes. He'd know that face anywhere.

The man has small slanted eyes and a flat nose melting into full, round cheeks. He's small, maybe five and a half feet tall, and light brown-skinned. He doesn't realize he's being watched until John speaks.

"Where you from?" he asks, eyebrows like daggers. The landscaper stops raking and stares up into John's eyes—a big move for such a small man. John has a good sixty pounds on him.

"Vietnam," the man replies. "North Vietnam."

John's pulse quickens. His fists clench. His throat ties itself in a knot and pulls tighter, tighter. The young soldier still trapped in John sees the enemy in front of him now, the first time in forty years. Here he is. Face-to-face again.

"North Vietnam?" he bellows, not believing the boldness, the gall of this man, admitting it with pride. Old bullet wounds on John's back open and ooze, tingling with phantom pain. "How old are you?" he asks. But he already knows; he's the same age as him. Blood and adrenaline rush to his head and it swells, making him dizzy.

"Sixty." The man looks back at John and recognizes the hatred in his eyes. He'd know it anywhere. So he adds, spitting salt in his wound, "I fought with Viet Mihn."

"I knew it!" John has this crazy half grin on his face, trying to shove the killer back. "I was in Vietnam too . . . *killing* your ass!" He's losing control and knows it. It's slipping, thrashing, a wet fish in his hands. Flashes of his best buddy Ernest's face, the one he's tried not to think about for all these years, flip through his mind like an aging silent film. "Clean up this pinestraw and get back to work or I'll shoot your head off!"

The smile is gone now. When John hears what he's said, how he let the rampage in his head out through his mouth, and how the landscaper hasn't crumbled but straightened taller, lifting his rake a few inches above ground, he backs up. He has to. He's worked hard over the years learning to control his anger with family, business, trying to assimilate back into civilization.

But this.

This is so completely unexpected it sideswipes him like a drunk. John unclenches his fists and closes his lips. He could kill the man right here with the sounds of the jungle closing in around him, his heart pounding in his ears like gunfire. It takes everything he has in him, but John Porter walks away finally, forty years older, forty pounds heavier, breathing hard. Oxygen fills his cells in case he has to dive from enemy fire like they taught him to so long ago.

Old instincts like old scars—some things never go away.

CHAPTER FOUR

The Soldier

Katherine Ann

So there we are sitting in this trendy tapas restaurant in downtown Charleston, a mural of an Asian temple covering the wall; the men are drinking mojitos, the ladies sipping champagne. My father has already complained that the people behind him are too loud, the table's too small, we've brought him to some "dang yuppie place," but Mama and I grin at each other anyway, intent on enjoying ourselves.

"To thirty-seven years," I say, holding up my glass. RC lifts his, too, and we toast my parents' anniversary with clinking and gratitude. And more than a little bit of amazement.

Mama is not your typical June Cleaver, but at least you know where you stand with her most of the time. My father, however, is a difficult man—to live with, to be around, to talk to. He's loud and emotional, at times embarrassingly so. He can switch from elation to anger on a dime. He's all at once the most sensitive person and the most callused. His unpredictability leaves those who love him always on edge.

His mojito is gone now and he's searching around for our waiter, swearing he "won't be getting a tip tonight," which is

17

absolutely not true. I've never seen him stiff a server. In fact he usually goes overboard, becoming best buddies with the guy by the end of the meal. And anyway, it's our treat tonight. It's a big occasion.

"Can you believe it's been thirty-seven years?" I ask my mother.

"No," she says, half smiling. "I can't believe it."

"She might even give me a kiss tonight," my dad announces too loudly, guffawing. "I get one smooch a year on our anniversary. That's it." He slurps on his straw and shakes his ice while my mother blushes and I shift in my seat. My husband stays quiet, wondering if it's true or not, and I squeeze his hand under the table to let him know Daddy's teasing. My parents have never been much for public displays of affection.

The tapas we order fly at us randomly. We devour each tiny dish like wild hyenas, afraid we'll miss out on tempura shrimp, skewered beef, a cheese plate, sushi.

Daddy orders a bottle of pinot noir for us. We eat more food. The place swells with people, making it louder, making us louder. I completely forget about Cooper and Tradd at home with the sitter. Any guilt I was feeling has left me now.

We're chitchatting, laughing, things are going along just fine, and then the owner of the place walks by, a stringy, well-dressed Asian fellow in funky glasses. Seeing him must have triggered Daddy's memory because all of a sudden my father begins to tell us that something happened to him recently. Something astounding. Disturbing.

Seems he was checking on a house of his and one of the landscapers was a former North Vietnamese soldier—he's never been face-to-face with one in all these years since the war. I can't believe it.

"I recognized him," he says. "Know him anywhere. I asked

him, 'Where you from?' and he looked at me, square in the eyes. Cocky little son-of-a . . . he knew who I was, where I'd been.

"Vietnam, he told me. From North Vietnam, can you believe that? It's the first time in forty years I've seen a gook."

Daddy's waving his arms, and I can't believe this is coming out of his mouth. I look around to see who might be listening. "*Gook*, Daddy?" Is he actually saying this word? He can see the offense in my eyes.

"That's what we used to call them in Nam! *Gooks! Charlie! VC!*" He points his finger from across the table as if aiming. "Let me tell you something. You ever been facedown in a rice paddy, hiding, scared to death and the man next to you crying, bleeding, got blood all over you—they'll always be gooks, I don't care how politically correct you are!"

"Sorry, Daddy, I just—so you really haven't seen one in all these years?" I reiterate, dumbfounded.

His face is getting flushed; he's becoming more agitated, a crazy look flitting in his eyes. "No! No," he says, going back to the moment. He relays word for word their interaction, how he told this man to get back to work or he'd *blow his head off*—

And I'm stunned. We all are. I've never heard him utter such words.

"So you actually went back to Vietnam then?" I ask him. "You flashed back, I mean?" Mind you, my father and I have never talked about his time in Vietnam. Ever.

Daddy grabs his chest. "Yes! Dad-gummit, yes. It all came back." His eyes show pain now, glassy. The room around us disappears into a white fog. I'm aware that Mama is still to my right and my husband to my left, but I can't tear away from my father's face. I've never seen this face. And all at once, he opens up, spilling uncontrollably.

"You have no idea. We were *killing* these people. If you didn't kill them, they'd kill you." He starts drawing a map with his index finger on the table and then pounding. "We were right here near the DMZ, see? Here's North Vietnam. We were right here. We'd go into these villages. I just can't tell you—women, children, everything." His eyes are tearing up now; he can't look at me. My eyes fill up too.

"I got shot and they evacuated me. I was still bleeding when I went back in there." He reaches over his shoulder and touches the scar through his designer shirt. Then he smacks the flat of his hand on the edge of the table. Our waiter walks over and studies our water glasses. He thinks of filling them again, but then moves away stealthily.

"So why'd you go back in?" I ask naively, genuinely curious. I can't fathom going back to the front line while not even fully healed.

He erupts then. Flames glow all around him.

"Why'd I go back in? For the man right *here*!" he grabs my husband's arm and shakes it. "And the man right *here*!" he says, tears streaming now as he points to my mother. "Let me tell you something, we weren't fighting for a country—that might have gotten us over there, but it's not what made us keep going. You do it because of the man beside you. The man *beside* you!" He's crying now and tears are streaming down my cheeks, but I can't blink my eyes. The world has disappeared except for us. I am connected to my father, a cord between us.

He continues, tells about his buddy who never made it home. "He was a great guy, another grunt like me. Like a brother. We were up in this mountain and—just like that—"

I've never heard about this man. How have I not known these things about my father? How have I not cared to know what lies deep within him, what tortures him?

I have no idea how the situation finally dissipates—how my father emerges from war and back to the table—but we're all here now, spent, shocked to death. We can't believe what we've just been through, how he took us back to Vietnam with him. I look at my mother, a woman who's lived with this often-difficult man for thirty-seven years, and I whisper to her, "See? That's why you love him."

I love my father more now than I ever have, and believe me when I say that my love has come a long way. At times growing up I couldn't stand the sight of him. But at this moment, I'd give anything to be able to crawl in his head so he won't have to be alone anymore.

While the men talk about the enormous bill that just arrived and my bug-eyed husband pulls out his wallet to pay, I ask my mother, "Have you ever heard any of that?"

She shakes her head and says to me quietly, stunned, "No. Never. He's never talked about it."

We stand to leave, and that same war voice exits my father's lips again—one more time from out of nowhere. "I may be an okay builder or an okay father—"

"You're a great father," I interrupt, trying to make this all right for him.

"—but I'll always be a soldier," he says.

He'll always be a soldier.

I watch as my father stands straight, pulling his legs together. I'm fearful he may salute, but he doesn't. It's over, for now, but I'm sure of it—something is happening here—something monumental. We leave the restaurant, bellies full, nerves rattled, and I have the distinct feeling we're walking along a fault line. At any moment it could open up and sweep us all out to sea.

CHAPTER FIVE

THE WISH

Five miles south of Da Nang, Vietnam, Spring 1970

Ernest

Ernest Marquette was a long way from Georgia, a long way from Mama's wide skirt to hide behind. There was no cow pasture to lose himself in, no religion of fireflies to sustain his faith.

Now Ernest had made an extremely foolish wish.

At first he thought it was peaceful, the muffled *whoosh* of the fish going by, of cool water surrounding him, cushioning him, suspending him. Of being in an altered state.

Then he realized what he had done. Panic set in.

The year was 1970. He was a first lieutenant in the 101st Airborne, second battalion, Bravo company. Army infantry. He'd spent three days in the bush searching, destroying, watching his friends peel away from the earth like dragonflies on the windshield of the family Ford going sixty miles an hour down winding two-lane roads. James, "Little Bill," "Mad Max," they were all gone. Ernest wondered why he was still here. In fact, he wondered about so many things.

Having been in Vietnam for nearly six months, he'd had an ear for spiritual talk, anything that could get him through another day—Buddhist philosophies, Hindu rituals, Jesus teachings that reminded him of home. At any and every spiritual gathering, Ernest was there, palms open for morsels to feed his soul and fight back the waves of nauseating terror that threatened to pull him under. Watching the tranquil fishpond at his feet, Ernest Marquette remained sick with fear. He remembered a conversation he'd had over a meal of C rations with Private Lu Tien, a Taoist. He'd told him "life is but a pool of water, and koi represent courage in adversity—the human spirit overcoming obstacles without fear."

Without fear. He envied those fish.

He'd just arrived in China Beach for a little R & R, but the guys laughing and girls in bikinis were making him sick—the carelessness of it all. The stench of death still clung in his nostrils. Ernest and his buddy, John Porter, jumped in a Jeep and sped five miles south of Da Nang, toward the Marble Mountains, named after the minerals within and the five elements of the universe: water, wood, fire, earth, and metal.

They'd climbed a hundred or more steps and entered a sanctuary carved into the mountainside. A huge white Buddha grinned, nestled in the rock. Incense swirled around the two men, emanating from a large urn, luring them like perfume. Candles flickered. Koi swam in a pond covered in lily pads blooming white and purple. It was like climbing the steps from hell and finding there really was a heaven—right there at the top.

Ernest's heart pounded with fear, adrenaline, fatigue, though he should have felt a little more at ease away from the combat. But his nerves were exposed. He couldn't get away from the bloodshed, the confusion—not after everything he'd seen and done. It clung to him like chiggers just under the skin. The memories, as he scratched them, were worse than the real thing. He wondered if he would ever shake them off. Wondered if his brother Randy, who'd survived the war and gone back home already, would ever be able to forget what he'd seen.

Ernest was standing at the foot of a small pond, listening to the waterfall, staring at his reflection in the dark water, his back toward civilization. It didn't look like him. Just some soldier staring back. A stranger. His buddy, John, was calling him to go look in another cave. "You gotta see this, man," he was saying. "Get over here."

But Ernest was lost in thought, his eyes transfixed on a large white koi that seemed to rule this pond. Smaller fish, orange ones, swam hurriedly, desperate for food, attempting to greet him—expecting crumbs or rice cake. Spoiled fish. Nothing to do but beg for a meal.

The big white koi waited back a little, either cautious or confident it'd be eating well soon; it was nearly twice the size of the others, almost eighteen inches. It lifted its ugly head out of the water and opened its mouth wide, gulping air. It looked at Ernest square-jawed, laughing almost, then darted down again.

Ernest clenched his fists, shut his eyes, and reached into his pocket, fishing around for a coin. He found one—a 1963 Vietnamese Xu. Ngo Dinh Diem's aluminum face was glaring at him, so he flipped it over to the bamboo side. The calmer side.

He could still hear the cries of children who'd lost parents, mothers who'd lost children, hear the explosions that rocked his very core. All he could think about was how to get out of this place.

It was then that he wished it—almost in a fleeting way. *Wouldn't it be nice to have the life of that great white fish, swimming in peace without a care in the world?* No worries, no clawing fear.

He opened his eyes. *Plunk.* The coin sent quiet ripples out in concentric circles as it hit the surface.

He did not hear the man now standing behind him. Didn't see the light shimmering off the blade or feel the coolness of the knife as it severed his throat. No, Ernest Marquette had no idea he was dying. The two events—the wish and the attack—had simply happened at the same precise moment. Funny how the universe works sometimes. As much as Ernest could tell, his wish had come true.

Without warning, the water cocooned him, swallowed him. Ernest gasped for air and water filled his mouth. One more time he inhaled. His lungs hurt. His body was being squeezed into a tube. Longer, longer, tighter. Another second and it was all over.

Ernest's body didn't hurt anymore. His lungs were calm and unbelievably, gloriously filled. An orange koi with white spots approached him, unafraid, unimpressed. It touched Ernest's face with outstretched lips, and he could have sworn he heard it say, "Welcome home, soldier."

Welcome home.

CHAPTER SIX

The War
Charleston, May 2008

Katherine Ann

"So he didn't say anything more?" Hilda asks, lifting her arms straight out to her sides and twisting. Water drips off her pudgy elbows. "Did he say he killed anybody? How many people you think he killed?" Her brown lipstick bleeds from the heat into the lines around her lips.

"He did not say, Hilda. Good heavens, what do you think, I'm just going to ask my daddy a question like that when he's never even talked about the war before?"

"Well, he said he was a killing machine, didn't he? I bet he killed a bunch of 'em," spouts Tillie, the oldest of our group. She hops on one foot and then the other, bouncing slow and awkward in the water as if running a race on the moon. I glare at her. We all do, shocked by her brazen, childlike honesty. We'll be listening to Tillie's revelations for years to come. Though she's eighty-five, she doesn't look a day over seventy. We each aspire to be in Tillie's kind of health when we reach her age. For a couple of us, that won't be much longer.

Tillie reaches over to the side of the pool and holds on,

catching her breath. "Well, what are you looking at me for? It's war, for goodness sake. In war, people die. There's no reason to pussyfoot around it."

"I, for one, have had enough of this war talk," says Mama, bristling. She straightens the straps of her fuchsia bathing suit as if they're itchy, and she clears her throat. "I didn't like hearing about the war years ago, and I certainly don't like talking about it now."

"You mean he talked to you about it? Daddy talked to you about Vietnam?" I ask.

"What? No, no, of course not. I told you he didn't. Not really anyway. There's just . . . it's always been a difficult thing for your father to deal with. No use bringing it out in the open again, Katie-bug." She shakes her head at me, a warning. "Nothing good can come of it."

I breathe in deep and stare at Mama. I don't know what to do with her sometimes. Like me, she can be a brick wall of a woman. She swings her noodle around from side to side and stares off into the water, avoiding my gaze. Then I look around at each of them. Tillie turns away from me and Hilda slips under the water. Only Connie looks me back in the eyes.

"My Leroy still has nightmares, you know. Wakes up in the middle of the night sometimes in cold sweats, runnin', hidin'. Scares me to death." She stares at the water and rubs the back of her neck. "Mm hmm. Says he still sees their faces." She wades over to Tillie and examines her brown-spotted forehead. "Time for more sunscreen, baby."

Fifty-six-year-old Connie Monroe is Tillie's nurse. Or live-in angel, if you ask me. She and her husband live in Tillie Archer's guesthouse, going on eleven years now. She's family to Tillie, helps her in immeasurable ways and quite honestly, she's become helper to us all. Connie's usually the only voice of reason in the bunch.

She sits on the blue-tiled edge and plops her dark, buoyant legs into the water so that she can apply cream to Tillie's face. Tillie's eyes are closed, her white skin now whiter, and she reminds me of a small child at the mercy of her mama. "Yes sir, mark my words," Connie says, "don't none of it go away. Try all they want to, the war never ends for those boys. It's a shame. Your daddy, he's just the classic example."

"Example of what?"

"Of PTSD. Post-traumatic stress disorder. Got all the symptoms, you know."

"You think?" She makes him sound like a disease.

"Shucks, all his great big outbursts, all that drinking too much, being funny all the time—even when ain't nothin' funny. Katie-bug, he's coverin' it all up. Can't cover it up though. Stuff slips out like sewer water, all over the place."

"Well, I, for one, think this is silly," says Mama. "Nonsense. That's just John for you. It's his personality. It's been forty years since the Vietnam War. John is successful, we have a very nice family, home, everything we could ever want, and I don't want to hear one more word about it. He does not have any disorder. Period. No use digging up old bones, pun intended. Now come on and grab your beach balls." Mama jumps out of the water and heads to the pool house. She returns with a sour look on her face and an armful of small colored balls. She pops them one at a time into the water, aiming at us. We each dutifully take them and hold them over our heads.

"All right then, what shall we sing?" asks Hilda, piping up in a scratchy tenor. "How about this? *Onward, Christian so-oldiers, marching as to waaaar . . .*"

"How 'bout, just stick it, Hilda," Mama stings.

So we march in place in silence, the others oblivious to the war beginning to wage in my head.

CHAPTER SEVEN

The Captive

Marble Mountain, Vietnam, Summer 2008

Ernest

The one thing Ernest's father had told him before he left for Vietnam was, "Just don't come back in a body bag, Son." Ernest always figured that's how it would happen. He'd return to the States with a dog tag around his toe, his mother in tears, his father let down. But not like this. Not this way. There are days, years that Ernest feels like a deserter, but he never would have done that to his brothers in arms. Desertion was not an option. Death, now that was an option. Survival, there was a slim chance for that, but desertion? To this day, what must they think of him?

It's taken some time to get used to it—his new life as lord of the fishes on top of Marble Mountain. At first he was happy in a sense, relieved. No more war, no more dying, no more waking in the middle of the night to the sound of enemy fire. But the mind, you know, it's a slippery and dangerous thing. Thoughts become reality if not properly contained. The war he tried to escape? It's never really ended for him. He relives it day in and day out. Over and over and over.

And koi can live for up to two hundred years.

His destiny is useless. He is perched at the top of a mountain in the face of smiling Buddha, never again to eat Mama's peach pie or drive his daddy's tractor in Norwood, Georgia. Just staring down the stairs to hell with no apparent pathway to heaven.

It's been nearly four decades—swimming, circling, nothing more than futile movements. In desperation now, a final plea for something more, something meaningful, Ernest Marquette hovers over the rusted coin he threw in thirty-eight years ago and makes a second wish: to be free of that which holds him captive. Then he nibbles on a slice of watermelon rind and waits for the monks or tourists to throw him his next meal.

BEFORE THE SUN rises, the monks begin their day with chanting, the lighting of incense and the ringing of a large gong. Ernest Marquette feels the vibrations and stirs from his slumber, though it's hard to tell when a fish is sleeping as the eyes do not close. No eyelids, you see. If the eyes do not close, can a fish ever sleep? This is the type of question for which Ernest still does not have the answer. His very nature is that of a human, and though his body is now slender and slick, he still feels like an outsider.

There is one particular monk who wears an orange robe and shaved head as do all the monks, who comes to the edge of the pond every day after sunup. Ernest has named this one Brother Chong. He wears round-rimmed glasses and has a scar across his cheek so that he appears to be half smiling all the time. After the monks are fed and humming intently, Brother Chong brings a bowl of fish food consisting of processed fish pellets, dried shrimp, and remnants of the monks' morning meal, typically rice or rice noodles, sometimes day-old cut fruit.

Ernest is always first to be fed. He's the quickest. His instincts are better than the other fish. Beating the fish at their own game? Perhaps. Or perhaps it's that Ernest still remembers what it was like to be the youngest of five children in a small yellow farmhouse in Georgia. How he'd have to belly up to the table first and be the last to leave in order to get enough food. Here, in this pond in Vietnam, not much has changed in the way of Ernest's eating habits. He does wonder though, suffering over the unknown fate of his family and friends back home. This place will never feel like home.

There is a waterfall at one end of the pond and when he first became cold-blooded, Ernest was drawn to it instinctively as one might be drawn to excitement or danger. He found sensual pleasure under that waterfall as the drumming pressure massaged his scales. He could find such little pleasure in those days. But sitting under waterfalls is for the naive, and soon Ernest was withering away. He was sitting under the falls while the others were being fed. It didn't take long for him to pull himself together and deny himself the excess. Now decades later, he is the biggest fish in this pond and watches the other smaller, newer fish do themselves in with the call of the waterfall.

A hand swoops down, ready to sprinkle rations over Ernest's head. He opens his mouth wide with anticipation. Ernest knows there's something different about this man, Brother Chong. He doesn't gaze into the water as the other monks do, searching for God in its depths. Rather, Ernest detects a look of dread or despise. Perhaps he was given the chore of feeding the fish as punishment for some earthly sin. Perhaps in a past life he was himself a fish and chose a loathsome task such as maintaining the fishpond to toughen his resolve about becoming a monk, or staying a monk, so that he could rise to a higher state of enlightenment. Far from being a fish.

Ernest looks up into his face billowing through the water and wonders if he might trade places with Brother Chong. Is it possible? It is this same desire, however, that led him to his current state, so he pushes the thought from his small mind and tries instead to think contented thoughts. Water is good. Water is nice. Water is forever. Ohm, and all that.

IT'S EVENING NOW. Brother Chong will soon be here to clear the waste from the fish, the debris from the tourists. Ernest sits under a water lily—or "lotus" as they are called in the Orient—and hides himself, plotting his escape, realizing its hopelessness, and finally dipping only his tail in the waterfall in order to forget his plight.

"What are you looking at?" he snips at a young white fish glaring at him. It seems all the fish glare at him. Ernest moves out of the way of the falls and says, "Knock yourself out," secretly hoping this fish will get hooked on the feeling, wither away, and die like so many of the others. Being waterlogged for so long has done little to enlighten his spirit.

Moments later Brother Chong appears with a large skimmer in hand, and as he nears the surface of the water, Ernest recognizes a sad look in his eyes. He appears waterlogged and drowning, much like Ernest. Ernest avoids his gaze lest Brother Chong be tempted to make such a foolish wish as he himself once did.

CHAPTER EIGHT

THE POOL
Charleston, South Carolina

Katherine Ann

This morning the sky is clear blue, not a cloud in it, and the water is rippled and shining white like diamonds. It's beautiful out here. I take in a deep breath, let it out, and breathe in the saltiness again. It's next to heaven, feeling the soft grass beneath my toes, watching egrets circle overhead and dive down to catch a fish every now and again. The air is cool and sultry, not bordering on hot like it will be in a couple hours. It's eight thirty, and I'm the first one here.

I don't even come through the house anymore; I just walk around out back, past the shrubs, persimmon tree, and flower beds. I don't bother Mama and Daddy. He's already gone anyway, at work, driving around, checking on his houses. He probably left two hours ago. Mama's been up since then too, but it takes her time to get ready in the morning, God knows why. She's just going to get in the swimming pool and get all wet, but she has to take a shower first and apply her makeup just so and make sure she hasn't gained an ounce since yesterday and still looks the same in her bathing suit. She's got a different one for every day

33

of the week. She buys more suits than I buy toilet paper. And there's a hat to match each of those suits, and shoes, if you can believe it. But whatever makes Mama happy.

There she is now, coming out of the house. She's wearing a white suit today—a one-piece, of course. "One never shows her midriff after having children" is what she told me. Drives her absolutely insane that I wear bikinis. One-pieces make me feel like a sausage.

Her hat is straw with a white ribbon tied around it, and her shoes are *clip-clop, clip-clopping* my way. Mama still has a beautiful figure. She's probably in better shape then she was twenty years ago. My body has work to do, I'm afraid. I don't have as much discipline as Mama does. I like my Jack's Cosmic Dog and french fries a little more. And RC doesn't mind. He loves me no matter what. He told me so on our wedding day, and that's a vow I don't take lightly. I often wonder if his hazel eyes are failing when he tells me I'm the most beautiful girl in the world.

It does make me sad, not being able to fit into the newest fashions. Mama will pick up a size four and then say she grew out of it, handing me stacks of clothes every now and again. "Here, honey, just one more thing. These are just way too big on me now." This is simply not true. First, Mama's size never changes, and second, it's apparent the clothes have never been worn. But I play along. 'Course, I'm at least a six, maybe even a size seven—nothing fits in the waist anymore or the hips. But I keep them in the closet because Mama gave them to me and because they're much more expensive than anything I could ever buy. And out of the slim possibility that I might just fit into them one day.

"Morning, Mama. Sure is nice out here today."

"Mmm hmm. Sure is."

I walk toward her and find a lounge chair. I sit down and pull my tennis shoes off, then my shorts and my top and walk them into the pool house, putting them in my designated cubbyhole with my name at the front, *Katie-bug*. Mama steps one foot then the other into the water, feels the coolness of it, kicks her feet around a little bit, and I come and do the same. Then we sit on the side of the pool at the steps with the silver rail in between us and just stare off at the waterway.

"Did you notice something was wrong with Hilda's lip?" I ask her.

"Mm hmm."

"Well, have you said anything to her?"

"No. Have you?"

"Well, no, but Mama, you should really say something to her. She's got to have that looked at."

"Why don't you say something to her, honey?"

I look at her. It's useless.

"Oh, I guess I will."

Mama doesn't like to talk about anything unpleasant. The subject of skin cancer, I imagine, is on her list of unpleasantries.

"You should have seen Cooper this morning," I tell her, smiling. "He's trying to dress himself these days. Had on pajama bottoms and a fireman's raincoat. I tell you, it was all I could do to talk him out of it before school."

"I know someone else who was just like that when she was a little girl."

"Really? I thought I had good taste. Remember those pink shoes I always had to wear and that bright orange dress with red flowers?"

"Oh, how could I forget? You had to wear it every day. It's just a phase though. Look how Tradd's coming into his own."

"I know it. They're growing up too fast, Mama."

"I'm sorry, sweetie. Children tend to do that." Mama crosses her arms and sighs. "You want me to watch the boys tonight?"

"Tonight? It's a school night."

"They're in preschool. It's not like they have homework or anything. Besides, you and RC need to get out. Need a little time to yourselves."

This sounds like a logical thing to say. Sounds like a wonderful blessing, but at the same time makes me wonder what she's really trying to say.

"I suppose it has been awhile . . ." I say, thinking of the pot roast already cooking in the Crock-Pot. "You think we need time alone?"

"All couples do, Katie-bug. Even the best marriages. And your husband just happens to spend time every day with physically fit women at the gym. I do not see how you stand that."

"Oh, please. RC's never given me the slightest reason to be jealous, Mama."

"Well, there's jealous and then there's just smart."

I sigh, loudly. "I'll ask her this morning," I say, changing the subject.

"Ask who? What?"

"I'll ask Hilda to go see a doctor. You just promise to back me up."

"Thank you, honey." She smiles so pretty. "And what about the boys? Can we watch them tonight?"

"I suppose so. They'll be thrilled. Thanks."

Tillie and Connie make their way slowly across the lawn, Connie holding her up with her thick arm. Tillie looks like a walking skeleton with skin on her. She reminds me of those high school science lab skeletons named "Mr. Bones." You can see her hip bones sticking out. You can see her leg bones sticking out past her hip bones. It's not like anything I've ever seen except in pictures of concentration camps from Nazi wartime. And there's hardly any musculature left on her body, yet she's always got this grin on her face. And Connie swears she feeds her, and the woman's got an appetite like a horse.

"Betty Jo," says Tillie, "you seen that pile of dog mess in your front yard? I'd call the pound if I were you."

"We've talked to him already," says Mama.

"I know it, but that dog is just nothing but trouble. He's dangerous. Connie, tell her."

"That's a mighty big dog," Connie says.

"And he's stupid too," says Tillie. "Big dogs like that, they don't have big brains, they got these little tiny pea brains with great big bladders, and they leave great big ole dog messes in our yards. I tell you what, if that dog comes in my yard and does that I'm calling the city to come get him."

"I'll have John talk to Mr. Lawson again, all right, Tillie? Now come on in, the water feels good."

She lumbers over and with Connie's help removes her flip-flops and cover-up. Then she holds on to the rail and eases down into the pool while Connie undresses and puts their things away. "I remembered a new step," she says. "You're gonna like this one."

Tillie wades into the water waist deep and then flops backward so that she's floating on top. She turns her head to the side and pulls in a mouthful of water, then spits it up into the air while flapping her hands, making a *slap-slapping* sound. Then she moves back to standing and asks, "You know what we called that one?"

We all shake our heads, calculating if we can do it properly and marveling at Tillie's abilities even at her age.

"We called that 'The Waterfall.' You get five, six girls doing the same thing, heads together in a circle, and it really does look and sound like a waterfall." She claps her hands together. "Want to try it?"

"Right now?" Mama asks. We all give her the evil eye because we know she doesn't want to get her hair wet.

"Well it *is* Wednesday, Mama," I scold. "I'd like to learn, Tillie," I say sanctimoniously, and I pull her to the other side to practice my new move.

Our annual event is what keeps us going, keeps us here when the weather is overcast, when our bones are creaking. Anyone within a five-mile radius of this place has heard of the Water Lilies' Synchronized Swimming Event. It's what's talked about over suppers of macaroni and cheese and spiraled ham and sweet iced tea. Highly anticipated. At least, that's what we imagine. We devote at least one morning a week to the planning and preparation of it. Today is that morning.

Tillie is our captain. She's the one with all the ideas, all the creativity. Tillie was actually a college champion in synchronized swimming back in 1943. Then she became a real-live mermaid at the famed Weeki Wachee Springs in Florida. Now, of course, Tillie has a hard time doing the movements that are under water—we can't stay under there too long because her breath gives out. But she's the brains behind us, no doubt about it.

Hilda's here now, slipping her noodle behind her neck. "I'll just rest my head on this and flap this way. Yes? Yes. It works."

Oh Hilda, God bless her, doesn't know how to swim, so she can't do anything without holding on to her big ole noodle. We tried giving her water wings one time, but that just became too cumbersome. The noodle, we found out, works best. If Hilda ever slips off of her noodle, we're sure to know it. All we hear is a slew of German curse words flying at us.

"*Donnerwetter!* Drowning here! Hey, you want me to drown today? Somebody get me the noodle. Throw me the noodle!"

I think Hilda can swim. In fact, I've seen her tread water for at least fifteen seconds before she starts to sink. I think it's all in her head. It has to be. You can't come out here to a swimming pool every single morning for years and not catch on to how to swim. But that's Hilda's hang-up and we love her anyway.

I move a little closer to Hilda and try to get a better look at her mouth. She thrashes around in the shallow end, water splashing. I just can't tell. Is that thing still on her lip?

Hilda's body is square and solid like a tank, like a Hummer coming at you from down the road. And she's way too brown. What she lacks in pool skills she makes up for on dry land, however. We all lean on Hilda. Hilda has been my mother's closest friend since I don't know how long. I think the two of them get along because they both have this serious streak, this no-nonsense side. Gumption. You should hear them go at it. Neither one of them takes a lick off of the other. The way they sound sometimes, you'd think they're not friends at all.

"Betty Jo, get your head in the water," she says. "It's Wednesday."

Mama whines, "But I just had my hair done. It did something right this morning. See? Nice and full?" She plumps her curls.

"I don't care if you got the Goodyear Blimp on your head. Stick on your swim cap, get in the water, and practice this waterfall thing. Okay?"

"I can see how to do it just by looking," Mama rebuffs. "Some of us don't need to practice quite so hard as some others."

"It's all about appearances and Southern pretense with you,

isn't it?" Hilda stands up now, brows melting together, water dropping off her chin. She throws her hands in the air. "You hear how she talks to me? Some friend she is. I won't be the one looking silly at our big event. You go right ahead and make a fool—"

"Hilda! We're thinking of teaching the boys German," I blurt out, trying to get Hilda to stop arguing and face me and nothing better coming to mind.

She turns to me, eyes wide and a smile forming. Yep. There it is, a pea-sized brown spot on her top lip.

"You are?" she asks, pleased, forgetting Mama.

"You are?" asks Mama, flummoxed.

"Well, we're thinking of it. Never know when it might come handy," I lie. "RC wants to, anyway."

"That's wonderful, dear!" Hilda squeals. "What would you like to know?"

In my peripheral vision I see Mama, who's got that look on her face like she's resigned herself to my crazy notions.

"Numbers. Can you teach me one to ten?"

"That's easy." Hilda holds up her right hand. "Tell them this: *eins, zwei, drei, vier, fünf*—" She pops up her thumb.

"Fünf?" I ask.

"Fünf. Then *sechs, sieben, acht, neun, zehn.* That's it. All there is to it! Now you try."

Oh boy. "Acht, neuf, ten . . . yes, I think I have it. Thank you, Hilda! The boys will be so excited! Oh, wait a minute. Hmmm, could you look here a minute? Look right at me?"

She pauses and gives me her best deer in a headlight.

"Do you have something on your lip?" I ask. "Looks like something right—"

"Oh, that's nothing. I'm fine. Just a spot. Should go away, no problems."

I look over at Mama for reinforcement, but she's squirming and appears to be considering sticking her head under water.

"Well, okay," I say. "But maybe you should have a doctor look at it? If it doesn't get better, you know."

She nods and wraps her noodle around her back, then curves it under her bottom and attempts to sit on it. "You just let me know if you need more German vords for the boys. I have many more where that comes from."

I smile at her and promise I will. Such a good heart she has. Mama's been there through Hilda's darkest times. In return, Mama knows Hilda loves her more than anyone else in her life. She's very protective of her. Hilda's husband, a pilot for a commercial airline, left her for a younger woman, a stewardess. It's so cliché, but when it happened Hilda was ready to pack up and go back to Germany. Mama's the one who talked her into staying.

I like the fact that Mama has friends. Sometimes I worry about her. What would happen to her if Daddy . . . well if something were to happen to Daddy? If he weren't around anymore? I wonder what Mama would do, how she would take care of herself. I think on some level, I stay with the Water Lilies for Mama's sake. To keep an eye over her. To be sure she's got a network of friends to fall back on if she ever needed to. Come to think of it, that may be why I'm with the Water Lilies—they're my safety net. When one of us is down, there's bound to be at least one who can bring the other up. We can't all be down on the same day, the odds are against it. That's the good thing about having a group of friends, not just one.

And being this close to Mama every morning, in a way, allows me to be her friend, not just her daughter, not just the one she bosses around, but to let her see me on a different level, as a woman. I can tell it means a lot to her that I'm here.

"Somebody lift my leg up," says Tillie, attempting the water-fall again with one leg dragging. "It won't seem to do what I want it to today." Mama puts her hand up and keeps Connie from budging. She glides over and lifts Tillie's ankle, straightening her leg out. "Thank you, dear," says Tillie as she turns her head to the side to pull in water.

"Anytime," says Mama, winking. And she means it.

Then she yelps.

"Tillie!" A waterspout originating from Tillie's lips sprays Mama's straw hat and seeps through the holes down her cheeks. "Cut that out!" she says, dropping Tillie's leg and pulling her hat down lower on her ears. We're all cracking smiles, and I detect a small one even on Mama's face. "Of all the nerve," she mutters.

On her way back to her station Mama asks me to turn up the music a little louder, so I hop out of the water and turn the little knob. The Temptations croon. I splash back in and see Mama out of the corner of my eye, bobbing to her own beat, grinning like the Cheshire cat. Mama's time with the Lilies is sacred, wet hair or not. She takes seriously the frivolity of our girl time—with no men in sight to thoroughly muck it up.

CHAPTER NINE

THE CONFESSION

Katherine Ann

My husband has the most beautiful body I've ever seen. It's not like his shoulders are nice or his rear end is nice, no. Every single bit of him is spectacular. And Daddy wanted me to marry another lawyer? Why? So we could talk law all the time and try to one-up the other in closing arguments? I married the man of my dreams, Daddy, thank you very much. He's gentle, he's smart, he's . . . he's taking my hand in his and looking at me with those gorgeous hazel eyes right now. With the sunset outside our window, his eyes appear green. They pull me to him.

"We should get out and do this more often," he says. "Just the two of us. I love this free babysitting thing with your parents."

I smile. I know he's right. I take a deep breath. "I just . . . ever since I had the boys, it feels like a part of me is missing or something whenever they're not around. Do you feel like that or is it only a woman thing?"

"No, I get it, I just don't get to have dinner with my beautiful wife very often. When there's no chicken fingers and ketchup involved, that is." His cheeks dimple and he strokes the top of my wrist, sending chills up my arm. Then he sees the look in my eyes. "Why don't you call them? It'll make you feel better."

"No, I'm sure they're fine. They love Nana and Papa's house. They're probably having a ball right now."

"Then what's wrong? You definitely don't seem like yourself tonight."

"Can I get you something to drink?" The waitress has appeared dressed in black slacks and a white button-down. Her hair is pulled back in a clean ponytail.

"I'll have a glass of your house red," I say.

"A Red Stripe for me," says RC. It's the same thing we drank on our Jamaican honeymoon. My blood tingles with the memories. The woman nods and walks away.

"Sooo?" RC prompts.

"So what?"

"Is something on your mind?"

"Oh. I don't know." I shake my head and pull my hand back from his, fidgeting with my overgrown cuticles. "I just can't seem to get Daddy's 'little episode' the other night out of my head. Can you?"

"It was something, I'll give you that."

"I just feel so bad I never asked him about the war. I mean, how selfish can I be? I'm his daughter. It was obviously the most shattering thing that ever happened to him in his life, and I never even asked."

"You're a girl. I doubt he would've talked war with you even if you had asked. A lot of vets never talk about the war."

The waitress returns and sets our drinks down. We ask for a few more minutes to look over the menu and she leaves us again. I turn to watch a boat on Shem Creek trawling slowly while birds flock and cry behind it.

"You want to know the worst thing?" I say quietly.

"Hmmm."

There are tears brimming in my eyes now. I look down at my empty plate. "I never wanted to know about the war . . . because I was afraid of what I'd learn. Daddy's never been the easiest person to love, you know, not for me. There were times, as a teenager . . . you're going to think I'm horrible for saying this."

"Come on, Katie, you know I won't." He gives me his reassuring Boy-Scout-trustworthy look and takes both of my hands, rubbing my palms that are resting on either side of my plate now. "Have I ever judged you before?"

"I always thought . . ." I blurt out. Then I whisper, "I *worried* that if I knew Daddy had killed somebody . . . you know, could actually picture him killing a man, that that's all I'd be able to see when I looked at him. Is that weird? Things were rough with us at times, growing up. My emotions, his emotions. I had a hard time dealing with boys because of it. I guess I thought if I had some concrete evidence against him—"

"Well, how do you feel now? Now that you know?"

"Just the opposite," I say. "It makes me love him more. I feel so guilty about how I treated him. I cannot imagine what my father has suffered over the years, knowing what he did. What he had to do. Everything he saw. The soldiers who came home from Vietnam were treated terribly in this country. And then he had to deal with a spoiled brat like me on top of it all."

"You about ready to order? Oh—" The waitress sees she's interrupted something and turns to go, but I stop her. "It's okay," I say. "We're ready. How about . . . bring me the seafood platter."

"Fried or broiled?"

"Fried. Extra tartar sauce, please." I hand her the menu.

"Fries or red rice with that?"

"Um . . . fries."

I know I've broken every cardinal rule about eating, but I need this food right now. I need comfort. I feel strangely out of control—like I was when I was sixteen, binging and purging in secret. I also feel the overwhelming need to check on my boys.

"I'll be right back," I say as RC orders his dinner. Then I slip off to the bathroom to call Mama. There is something like heartburn beginning to nip at my chest, and I fear my romantic dinner with RC is beginning to spin down the drain. My fault, of course. There is a gorgeous man who loves me waiting in the other room, and I can't even focus on him. What's my problem?

The calm, cool, together person I've grown into feels strangely insecure like the pimply teen she once was. I picture my spine unraveling at the seams. I take a deep breath and dial my mother's number.

CHAPTER TEN

The Boat People
Georgetown, South Carolina

Lisa

I have my father's tree trunk legs and big nose. It juts out with a hump on top, very unlike my mother's, pressed flat against her face.

"Lisa, *con gai*, you are beautiful. No worry. Face beautiful. Just like your father. Okay?" Every night of my life my mother would grin and tell me this while tucking me in bed. She'd use her forefinger to mush my nose, then straighten it, then touch her own. Every night she seemed astounded that I came from her body. After she'd gone I'd lie on my face, nearly suffocating in my pillow trying to flatten my nose. Then I'd roll over on my back, feeling my bump, willing my nose to shrink on its own.

I close my eyes now and sit on the floor of my shower. I let warm water run down over my head, over my thick legs. I feel it on my scalp, dropping over my eyelids, pouring off the tip of my telltale nose. Listen. That's the sound of our history. When my eyes are closed and I'm wound up tight like a ball, cradling my knees, drenched in rain, I am in my mother's womb again. I am in her womb and safe like a tiny boat on an evil sea.

"So many!" my mother would tell me, weeping. "I don't know how we make it. We run out of food, people sick, they die. Just like that. And then the pirates. *Choi oi!* I say, maybe I can't live! Maybe I try to jump into water, but *Ahn Dien*, he say no. I have a child. No honor in taking another life to grave."

I don't remember the voyage to America. In fact, I don't remember a thing of my life before America. From what I've heard from Ma and Uncle, I consider this a blessing. As far as I'm concerned, I was born at age five in a refugee camp in Florida, and my soul was formed in Vietnam. As to when my life will begin, that is something yet to be seen. When does life really begin? Conception? Birth? Sometime much later?

I don't want to get out of this shower. I don't ever want the rain to end. Though I don't remember Vietnam, the sound takes my soul back to the *mua* season when the rain would douse the earth for days, flooding everything. I want to stay in the rain. I want to rewind time, to take *Ma* back to a time when she was happy. And beautiful. But time doesn't rewind for anyone.

I open my eyes and see-feel the blurriness of my life. I'm neither here nor there. I'm waterlogged now. My fingertips are wrinkled. The water is turning cold.

I dry off and enter the cold air of my life. I shiver. Look at her there. She looks much older than her fifty-nine years. Her hair is stick-straight, pepper-white, and pulled back loosely behind her neck. In the glare of the television, her heart-shaped face appears lined with deep crevices, her skin puffy all over. My mother's eyes are tiny marbles supported by thick orange wedges. They glisten in the light, reminding me she's still alive. Her top lids are heavy and her right eye is forced shut. She hasn't been sleeping well. Ma stares straight ahead at the television, watching commercials, searching for pieces of her life.

"Why no Vietnamese actress on TV?" she would complain when I was younger. "Lisa, *con gai*, you should be a TV star. You look like that big girl on *Guiding Light*, no? Bigger nose? *Choi oi!* Maybe radio star is good for you, okay? You like listen to radio, no?"

My mother could talk for hours about nothing. As an adolescent I mastered the art of tuning her out, saying, "*Vay a?*" every minute or so to make her think I was still in the conversation.

She is completely silent now. Ma spoke her heart every year of her life, yet in the last six months since Uncle passed—her last vestige of home—she does not say a word. I'm here with her some of the time, speaking her native tongue, but I can bring her no joy, no peace. Look at me. I am the spitting image of the bad luck that has befallen our family.

I tried to believe my mother—that I was beautiful—but I wasn't. I wanted to please her. Be like her. As I got older, graduated from college, I felt a need to fit into my mother's world, to help her feel like she wasn't so alone—especially now that Uncle is gone. I've found my link to my mother's life, my Vietnamese half, through food. And it shows. All over. I've eaten myself silly in the past few months.

I move through the doorway of our tiny kitchen and reach under the cabinet for two pots. Then I open the fridge and pull out the ingredients I'll need to make Ma's breakfast, *pho* or beef noodle soup.

I can hear laughing coming from *Good Morning, America* while I bring the stock, spices, and beef to a boil. The water for the rice noodles boils first, so I cook, drain, and divide them between two bowls. When the beef is ready, I pull it out and slice it thinly on my bamboo board, laying the slices over the noodles, topping the whole thing with savory broth, onion, and cilantro.

The steam hits my chin when I set the bowls on the table in the breakfast nook, then I walk into the living room and put my hand on Ma's shoulder. "Breakfast's ready, Ma." It takes her a moment to pull her eyes away from the television, and she rises. We walk arm in arm in silence to the table. I seat her in the chair that faces the window, hoping to give her a view of the real world.

In fifteen minutes my stomach is full and Ma has only sipped her broth, eating none of the meat. She pushes it away and then walks back to her favorite chair, ignoring my sighs of protest. The *pho* will not hold. It's just not good if it's not fresh, so I slurp up the rest of hers, stuffing myself now. I wash by hand and put away the dishes.

It's 8:24 a.m. I don my chef's clothes so I can head to the restaurant to cook and eat some more. Before the door shuts, I say "*Chao, Ma*" to a motionless old woman who was once my mother, propped up in front of a glowing American idol that's become her window to the world.

PART TWO
EARTH

Ác giả, ác báo.

What you reap is what you sow.

—Vietnamese proverb

CHAPTER ELEVEN

The Edge
Charleston, Memorial Day

Katherine Ann

"Hey, Katie-bug!" Daddy barks, standing in front of his media center and turning the volume up. "Are you the one that gave me this flamingo music?"

"*Fla-men-co* music. Yeah, that was me," I say.

"I like it. It's nice. You like it?"

"I can't stand that music," my mother whispers, grazing my arm with a tray of fresh-cut fruit.

"It's real nice," I say, listening to the strumming guitars, watching the excitement grow on Daddy's face. He's happy tonight. He's always happy when he's entertaining. When he's king of his domain. When he gets to drink.

"What are we drinking, Nana?" he asks. "White, red, or champagne? How about champagne?" Before getting Mama's answer, he reaches into the wine cooler and manhandles a 1999 bottle of Dom Pérignon.

My mother gives him that exasperated look—the one she's perfected just for him. "I was going to say red," she says as he pops the cork, letting the bubbles dribble onto the counter. He's in heaven.

53

Daddy pours four glasses and hands me one. RC grabs his and takes a sip immediately. My boys are playing in the backyard with plastic yellow dump trucks in the gravel around the fountain, next to the pool. The marsh is a watercolor painting in subdued greens and blues behind them.

"Here's to you," Daddy says to us, holding his glass in the air. My mother, husband, and I clink glasses with him and say, "Cheers."

"And Happy Memorial Day," I add stupidly. Are you supposed to say "happy" when you refer to Memorial Day? A day about remembering lost soldiers? What an idiot.

Daddy nods his head and clears his throat. Just the mention of the word "memorial" has made his eyes water. "Thanks," he says. "Yeah, here's to that."

Out of the corner of my eye, I see my boys. They're too close to the water. I run to the sliding glass door on the sunporch and throw it open. "Back away from the pool! Cooper! Tradd, you should know better. Your brother can't swim!"

"But he came over first. We were looking for frogs," Tradd whines, thinking of crying.

"I don't care who did it first. You're older. He does whatever you do! Now move away from the water or you're coming inside. For good. I mean it." I have my hands on my hips and he knows I mean business. I watch as my four-year-old pulls my two-year-old by the arm, and they return to their dump trucks and plop down. I'm surprised they didn't put up a bigger fuss.

When I make my way back to my champagne glass, the mood has changed in the room. It doesn't feel like a celebration anymore. My father and RC are sitting in front of the TV watching a golf game while Mama busies herself at the sink.

The boys traipse in after me a few seconds later, the sound of the sliding door opening and slamming shut, then opening and slamming shut again. They have these explorer looks on their faces, the ones they wear when they're looking to get into something. The boys always love coming to Nana and Papa's house where everything is new and exciting.

"Can we ride on those scooters?" Tradd asks me, tugging my pants, referring to the electric death contraptions Daddy bought just in time for summer.

"Go ask your papa," I whisper. So he does, with Cooper in tow.

"Yeah, sure, come on!" Daddy says, rising from his recliner. I'm fairly sure he's more excited about being asked than the boys are for actually getting to ride on the things. "Let's go!"

The four boys—Daddy, RC, Tradd, and Cooper—head to the garage while I help Mama put the fish in the oven and set the timer. Precisely six minutes and seventeen seconds later, we hear wailing coming from outside. I don't even move—the men can handle it—though my nerves fray just a little. Then the whole screaming circus bulldozes into the house, right to where Mama and I are standing as if we're magnets. Our peace is thoroughly broken.

"Haaaa wollova fooooo!" My son Tradd reaches his lung capacity and lets us have it. My father is carrying him, one arm under, the other cradling his foot.

"Why'd you jump off? Why the heck'd you have to jump off? I told you I'd slow down!" Daddy looks at me, pleading his case. "I told him I'd slow down—"

"Waaaaaa! Ran ovaaaaa!"

"Hold on, just hold on. Are you all right, baby?" I move to take Tradd from Daddy's arms. Tradd reaches for me and points to his bleeding foot, which obviously has been run over by the scooter.

"It'll be all right, Tradd honey," I say. "It's just a scratch, and Papa didn't mean to."

"Yes, he did!"

My father puts his finger within inches of my four-year-old's face and yells, "I did not! It was *your* fault. This is all *your* fault!"

Oh good gracious. Did he just say that? Who's the four-year-old here? I grab my son and pull him into the other room, away from his grandfather. His grandfather, of all people! What did he just do to my child's young psyche? For that matter, what in the world did he do to mine for all those years of raising me?

Life has not always been easy, being the daughter of a builder. I can remember times when the money just wasn't there. People weren't buying houses. They weren't building custom houses. They certainly weren't buying houses from my father. Daddy hates people; that's what he would have you believe. Truthfully, he just doesn't know how to handle people, cater to them, coddle them— things born and bred in every other Southerner. Maybe that's the problem. He's not originally from the South. Perhaps it's something in his genes.

His ability to deal with children is severely hampered by his inability to contain his emotions. And my father's outlook on life, his bearability, is directly proportional to the amount of cash in his pockets. I remember when I was seven years old, we'd just moved into a mammoth house on the beach. Our ship had come in, so they say. Daddy's business must have been doing well because I distinctly recall him standing in front of the fireplace with wads of dollar bills in his hands. He yelled, "Hundred dollar pickup!" and I scrambled on the floor, reaching into the air with wings, grabbing as many bills as I could and stuffing them into my greedy hands, thrilled there was a smile on Daddy's face.

I didn't even know what money was. What it did. I do know I developed a taste for it early on.

Was Daddy trying to buy my affection?

For my father, money truly does buy happiness. The only problem is: money is my father's fickle lover. She comes and goes as she pleases—taking every ounce of perceived happiness with her and sucking us dry as she goes.

After things have cooled down a bit and our Memorial Day dinner has been eaten, RC and I take the kids home early. And as we head out the door and I realize Daddy is ignoring us for the TV set, I make a mental note to ask my mother if they're having money problems. Daddy, obviously, is losing his edge.

WE'VE BEEN HOME for an hour and the boys are bathed and dressed. I can hear RC telling Cooper a Diego story in the other room. It's part of his bedtime routine along with prayers, ABCs, and his blue frayed blankie. He has to have it to sleep.

I lift Tradd's bangs and run my hand over his forehead, then bend and kiss him on his little nose. He's lying on his pillow, foot sticking out of the covers for fear it will hurt if it rubs against them. We've read a book, and the lights are out except for his sailboat nightlight, shining near the closet. "You ready to say your prayers?" I ask.

Tradd turns his head and stays quiet.

"Honey? You want me to start?"

He nods.

"Okay. Now I lay me . . ."

"Down to sleep," he says.

"I pray the Lord . . ."

"My soul to keep."

"Bless Mommy and Daddy . . ."

I wait for Tradd to bless Nana and Papa, but he stays quiet.

"Bless . . ." I prompt him. He pinches his lips tight. "Tradd, let's bless Nana and Papa now."

"I don't want to."

The silence in the air grows thick with meaning. "Well, they need blessings too," I say.

"In Jesus name, Amen." Tradd's voice is small but final. I can hear the hurt still in his voice. I give him a long look then kiss him again and whisper, "I love you, punkin. Sweet dreams. See you in the morning." Then I head out into the glare of the hallway, wondering how long it will take my little boy to get over his granddaddy's screaming tonight. I know as a child I used to hold onto it for days and days . . .

RC passes me as I head for Cooper's room to say good night, and a wave of gratitude rolls over me. I'm so thankful my children have RC in their lives—his calm, steady nature, his long-enduring patience. For that matter, I'm thankful I have him too.

Just after I kiss Cooper, the fire alarm blares. It only lasts about thirty seconds, a false alarm, but the damage is done. The kids are out of bed again, my heart is pounding, and my nerves are frayed like split ends. How appropriate. A perfect ending to a lovely Memorial Day.

CHAPTER TWELVE

The Visit

John

John sits in his recliner and tenses his arms as Tiger readies for the putt. When Tiger Woods first came on the scene, John had sworn him off unconsciously either for the sin of being a newcomer, being a youngster, or for the color of his skin. Once he came around to the fact that Tiger was no fly-by-night, that he was here to stay, John rallied for him, became his biggest fan. He works hard not to miss a single tournament. Loyalty for people or things or countries is hard for John to muster, but once his allegiance is earned, it never dies.

John's eye twitches when Tiger's caddy takes his putter and stuffs it into the bag over his shoulder. John looks at the man and almost envies him—his ability to feel the cool air behind the television screen and see the green from that close up. Smell the grass. Memories of his days as a caddy leave him warm and his brain flooded with endorphins. It's this letting down of his guard that leaves him utterly unable to stop what's coming next.

He is no longer sixty in a recliner watching golf in Charleston, South Carolina.

Thirteen-year-old John Porter stands in front of his seven sisters, the youngest in his arms resting on his hip, red-faced from crying. The police are here, at his home in New Jersey. They are taking his parents away, handcuffed, in separate cars.

"You're the man of this family now! Take care of your sisters for me," his mother wails as they push her head into the car. Before the door shuts, he hears her say, "Never stole a penny in my life!"

John's heart is not racing. It's stopped. A panic has seized him from his ankles to his chin. His young mind races to the money he's stashed in the closet from mowing lawns. Will it be enough to feed his sisters? How many lawns does he need to mow in order to make it? Let's see, one hundred lawns at seventy-five cents a piece is . . . So maybe five hundred lawns? But what about school? When will he find the time?

His face begins to fill with fear at the sounds of his sisters' collective crying. They tug on him, cling to him. Then a third car comes, this one with no police markings. Now a fourth. These are the social workers. John won't have to worry any more about being the man of the family.

He is losing control.

In groups of twos and threes, the children will soon be divvied up between foster homes. John feels something like steel framing up his spine. He hates how poor his family is, hates his parents for having so many children while being so poor.

As he's driven away, watching his cement block house and freshly cut lawn grow smaller and smaller, he makes a silent, angry, terrified vow: *My children will never have to go through this.*

His foster home is not much better than the one he grew up in. He has a roof over his head, two of his sisters with him, and abusive adults rationing one meal a day for each. He forces himself to forget about his parents. To forget about his sisters living in other people's homes.

He finds an after-school job three miles away at the municipal golf course. As a caddy, he can pretend to be one of these men who has time to golf, has enough money to golf. He holds their bags and *yes sir*'s them so well that his tips become larger, the pats on the back more frequent.

By the time he is fifteen his family is brought back together intact under one roof, but there is no rejoicing. John Porter has so utterly removed himself from family that his brain thinks of nothing else but escaping to the golf course and listening to the men curse and tell their dirty jokes. He is a man among these golfers and has his first beer with them. He stays as long on the course as possible so that he doesn't have to see those strangers at home.

At age eighteen with the draft in full swing for Vietnam, John Porter doesn't wait for his number to be called. Instead he volunteers, not quite good enough to become a professional golfer, yet ready to escape the hell back at home.

Tiger is getting ready to tee off again. John Porter is back in his recliner now, reaching for a half-empty bottle of beer. He takes one long swig to finish the bottle and erase the past and has no idea that he isn't alone in this room. There's someone else with him now.

Ernest

Ernest Marquette's second wish is beginning to take effect. His desire to be free of that which holds him captive is the true longing of his heart. And since no heart is truly separate from another, the visitations are beginning now. It's the first time this has happened to Ernest—this new connection with John Porter, the ability to leave his pond—whether in body or spirit—Ernest doesn't know. Doesn't question it now. He simply feels for John, wonders how in the world he can be privy to this vision, privy to the thoughts in his head, and he wishes he could ease John's suffering. He didn't know all that stuff about John's life before Vietnam. John simply had never talked about it.

Ernest doesn't know how to feel, seeing his best friend after all these years, sitting in his den. He looks old, truthfully, seems to have done well for himself what with the house and all, but before he can think too hard, he is swept back into his slimy fish body at the top of Marble Mountain.

Was it a dream? An out-of-body experience? His mind is reeling. Had he escaped from Vietnam for a moment?

Of course there's always the possibility he's going mad. But Ernest knows now that John Porter is alive and well. He knows that life exists outside of this pond, outside of this godforsaken country—and nothing and no one will be able to keep his spirit still.

Ernest wonders if he should visit the eldest fish, the one that sits farthest from the waterfall. If answers are to be had, surely they'll come from him. Perhaps, other than dying, there is indeed a way to escape this place once and for all.

CHAPTER THIRTEEN

THE FAIRY TALE
Georgetown

Lisa

The first time I heard the word *super-cali-fragi-listic-expi-ali-do-cious*, I knew I was in love. In love with the English language. In love with America. My life at home with Ma and Uncle was a cocoon of Vietnamese culture that sheltered me, swallowed me. To leave the house each day for school and wait for the school bus, listening to car radios as they whizzed by—it was like visiting a foreign country. Every day.

When I first heard Mary Poppins sing that song, the one with the superlong word, I was enamored. I wrote it down on my notebook over and over like I would do Sam Johnson's name just a few years later. I memorized it. I sang it aloud as I jumped off benches with my umbrella, hoping to fly. English. What an incredible, artistic language it was, a sharp contrast to the monosyllabic world into which I returned each afternoon.

My mother and uncle made a point not to speak any English during meals when I was young. I was like a secret agent, putting on a new persona when I walked out the door. Leading a dual life. Not an exciting one, just a dual one.

Growing up, the Vietnamese language to me was boring. It's made up of single syllable words spoken in mainly six tones. One word can have many meanings based on the tone in which it's delivered. For instance, the word *vo* can mean skin, martial arts, a sock, or even a wife. Said a different way, *vo* can mean to enter or to be broken. Vietnamese is an efficient language, I'll give it that, but it can't match the beauty of some American words, the way they flow off the tongue in flames.

Like persimmon. I love this word, persimmon. Say it, per-sim-mon. In Vietnamese? *Hong.* Lemongrass? *Sa.* Avocado? *Bo.* Papaya? *Du du.* Need I go on?

But my Vietnamese upbringing did offer me some things that I cherish to this day—things that I could wrap myself in, lose myself in—the fairy tales. Vietnam is chock full of legends about how things came to be and tales with moral lessons attached. My favorite Vietnamese fairy tale was the Cinderella-like story about Tam and Cam. As a child, I'd ask my mother to recite it for me before bedtime. It was much more vengeful and gory than the American version—and, it seemed to me, more magical.

I lift the covers over her and sit down on the edge of the bed next to my mother whose eyes are already closed. I run my hand over her forehead and long to reach inside and pull her out of her shell. Instinctively, I open my mouth and use my Vietnamese words and long-ago fairy tale to take Ma back to a simpler time.

"Once upon a time, there was a young girl named Tam whose mother died. Tam's father remarried a terrible woman in his grief, and months later he and the new wife had a daughter named Cam. The stepmother wanted all of her husband's favor to go toward the new child, so she told him lies about Tam."

I see Ma's eyes move behind her eyelids and know that she is listening.

"One day, the stepmother sent Tam and Cam to the river to fill their baskets with fish, but while Tam worked, Cam lay around, lazy. When it was time to go home, Cam tricked Tam into washing in the river and stole her fish. Finding that her basket was empty, Tam wailed at the thought of what her stepmother might do to her.

"'Don't worry, child,' said the Goddess of Mercy, suddenly appearing at her side. 'There is one more.' Tam looked in her basket and saw a golden fish. 'Take this home and care for it. Feed it every day and you'll have anything you want.'"

Ma's features smooth as if she's relaxing.

"So Tam fed the fish secretly every day until the stepmother caught it and cooked it up, throwing its bones out the window.

"When Tam realized the fish was dead, she cried until the Goddess of Mercy told her to find the bones of the fish and bury them in a hidden place. 'Once you do this, your wishes will be granted.' Tam obeyed, and soon there was a great gala in town. Her stepmother and Cam dressed in their finest, leaving Tam at home in rags. Tam went to the hidden bones and wished for nice clothes. Suddenly, she was robed in a beautiful *ao dai*, so she went to the gala and met the king, who instantly fell in love with her. Tam and the king were married."

This, of course, is where the original Cinderella story would end, but not in our Vietnamese version. Ma rolls over on her side and takes a deep breath, preparing for what is coming next. I rub her back softly and continue, unable to see her face anymore.

I tell Ma the part about Tam climbing the betel tree and how her stepmother cuts the tree down, and Tam falls to her death. Ma's leg twitches and I stop rubbing her back. I speak softer now.

"The stepmother introduced her daughter, Cam, to the king and he married her in his sadness. But the Goddess of Mercy turned the spirit of Tam into a nightingale, and she flew to the king. Cam killed the bird out of jealousy so the Goddess of Mercy turned the spirit of Tam into a great tree. The tree dropped a large golden fruit to the ground and an old woman picked it up and took it home.

"The next day, the woman's house was cleaned and food prepared. She peeked through the window to see who was doing these things and saw a beautiful girl climbing out of the fruit.

"Are you asleep, Ma?" I ask. She doesn't answer. I whisper now.

"You know the rest. This is the good part. The king walked by the old woman's house, so she gave him a betel nut out of respect. He ate it and said it was exactly how his beloved wife used to make them. Then he asked who had prepared the food.

"'No one but a worthless servant,' the woman said. When the king asked to see her, he knew it was his Tam and took her home, marrying her again as his second and favorite wife. Cam was again jealous of her sister, especially of her beauty, and asked Tam how she could get her skin as white as hers.

"Tam told her stepsister to jump into a pot of boiling water and Cam complied, dying instantly. Next the evil stepmother died from grief. And the king and Tam lived happily ever after. Because why?"

My mother's body goes rigid and she seems to be holding her breath for my answer.

"Because they got what they deserved," I whisper. Then I turn out the light and leave my mother to rest in peace, dreaming of all the wonderful things that she, herself, deserves.

CHAPTER FOURTEEN

The Symptoms
Charleston, June

Katherine Ann

"So how are you and Daddy doing?" I ask my mother in the pool house after pulling off my sweatpants. I found her dressing out here this morning, which is odd. She stands next to me, checking the fit in the rear end of her new lime green suit.

"Fine, just fine," she says, smiling absently and moving to smooth cream on her arms.

"That's good." I hesitate. "But, I mean, is everything all right . . . building wise? Money and all that?" I know it's prying, but I just have to know. Lack of funds would explain Daddy's recent flare-ups.

"We're fine, dear. Your dad's building like crazy. He's got more work right now than he knows what to do with. Why?"

"Oh, no reason," I say. "That's good. The business and all. It's good."

"Honey, are *you* all right? The boys? Why the sudden interest in our finances? You and RC need help or something?" she asks, clicking the sunscreen shut and setting it down on the bench.

"Oh, no," I say quickly, "we're all fine, it's just . . . I don't know. I'm not doing so well, I guess."

"What's wrong?" She's sitting now on the long bench next to me, holding one sandal in her hand with her foot still dangling in midair.

I consider keeping my mouth shut but a wave of anxiety sweeps over me, and I spill it. "I think I might have health problems."

Too late to turn back now.

"Whaaaat?" Mama sets her foot down and gives me her full attention.

"My heart. And stomach, well, maybe. I thought I'd save all my issues for my yearly gynecologist check-up—save money, you know—and I guess I sort of bombarded her. Not sure she knew what to do with me. Apparently, she does think the on-again, off-again pain in my left breast is dire enough to warrant a mammogram. A mammogram, Mama! That's on Friday. Till then, I just take two Zantac per day to try and eliminate this pain and bloating in my abdomen." I hold my middle and burp. "And belching."

"Goodness gracious, honey, can't all that be wrong with you," she says, trying to pooh-pooh it away. It *is* unpleasant after all. "Are you sure? Have they done any tests? I just don't understand."

"Look." I scoot closer to her and lift my left breast, much to her horror. "When I press on this very particular spot under my ribs, I feel pain. Distinct, put-your-finger-on-it pain. This can't be normal."

"Maybe it's an ulcer?" she offers, staring at her feet.

"Gracious, I hope it's an ulcer and nothing more serious like . . . stomach cancer."

"Katie-bug, cancer? For goodness sakes."

"Well, I don't know how to explain it, I'm just so upset all of a sudden."

"Sounds like you're falling apart," Mama says, her face crisscrossing with worry lines.

"Well, I'm sure it's nothing. Really," I backpedal. "I'll just ask about it at today's appointment with my regular doctor. So much for saving money. They're giving me an electrocardiogram."

"Electro-what?" asks Tillie, now standing in the doorway and blocking just a sliver of sunlight. Mama and I turn to acknowledge her presence.

"Oh, it's nothing," I say. "Standard stuff, I'm sure, but my heart has been skipping beats lately."

"Well, that's normal," she says. "My Fred had some of that before he died."

We stare at Tillie, unnerved and mortified at the possibilities.

"Oh, but that's not what killed him. No." Tillie tee-hees at her proximity of words. "What killed him was the heart attack. Those skipping beats didn't do a dad-gum thing but annoy the heck out of him."

"Well, that's a relief," Mama says, rolling her eyes and turning to me again. She whispers now. "Honey, this sounds an awful lot like . . . Didn't this happen years ago? I seem to remember . . . you were in high school. What did they say it was then? Nerves? When does this happen, Katie-bug? These skipping beats and all."

"Mostly when I'm trying to relax. Mostly when I'm propped up in bed reading, and RC is lying next to me reading or sleeping or watching TV. It's then that I feel it the most."

"Sounds like RC's the problem," Connie says, sneaking up behind Tillie and emitting a low, sultry laugh. "Maybe he needs to be doing something else in bed other than watching TV."

"What? Oh, no. Well, how could he anyway, what with the bloating and all."

"Bloating?" asks Tillie, subconsciously rubbing her own navel.

"Lots of bloating! Look at this!" I turn to the side, and the women study my figure as if I'm a lab specimen. "See? My stomach is enormous! And no, Connie, I am not pregnant." I see her cocking her head to the side and elbowing Tillie like I'm some inside joke. "Trust me. No worries there."

I AM SITTING on crumpled white paper spread over an examination table, a green immodest gown tied behind my back, and Dr. Landry asks me, "Have I seen you here before?"

"Yes," I tell him. "Last year when I broke out from shingles. Due to stress."

He pauses and looks at me, trying to place me. "Let's just look through your records."

I think I might be a hypochondriac. I bet right now the doctor is typing away on that little computer notebook thingy with his pointy little poking instrument that I'm suffering from a severe case of hypochondria. How embarrassing. I once was a high-powered lawyer handling cases on medical malpractice, and now I'm just a whiney little woman taking up this doctor's time.

The nurse did an EKG on me twenty minutes ago. Four lines with spikes run lengthwise across the page. I can see the lines there, next to the doctor.

"How do you get along with your husband?" he asks me.

"My husband? We have a great relationship." Kind of a personal question, don't you think, doc? "RC's wonderful. Well, except he just called me three times since I've been sitting here for the past hour, wondering when I'm coming home. My youngest, he gets upset when I'm not there sometimes." My heart aches, remembering Cooper's cries for Mommy over the telephone just minutes ago. I try to wipe it from my mind.

He's writing something again. What is he writing?

"Normal bowel movements?"

"Uh, yes."

"Any unusual stress?"

"Unusual? I don't think so. I do have a two-year-old and a four-year-old. Boys."

"That'll do it," he says. "Is the Zantac helping your stomach at all?"

"A little," I say. He finishes tapping away and then looks at me. "We're going to have you wear a monitor for the next twenty-four hours to rule out anything with your heart, all right?"

Really? "Well, was the EKG okay?" I ask, nervous now.

"Perfect. We're just going to do this to rule anything out. If there's anything there, we'll find it. The nurse will be in to hook you up for the monitor in a few minutes. Any questions for me?"

I run through my list of pressing questions and then the doctor smiles and walks out of the room. Now I wait for the nurse again. Here she is, a grandmotherly type with glasses.

"We don't do many of these around here," she says, holding a large plastic package, "but luckily they've provided good instructions with pictures. See?" She actually shows me the pictures.

Oh. Wonderful. Really? This is who's hooking electricity up to my body?

After twenty minutes of naked breasts, vigorous skin cleansing (might as well be a Brillo pad), searching for ribs numbered two, four, seven, et cetera, and sticking these little round things on my skin, then pulling them off again and sticking new ones on in slightly better places, I am finally hooked up to the wires.

"Let's see," says the nurse. "Brown goes here. Red goes here . . ." She does the same with black, white, and green. With each wire, I'm picturing the headlines: "Former malpractice lawyer dies from crossed wires." Just when I think it's all over, it's time for the tape.

I swear, when I leave twenty minutes later, I am mummified, cross my heart, and my chest is hooked up to a large Walkman with wires strapped across my body. My chest is attached to my stomach, and I can't stand up straight or take a deep breath.

Note to self: Do not walk into a bank, as it appears I'm wearing a bomb.

Oh, and I'm supposed to click a little button when I have an "event" and write everything down in this handy-dandy diary. No problem.

At home RC is waiting for me outside. He's brought the kids over to the neighbors' house to play with their kids per my instructions. It's a sure-fire way to console Cooper. I am strapped to a machine and really don't feel like explaining my situation just now to the neighbors, so I roll down the window.

"Can you bring the kids home now?"

RC hangs up his cell phone and comes to my car.

"Cooper was hyperventilating for forty minutes! I swear it's never been this bad. And work called. It was not a good day to be watching the kids."

I turn to glare at him. Five seconds home and I'm stressed already. "I couldn't even go to the doctor—"

"What is that?" he says when he notices the wires coming out of my shirt.

"It's to monitor my heart. Apparently I'm under a lot of stress."

"Stress about what?"

"I don't know, honey. You tell me. You called me three times in the doctor's office."

"I'm sorry, but David and Jan called in sick and everything's going haywire! I've got to go in and cover their clients too." He stops. "Did they listen to your heart and do this because something's wrong?"

"No, they're just checking." He stares at the bulk beneath my shirt.

"You want me to bring the kids over here before I leave?" he says, trying to appease me.

I look at him. I'm exhausted already. "Please." Then I turn around and head into the house, wondering how in the world I'm going to keep the children from disconnecting my wires for the next twenty-four hours. Maybe more importantly, how am I going to spread my lungs and breathe?

As claustrophobia begins to get its clutches around my throat, I wonder, how did I ever have the nerves to argue cases in a court of law? Seems like it was another lifetime ago. Well, at least the mammogram's not for another few days. Surely I'll be able to relax by then.

CHAPTER FIFTEEN

The Mentor
Marble Mountain, Vietnam

Ernest

It is midday. Lunch is being served in a pagoda outside the cave. Ernest knows what time it is, not only because the monks are all absent but because the sunlight forms a chiaroscuro of black and white right down the middle of the space. Buddha's face is the center of the cave, so at noon his face splits in two like Jekyll and Hyde. There are no tourists throwing bread crumbs in at the moment and the fish are swimming lazily around the pond, waiting for the monks to finish eating and Brother Chong to show his face again.

Now is the perfect time to speak with Eldest fish.

Ernest finds him fairly still, only making slight movements with his dorsal fins to keep in the same position. Forward a millimeter, back an inch, and so on. The utmost discipline. The relationship the two have had over the years has been one of mentor and pupil. Eldest fish has taught Ernest tips for survival, in body, yes, but mostly of the spirit. And much of what he's learned has come from nearly a century of studying the monks.

"You must harness the power of your spirit, keeping it under strictest control," he had told Ernest after he first joined the pond dwellers. "Otherwise, you will go mad. I have seen it in countless fish over my lifetime."

Ernest knows that Eldest fish will not look favorably upon his questions today. He can almost hear word for word his admonishment and he turns, thinking better of his actions.

"You have something to say?" Eldest fish says, apparently noticing Ernest's trepidation.

"Yes," says Ernest. "Something has happened."

"Go on."

"I don't know how to explain it, exactly." Ernest watches the light flickering on the surface of the water. "I was with my old friend yesterday." He waits to see the reaction of Eldest fish but there is none. "I was with him in his home. I saw him there just as I'm seeing you now. But not only that, I was in his head. I could feel the pain from his childhood memories."

"You could see and feel your friend?" Eldest fish repeats, turning now to watch a group of young fish laugh and dart through the waterfall.

"Yes. He's much older now. Do you know what this means? Can you tell me how I was able to leave this place?"

"Perhaps it was a dream. The mind is a powerful thing."

"It was not a dream," Ernest says with finality, staring the old fish in his good eye, the one that is not so clouded over.

The fish seems to consider Ernest's statement with much care. Finally, his mouth moves.

"Then your souls have become connected," he says.

"But how? What does this mean?"

"I don't know. Perhaps your souls have always been connected. Perhaps something is rising in the earth—the spirits. But you are not of the earth anymore. You are of the water. You must focus on holding your spirit as still as possible."

This is exactly what Ernest had anticipated, a warning. "There's something else," Ernest says. "I almost . . . felt like my old self. The self before I came here."

Eldest fish moves his fins and glides to the top of the water, opening his mouth wide to gulp air, and then lowering again to Ernest's level. A trail of small bubbles floats above him. "Then perhaps you are becoming human again."

"But—"

At this, the eldest fish darts away and joins the others who are now feeding on pellets and scraps that have dripped down below the surface.

Becoming human again. Ernest's gills flood and he nearly chokes, feeling a strangling sensation. If only he could be human again. Ernest feels he may burst at the thought of it.

CHAPTER SIXTEEN

THE FLOOD
Charleston, July

John

His mind is swimming, and though he fights it, a torrent of images washes over him like the Great Flood—John Porter is remembering the first man he ever watched die.

The man was lying on his back with his hand lifted way up over his head like he'd been trying to reach for something—like whatever it was might save his life—but he couldn't reach it. It was a picture of his family, pretty woman, couple kids. Before the man could grab it, his eyes closed. His hand loosened. The blood kept trickling out of his chest and onto the floor of his hut. John will never forget that, how the blood wouldn't stop. Never forget this man, how he'd never see his family again.

John Porter was twenty-two in Vietnam. Had only been there ten days before he went out on a search-and-destroy mission into this village near the DMZ. Charlie'd just been through there. What he left behind was so ugly, words can't describe. The horror nearly blinded him.

John had seen one beautiful thing in that hamlet though, a young woman with a face shaped like a heart and black eyes that were cavernous and betrayed her despair. He'd always remember that face. She was rocked back on her rear, hugging her knees in the corner, a bamboo rice steamer on its side next to her, and white rice, still moist, fanned out on the floor just inches away from the blood of her mother and father.

John looked at her and felt sick to his stomach. His buddy Ernest melted into tears for an instant and then sucked it back up. John approached the woman carefully, summoning a rare gentle spirit. Then he lifted the woman and cradled her like a child. She let him do this. She put her head on his shoulder and wailed with no sound. It was a deafening silence—one that still haunts him.

A FEW YEARS later, back in the States, John had remembered the face of that Vietnamese woman when he saw something else beautiful, his little Katie-bug coming to life. She stretched her arms when she entered this world. She was wrinkly, purple, the most gorgeous thing he had ever seen. *My Purple Heart*, he'd called her.

John was afraid to touch his own child. Afraid he'd hurt her or break her, do some permanent damage. And he told his wife Betty Jo this, but she made him hold her in his arms just the same, and a smile came over his face, a smile he had no control over. That's what Katherine Ann did—made him lose control in a good way. Not the bad kind of losing control where he was leading his men into the trenches and a third of them, he knew, weren't going to see the light of day, weren't going to make it home to their pregnant wives, weren't going to spend Christmas with parents and in-laws. No. Holding his baby in his arms was like letting go of all that for just a minute.

The beauty in this world outweighs the ugly. The problem is beauty goes dull like a diamond. You've got to buff it in order to see the true color, see the deep shine. Ugly? Ugly doesn't take much work. It just is. And it follows you around like a bad odor, like the stench of a stink bomb that you set off when you were seven years old and you told your mother, "It wasn't me." But she knew you were lying, so she whooped your hide with your father's belt while he watched and laughed. It's that stink that follows John Porter to this day. Follows him forever.

That six-pound-seven-ounce creature was the most powerful force John had ever come up against—mother, father, war, nothing. He clung to her, hoping she could stomach the stench that surrounded him. But the years have put distance between them, and he feels he barely knows her. That baby who came into this world to save his soul? She's too far gone. She can't save him anymore.

He looks at her there, his baby all grown up. She's still beautiful. The Water Lilies don't let John in that pool anymore, but he sits here in his big house just the same, holding a beer, peeking out the windows at them splashing around in the water. Looks silly if you ask him—bunch of old women. But what does he know? He's just a crotchety old man. Turned sixty this year. Sixty. *Hard to believe*, he thinks, running his finger along the woodwork of the window. He doesn't feel sixty. Heck, doesn't feel fifty. And the war? Still feels fresh like mud on his government-issued boots after a downpour. Fresh like the faces of just yesterday burned behind his eyes.

He remembers his buddy now—the last man he ever watched dying. He had no idea who was standing right behind him. He hopes to God he never felt the knife. *Oh, Ernest.* John's so sorry it had to happen that way. Just the thought of it makes him sick to his stomach, even after all this time.

John turns from the sunlight and squeezes his lids shut, then moves to the granite and glass-laden bar in search of a much stiffer drink.

CHAPTER SEVENTEEN

THE PHANTOM

Katherine Ann

Men. Boys. I've lost it. Completely. My throat is still sore from screaming at my sons. They've been at each other all afternoon, picking, whining, fighting. Maybe it has something to do with the heat. I can't take it anymore! I think I'm going to lose my mind. I've tried to separate them a million times. We've had lunch. We've played outside, been to the playground. I've tried to appease them, discipline them, read books to them, but they just keep nagging, crying, hitting . . .

I think I'm going to blow from the pressure. My head is splitting. When I yelled, it was if someone else had taken over. Someone else's voice. Someone I have no control over. My yelling is escalating. Deeper rage. Capital *R* rage. I cannot imagine where this has come from. I've always been a single child. No fighting with siblings. Nothing.

I quit my job, my *career* to do this—to stay home so I could be here for the kids—and this is the best I can do? I am a complete failure at mothering. I am a complete and utter *failure*.

My mother never raised her voice to me. Never. So what the

heck am I doing wrong? Why can't I handle this? What in the world is wrong with me?

My doctor said nothing was wrong with my heart at all, but now I'm starting to wonder. Maybe it's growing cold and hard. Insensitive.

I count to ten, wipe my tears, and open the door again, seeing them petrified and crying before me. I go to Tradd first. "Listen, I'm sorry I yelled, honey, but y'all are driving Mommy crazy. Do you understand? You stay over here and don't play with your brother for a while, okay?" He nods yes. I wonder if he really means it this time. I tell Cooper the same thing. "Stay away from your brother for a while, all right? I mean it. I love you." He sniffles and hugs me as if I'm going somewhere far away.

I give a tiny, exhausted smile before I go in my room and shut the door—quietly this time. Then I sit in my rocking chair, stunned from the anger. Stunned from the silence. They're quiet now. Maybe my screaming has scared the kids into behaving finally. I know it's scared me. In fact, I've never been so freaking terrified in all my life.

Then it dawns on me, almost like peace or acceptance. No. More like anger. I bet Daddy has something to do with my decline. I think back on the Memorial Day dinner and the anniversary dinner and all the other family events over the years. There is no doubt in my mind. I would bet my left leg my crazy father is a direct cause of my failing health and parental skills.

I rock and rock until my breathing has settled down. Until my stomach has stopped hurting. Until I hear the sounds of little boy laughter coming from the other room and all is normal again.

Then I stand up, convinced it's time to intervene in Daddy's life. The only question is *how*.

My fingertips graze the cool bottom of the pool as I try to stay inverted, my feet straight up in the air, my lips shut tight. I open my eyes and see the swirly white figures of Mama and Hilda, of course clutching her noodle, and Connie's large bosoms suspended, sans gravity, in water. We're all kicking and holding our breath except for Tillie, who walks around to each of us, straightening our legs or moving them for us.

In the still of the water I close my eyes and remember my voice as I yelled at my boys yesterday. Then I hear swishing noises and open my eyes to see Tillie's pasty sticks walk by to attend to Connie. I can't wait for her any longer—I think my chest might burst. I pop up like a bullet.

"Huuu-uhhhh," I gasp, hunched over, trying to catch my breath.

"You all right?" Tillie asks.

"Uh-huh. Just needed some air." Or rather, felt like I was suffocating. Like I was dying. Like I might implode with all that water closing in on me, my ears, my nose. *Mind over matter, Katie-bug. Get a hold of yourself. That was yesterday. Today's a new day.* I take another slow deep breath and work on relaxing.

The other ladies right themselves, and Mama slicks her hair back behind her ears, turning around to wipe her nose. Today is Wednesday, and for the past hour we've been practicing for the big event. Under Tillie's tutelage, we've learned how to do scissors with our legs in the air, how to dive from opposite ends of the pool without hitting one another (which took many tries, curses, and mangled limbs), and how to link arms and flutter Rockette-style.

"Y'all ready to call it a day?" Mama asks, stepping out of the pool to make her point.

"Reckon so," says Connie, leaning her folded arms on the edge of the pool. "Quite a workout today."

"You done good, girls," says Tillie, wrapping a fluffy white towel around her shoulders like a queen. "You make me proud."

I ascend the steps, feeling the water drip off of me, and move to a chaise where my towel awaits. When I bend to pick it up, I see something out of the corner of my eye. I stare up at the house and behind the glare of the sunlight, see my father moving away from the window.

"Is Daddy home?" I ask Mama.

"No," she says. "Left hours ago."

"Huh."

"Why?"

"Oh. No reason. Just wondering."

I wrap my towel around my waist and change my clothes in the pool house. While Hilda is showering and Connie, Tillie, and Mama are discussing the merits of a well-seasoned skillet, I slip away and head for the house.

"Daddy?" I call, pulling the sliding glass door shut behind me. The house is dramatically cooler than the outdoors, and I shiver. "Daddy, you home?"

I don't hear anything, so I go to look for his truck in the garage. It's not there.

That's strange. I could have sworn I saw Daddy in here. I walk to the kitchen and fill up a glass with water and ice from the refrigerator door and take a sip, then turn back to head for the pool house. As I walk past the window where I thought I saw Daddy, I stop. A beer can is resting on the bar counter. I pick it up and feel the cool wet condensation on the outside. I swirl it in my hand and feel the weight of it. Daddy *was* here. And in all my life, I can't remember my father not finishing a beer. In his book, it's something of a cardinal sin to waste the stuff.

I look at the clock, 10:39. My father was not at work, but

here, drinking alcohol—before noon. I pour the beer down the sink and flush it with the water and ice from my glass. Then I flood the drain to eliminate any smell of Daddy's being at home. I don't want to cause trouble for him with Mama. A man not working is a man in her hair. And a man drinking before noon is . . .

My stomach knots as I head for the door and wave to Tillie, Connie, and Hilda, who are making their way around the house. When Mama walks in the door, I smile at her, concealing my concern, and hand her a fresh glass of ice water.

"I'm exhausted," I say. "I'll see you in the morning?" I hope I look and sound as if nothing is strange.

"See you then," she says. "Give the boys a hug for me."

As I step into the warm air, I picture Daddy's ghostly figure in the window, see the beer can he didn't finish, remember him crying in the restaurant awhile ago. Something is not right. Good heavens, what's wrong with him? It's the war, I'm sure of it. It's all coming back for him.

Well, I'll be darned if I let him go through this alone. His mental health is my mental health! All my anger, anxiety, and illnesses, real or conjured, I can see so clearly now. If I don't help Daddy deal with his past, my future and the future of my children look bleaker and more morose every day.

I clutch my stomach which has completely tied itself in a bow, and I close my eyes to wish away an ulcer. It's surely pitting its way through my insides this very minute.

I've got to find a way to make Daddy well—and me—before it's too late.

CHAPTER EIGHTEEN

The Shrine
Georgetown

Lisa

My mother is still in bed. This is highly unusual, even in her recluse state. I stand outside her bedroom door and listen for sounds of life. After a minute, I turn the knob slowly and see Ma still bundled, her sheet and blanket tucked tightly around her shoulders and covering half of her face. She hasn't said it, but in her own way, she's been complaining of being cold at night. The thermostat will inch its way up to where I'm nearly roasting. I can't see how she could be cold—it's July here in the South.

I move closer to her and check to see if her covers are moving up and down with her breathing, and they are. I inhale slowly and walk toward the window where the light is coming through little slats in the blinds, giving a striated effect to my mother's ancestral shrine.

There is a long stick of incense, extinguished, lying in a red tray. The faint smell of it lingers. There are candles, short and colored, in a neat pattern on her dresser, surrounding two picture frames in red and green bamboo. I reach out and touch the one of Uncle. He is smiling again, the lines around his cheeks form a caricature, a happy cartoon of his younger self. Uncle was a good man. He shunned Ma's sternness and chose to be the voice of optimism and contentment in our home.

Though my mother spoke of Vietnam with heartsickness, remaining in mourning for all that she had lost—the village, her family, her old way of life—Uncle said not a word of the old days. He said nothing of the war, nothing of what he had seen or done as a soldier. Nothing of the voyage to America. It was as if when Uncle's feet hit American soil, he buried his past and put on a face of joviality. Whether this was out of relief from being removed from danger or whether it was a mask to cover the deep-seated pain within, I do not know. All I know is that I loved Uncle. He was the only father I've ever known. And Ma loved him. He was to her a brother, a parent, and a husband. And when he died, he took with him the happiness with which he filled this house.

I caress his face.

I miss you, Uncle. Wherever you are, please bring Ma back to me. I feel her slipping further away. If she leaves me too, I will be all alone.

The Vietnamese believe that the spirit goes on to live after death in another world, somewhat parallel to ours. To prepare loved ones who have passed to that world, miniatures of all that they need are given to them at the altar—furniture, food, clothing, even paper money burned for their prosperity. Ancestor veneration is of the utmost importance as departed loved ones have much to do with the lives of the living. If an ancestor is unhappy or dishonored, it may bring bad luck on the living. On the other hand, if the ancestor is appeased, good fortune flows to the ones who remain on this earth.

Ma has many rituals for honoring our ancestors. If the house were burning and she could only save one thing, it would be this ancestor altar in front of me. Not a day goes by without a candle being lit for someone she's lost. Sometimes flowers are stuck in a vase. On important days, death anniversaries, or festivals, food and drink are set out for our ancestors' spirits to feast upon.

At the front of the altar on a crocheted doily, there is a small wooden box that contains a torn black-and-white photo of my grandmother and grandfather. It was carefully taped back together and placed in a place of prominence. Other than this one and Uncle's, Ma has no other photos of our Vietnamese family. No photos survived the destroying of the village, yet there's a candle for each sister, brother, nephew, niece, and grandparent. I've watched Ma in her rituals and as a child would participate in them, saying prayers as she lit the candles for each. There would be silent weeping. Lips would move with murmured pleading.

My hand strays to the other photograph framed by red bamboo and glass. I pick it up and study the lines in his face, his masculine nose. I study his eyes, amplified and staring back at me through round coke-bottle lenses. He is wearing an American uniform. He is smiling with one foot propped up on a sandbag wall, his hand grasping a beer can. Behind him, soldiers laugh and joke, and to his side, a blurry soldier runs into the frame just as the camera snaps.

I pull the photo to my chest and hug it. I know who this is. Growing up, my mother had me honor him each night.

"Your father would have loved you," she would tell me. "Had death not stolen him from me, he would have returned. We would have been together as a family."

For some people, life is clouded with the what-ifs of what can never happen. My mother makes me sad in this way. Her glass is always half-empty. It is the emptiness on which she chooses to dwell. Never having been a real family. Never again able to watch the seasons turn in Vietnam. But for me, it has always been hard to mourn the man in this photo. Never having known him. Never having called him Father. But the little girl in me always wondered. Not knowing how he died, I imagined it was during an act of heroism, covering his buddies as he single-handedly fought off a Viet Cong ambush, or—

In a way, perhaps I do mourn. He is half of me after all, half of my blood. With Uncle gone and Ma disappearing, my body now aches for the father I will never have the chance to know.

I put the picture back in place and lean down to kiss my mother's forehead. "I'm leaving now, Ma," I whisper. "Going to work. Fresh rice cakes are in the kitchen."

Ma opens her eye and catches my face, and I'm not sure if I'm imagining it or not, but I choose to believe there's a smile beneath the sheet and blanket that mask her.

CHAPTER NINETEEN

~~~~~~~~

THE TICKETS
Charleston

Katherine Ann

Just over the Charleston Ravenel Bridge in Mount Pleasant is a lush area of trees and luxury condominiums and a place along the waterfront called Patriots Point. Docked in the waterway is an enormous aircraft carrier, the USS *Yorktown*, which served its time in both World War II and Vietnam. Tomorrow night, something special is happening on top of the *Yorktown*. Come hell or high water, Daddy and I are going to be there.

"You see this?" I ask a pre-showered RC, whose hair is sticking straight up in the back, reminiscent of Alfalfa. The kids are still asleep. Normally, RC gets up an hour before I do and scours the newspaper, drinking his milky-brown coffee in peace before he heads off to work at the gym. But not this morning. I couldn't sleep. And now I know why. I plop a folded local section of the *Post and Courier* on top of his national news and wait for his reaction while crickets chirp outside in the blue dawn.

"Huh," he says and shoves it off toward me. His eyes rest on the news again.

"Did you read it?" I ask. "They're having a gala on the *Yorktown* tomorrow night. See?" I point to the headline. "It's for the Medal of Honor recipients, honey. Medal of Honor . . . war heroes . . . Vietnam . . ."

He stares at me blankly.

"And?"

"And . . . I want to go. With Daddy."

RC scrunches his brow and pulls the paper to him again, studying it this time. He sits back and his eyebrows rise. I detect a slight shaking of his head.

"First off, your dad isn't a war hero, is he? He's not one of those award winners, right? And second, are you serious? Did you see how much tickets are?"

I'm steeling myself now. "I did see. But I think this would be good for Daddy. He's been going through something lately. You've seen him. Remember the restaurant? He's like, cracking. He's got to open up somehow. Don't you think this would be good for him?"

"Your father has been cracking ever since I met him. And the tickets are three hundred and fifty dollars, Katie! Absolutely not. We do not have that kind of money to spare these days. Do we? I mean, come on. The house, preschool . . . your doctor visits alone are going to kill us."

I raise an eyebrow.

"I mean, not that your health isn't worth it . . . it is."

I grit my teeth. It is a lot of money. I feel my bottom lip puckering, and I think I might cry. Here it was, the perfect way to help Daddy and it's out of my reach. What was I thinking anyway? The party's tomorrow. It's so last minute. It's seven hundred dollars!

I turn and walk away from RC, pouting—I know he's right. But I cannot help imagining my father, dressed in a suit, laughing and backslapping men with whom he can actually connect, and me, watching him proudly, being the one to have helped him finally deal with his scars. Daddy's never attended a veteran's reunion, never a memorial parade, nothing. Well, what's not to be is not to be.

AFTER ONLY TWO bouts of spilt milk and one crying fit, mine, I send the boys off to preschool in RC's truck. Then I breathe in peace to calm my nerves and slip on some flip-flops to head over to Mama's for swimming with the Water Lilies. I don't even feel like it. I am completely distracted.

"Hey, Katie-bug."

"Mornin', Katie-bug."

"Hey," I murmur. Not meaning to, I sigh loudly, only realizing it after the fact.

"Something wrong?" Connie asks me, rubbing sunscreen onto her face and neck. She takes her lubed hand and smacks a mosquito on her thigh, then scrapes it on the concrete, disgusted.

"Nothing's wrong. Just one of those days, you know?"

"Feelin' blue for no reason? Hormones," says Tillie. "Why, I can remember when I had me some o' them too." She giggles, and Connie grins at her, motioning for her to turn around so she can lotion her back.

"You are too much, Miss Tillie," she says. "Always telling it like it is."

"That's the only way to be," says Tillie.

"Ain't that right."

We slip into the water, Hilda, Connie, Tillie, and me, and then Mama strolls out from the house like Barbie wearing a white cover-up unbuttoned and blowing in the breeze and a floral suit that amplifies her perky bosoms. Her hat today has a wide floral ribbon in greens and purples to match her suit. She could top a cake.

Me, I'm un-showered and still bloated. I realize I forgot to take my Zantac this morning. Watching Mama makes me feel like a slug.

We do some water aerobics to the sounds of Art Garfunkel, then James Taylor, and my mood grows more somber even though I've got "Carolina In My Mind." When it's time for free swim, I breaststroke slowly back and forth, back and forth, feeling the pull on my inner thighs and the sun on my forehead.

". . . awfully quiet," I hear Mama say from the other end of the pool.

"Just her time of the month," says Hilda.

"Probably worried about that mammogram coming up," says Connie. "It's tomorrow, right?"

When I step out of the cool water, my body gains a hundred pounds and I slop back to the pool house to change. I peel off my wet suit, dry my body, and dress again. I am slipping my flip-flops back on when I notice a red light on my cell phone. I lift it to my ear and when I hear his voice, a sensation sweeps over me, much like tugging, from my feet to the hairs on top of my head.

"Hey, it's me." RC clears his throat. "Listen, I'm sorry about this morning. I've just been working so hard, covering everybody's shifts. It's starting to wear on me. But, I was thinking. I think you should go to that *Yorktown* thing tomorrow. With your dad, you know. It's just money, not like we have any but . . . yeah, it's probably worth it. Just be prepared to eat Hamburger Helper for a month. Anyway, love you."

Shame pricks at my chest as I think back on all those nasty

things I called RC in my head. Well, I take them all back now. He's a good provider. He's a good father and a good husband. I, Katherine Ann Porter Banks, have married the most wonderful man on earth. My spirit lifts to somewhere around my ears, and I feel so much better physically, it's as if I've been chest-paddled back to life.

Now, do I tell Daddy or surprise him? No matter. I've got to hurry! I have to pick up the tickets before I get the boys from school. And oh, what to wear!

My husband. What a gem of a man. He's quiet, for the most part, and unobtrusive, the opposite of Daddy, really. And he puts up with me. Loves me even, God knows why. My stomach flutters at the thought of thanking RC in person. He's finally on board with my Daddy theory. Now let's just hope I'm right . . . for all of our sakes.

CHAPTER TWENTY

THE RESTAURANT
Georgetown

Lisa

I work in the restaurant my family has owned for more than thirty years, Le's Kitchen. Being that we're in the Deep South and nestled in the middle of mills—steel, paper, and textile—Ma and Uncle decided the best thing to offer would be fried foods. Give them what they want. We make the best fried flounder this side of the Georgetown Bridge. We also serve french fries, hushpuppies, fried shrimp, chicken fried steak, and country fried chicken. All fresh. You name it, we fry it.

I'm the manager now, the head chef, the bookkeeper, and basically the only one who gives a hoot about how things are actually run around here. When Uncle got sick, Ma took to staying home to care for him. It all started with his leg. Uncle woke up one day and it had gone lame. He couldn't walk, couldn't get around. The doctor said it was all in his head, that somehow his stress or anxiety had caused it. Uncle couldn't understand what kind of anxiety he was talking about. "The restaurant isn't stressful, or no more so than it's always been," he told the doctor. "I'm as happy as ever."

But the next week he was having chest pains, and he died instantly when a clot from his leg struck his heart.

"Hello, Donnie," I say. Donnie's a regular here. Bushy gray eyebrows, lines around his eyes and always a NASCAR cap pushed forward and straight up on his head. He takes it off when he eats though. He has manners. He's been working at the steel mill for twenty years and has lunch here every day before his shift starts. I always say a secret prayer over Donnie and each and every mill worker who walks in the door. I've seen the smoke billowing up from the mills like dragon's breath. I pray for the men who walk directly into the dragon's belly that they'll come back out for one more day.

If the dragon doesn't kill them, this fried food surely will.

I send Charlene, our youngest waitress, just seventeen, over to Donnie with his fish and chips platter, extra biscuit and sweet tea, just like every day. He nods at her, slathers on some tartar sauce and commences to eating, but not before he closes his eyes and murmurs something. Donnie is a praying man. Most men around these parts are. When Ma was working here, she'd squat down in the kitchen in the corner and shell butter beans or peel shrimp with a bucket between her knees, oblivious to the Holy Spirit at work in the other room. The customers would always peek over the counter and tip their hats, saying, "Hey there, Ms. Le. Howdy-do today." And she'd smile, nod, and say, "Just fine. Nice day."

I miss Ma being in this kitchen with me. The corner where she used to squat only has her bucket now. I hate to move it, in case she decides to join me again.

"Two number threes and a five, extra crispy," Charlene trills, sliding her orders on the steel counter for me to see and wiping her hands on her green apron. She's working out pretty well. Waitresses come and go, you know. We had one waitress, Maggie, who stayed with us for nearly twelve years until she succumbed to cancer. Ma loved Maggie, though she was a rough, manly woman who smacked gum, called all the customers "hon," and tried to mama me when Ma wasn't around. It wasn't until I was about twenty-one that I realized what Maggie meant to this place and what this restaurant meant to her. I was sad like everybody else when she passed away, but also just a bit relieved. I know it's selfish, but when Maggie left the restaurant, I was finally allowed to start rising in the ranks. I moved from bussing tables at night and in the summers to actually waiting tables and talking with customers.

"We sure miss Maggie," they'd tell me. And I'd nod and put my biggest frown on and say, "Oh, I do too. Well, you have me now," as if I were some consolation prize. "I'll do the best I can. Now what can I get you, sugar?" The customers liked that answer, and after a while, Maggie's name was rarely mentioned except on the occasion a customer would grab my elbow, lean me down to his ear, and whisper, "God rest her soul, Maggie never gave me my food without a piece of bad advice I didn't ask for." Or, "Don't ever repeat this, Miss Lisa, but you're so dad-gum fast, you're like two Maggies rolled up together."

I face the hot fryer and set two battered flounder fillets into the basket and lower it. The cricks and crackles of the oil devouring the fish soothe my ears. I scoop some hush-puppy batter into another vat of oil and watch each spoonful plop and fizzle, plop and fizzle in neat, round drops. I get the same size every time and the same golden brown result. I should, I've been doing this for almost thirteen years now. The only thing that can screw up a hush puppy is old oil and batter that's too runny or too thick. But I run this place like clockwork. Nothing varies. It's always the same. The food's the same, the customers are the same, and the smell of fried food is always the same, clinging to my chef's clothes each night.

As I set the browned, steaming flounder fillets on two white oval plates and garnish with fresh cut fries and sprigs of parsley, I fight the urge to spoon *Nuoc Cham* dipping sauce around the fish. As if I had any in here. My mouth waters at the prospect, but I shove the thought away. These folks would never be able to stomach Vietnamese food. Their tastes are too bland. Their tongues would catch fire. They'd never be able to appreciate the salty, spicy goodness of a bowl of *bun thang*, now would they?

As I pan fry a flattened chicken breast in butter, I look down at my hand and remember my mother cooking for me when I was a child. When Ma would cook Vietnamese food for Uncle and me at home, she would hum and sing traditional songs, but here, cooking Southern food in this kitchen, I never once heard Ma breathe a note of music.

"Order's up," I say, just loud enough for Charlene, but not too loud for the customers to hear over their clinking cups and silverware. Charlene is a single mother with a one-year-old at home who stays with his grandmother. She quit high school when she found out she was pregnant and lived with this young man for a few months until he ran off. He never even met his child. The grandmother brings the baby in about once a week and everybody ogles over him. I feel for that baby. Charles is his name, though they call him Charlie. As long as Charlie is around, Charlene will have a job here at Le's Kitchen.

I look up when the bell on the door jingles. As Mayor Cummings and his good ole boys press in through the front door saying their howdys, I'm already reaching into the cooler for shrimp, flounder filets, and the mayor's favorite, chicken fried steak.

Another day and dollar at Le's Kitchen, so comfortable, so uneventful, I hardly have to think anymore.

CHAPTER TWENTY-ONE

THE MOON
Marble Mountain, Vietnam

Ernest

When the full moon rises over Marble Mountain, Ernest Marquette stares through a glaze of water, watching it shimmy as if it were a living, breathing being. His life as a fish is this way, giving a rippling effect to everything on the outside, the real world. To the extent that Ernest peers into that world, the effect is nauseating, much like the roller coaster at the county fair that would come once a year to his little town in Georgia.

Ernest longs to touch the moon.

He uses his fins to back up, pressing against the edge of the pond, taking note of all the other fishes' stillness. Then he swims with all his might and breaks the surface of the water. In that split second of being airborne, Ernest sees the moon clearly. It doesn't move. He is the one moving now much like the earth orbiting the sun. As Ernest descends into the pool, he sees to his left the unmistakable figure of Brother Chong.

The water slips out in circles above him, and Ernest darts beneath the green shade of a large lotus leaf. After a few moments, a man's hand drops below the surface. The fingers are still and nearly glowing because of the lunar light.

Just the slightest movement then, an involuntary twitching, Brother Chong appears to be testing the water.

Curious and safely on the other side of the pond, Ernest rises to the air and opens his mouth wide. He watches Brother Chong, and Brother Chong, in turn, watches Ernest. Finally, with a sigh, the dripping hand is withdrawn and fingers wiped lethargically upon his robe.

Ernest submerges again and waits for Brother Chong to leave, yet he doesn't. Through the water he sees the rippling man bow his head, eyes closed, and then do something Ernest hasn't seen for thirty-eight years: Brother Chong moves his right hand from his forehead to his sternum, then to each side of his chest. The sign of the cross? By a Buddhist monk? Surely not. Mystified, Ernest slowly ascends so that the top halves of his eyeballs are exposed above water, and as he catches the man standing and turning away, he could swear he hears a hushed, "Amen."

ERNEST'S MIND ECHOES with the symphony of amens he used to hear around the supper table. After the plates had been set and the food prepared and Mama and Daddy at their respective heads of the table, the amens would ring out, creating a Pavlov-like effect. Ernest's mouth would water with the closing of prayer. His mother's head would remain bowed long after the forks were picked up and stabbing things. In fact, Ernest's mother was usually the last to move after everyone else had upped and gone about their way.

Growing up in the little town of Norwood, Georgia, Ernest's mother was the fat lady. You know the real fat lady who sits in the general store and greets you? Everybody loved Ernest's mama. That wasn't the problem. The problem was that she couldn't move. She couldn't go anywhere, and that just made Ernest sad, how she'd sit there, happy to see Ernest and the kids when they'd ride in on their bicycles, and later, happy to see them when they were teenagers coming in for a Saturday night soda. There she was, still sitting in that chair with a smile on her face, not seeing anything of life other than the back of the cash register—and seemingly happy to do so. Ernest would look at his mother secretly, guiltily, and swear he'd never be bound to a chair like Mama, never be bound to a store like Mama, never be bound to a town like Mama. It's one of the reasons he joined the army and volunteered to go to Vietnam. It was a way to see the world. Well, such are the silly dreams of children. Life—and afterlife—can have a binding effect if you happen to wind up stuck in the wrong places.

Ernest longs to know how his mother is doing. Aches almost. Is she living? Did she die? He'd give anything to be able to wrap his arms around her warm molten body and dig his face into her side as he once did. And what about his father, his brothers? The not knowing, he determines, is the worst part of it all. *If there is such a thing as hell,* Ernest thinks, *it's being cut off completely from everything and everyone you love. This must be hell,* he figures.

Ernest glides through the water now to the coin he threw in thirty-eight years ago and hovers over it, hoping to be transported to Georgia or back to John Porter's life for an instant, anywhere but here. He hovers and he waits. But nothing happens. Nothing. He goes nowhere. Then resembling something akin to sleep, with his eyes wide open, Ernest stills his earthly body and feels hope sifting away from his scales like falling sediment.

The moon continues to glare over Vietnam, completely out of his reach.

CHAPTER TWENTY-TWO

THE PENDULUM
Charleston

Katherine Ann

"Why the heck'd you pay that kind of money?"

"I thought you'd like to go," I say, my spirit retreating into its shell. Daddy stuffs some large tools in the back of his truck and closes the hatchback, using all his muscle.

"Yeah, but three hundred and fifty dollars?" Daddy seems to let the weight of the figure settle into his brain, and he looks at me now, leaning against the truck, as if he's only just realized the sacrifice of it. His eyes go moist and he turns away, jiggling the keys in his pocket. "Well . . . what are we going to do? Where is it again? The *Yorktown*? What about your mother? She going too?"

"I thought it could be just the two of us . . . what with the tickets being so much and all. Unless . . . you want to take Mama instead, she can have my ticket—"

"No." He reaches over and kisses me gruffly on the cheek, his stubble chafing me. His voice wavers when he says, "I'll see you tonight then. Your mother's going to . . . Shoot, don't know how I'm going to do this. What the heck'd you get me into?"

"You can do it," I tell him, hope rising again, a pendulum on the upswing. "I'll be there. It'll be fun."

LET ME TELL you how much fun it is to get a mammogram. Well, it's not exactly fun, but it's not too bad either. After leaving Daddy, I drive to the hospital. I check in at the front desk, walk into a little dressing room, and pull the curtain closed behind me. There's a hook on the wall for my shirt and bra and a lovely printed gown that slips on and ties in the front. I feel so chic. I can hear other ladies in similar dressing rooms doing the same. I open up a little wet nap and clean off any residue of deodorant so it won't interfere with my mammogram results. I don't feel like having to come in and do this again anytime soon.

A young, blonde lady takes me to a clinical room with "the machine" up against one wall. She explains the procedure and is very good at what she does because she has me so at ease I'm almost looking forward to it.

"Now this might be a little uncomfortable so you just tell me if it starts to hurt." She pops these little round stickers on my nipples and guides me sideways into the machine. Next, I'm holding my arm perfectly still and my left breast is being squeezed from top to bottom in ways I never knew possible. "That's good," I say, when I'm sure any more pressure will cause it to pop.

I stare straight ahead and the woman leaves my side and goes behind me to snap the X-ray. It's quick and relatively painless. Then we do the other breast, same procedure, and I tell her when to stop pressing.

And voilà, it's over. Just like that. What I absolutely love about the whole affair is that the results will come back immediately. "I'm going to have these looked at by the radiologist," the lady says, "and if she wants more done, we'll go ahead and do them now. Okay? You will leave today knowing your results. Sound good?"

"Are you kidding me? Results from a doctor in the same day? This is great!" I say, a little too enthusiastically.

When the girl leaves, I'm left reading a *People* magazine and wondering about my fate. I stare at the beautiful faces of movie stars and singers and . . . it's all in the face, I realize. If the technician comes back in the room with a concerned look on her face, my whole life will change instantaneously. There will be surgery and chemotherapy and sick days and loss of hair and . . . oh, why haven't I gotten a hold of my temper? *It's the anger, the frustration, the daily yelling at the kids, Katie-bug! Why can't you calm down? Your anger is only hurting yourself and the ones you love the most in this world!*

I'm panting now, clutching my chest, as I remember the gala tonight. I'm taking Daddy with me, like it or not, and forcing him to be a man and face his past. He has skirted this issue long enough. Enough is enough, I say! His unpredictable temper has seeped under my skin like osmosis, and now I'm this twisted, neurotic woman who's getting ready to learn her sad fate. I have breast cancer; I just know it! My children will be motherless!

I cannot breathe. Breathe! I need some air. I jump up and grab the door handle, but as I turn it to escape, the perky young lady steps back in the room with a smile on her face. A smile.

"The radiologist says everything looks good. There's nothing to worry about."

"Whew!" I exclaim, nearly bursting into fits of laughter, relief.

"She *would* like me to do just one more on your left breast. Just to get a better look. This is very normal." She smiles to show me how normal it is. "Just move right over here, and we'll take this one last picture."

Are you kidding?

I thought we took this picture already, right? The nipple, the squeezing, the . . . oh, no, I think my heart has stopped. I'm melting, meeeeelting! My life is over. *Oh God, please make this go away. Please?*

The next few minutes slosh by me while my head and hope spiral downward to the floor.

Daddy. What about Daddy? This was going to be his night. This is his day. Not mine. No matter what the results, I will put on my poker face now, and when the time comes I'll tell everyone I'm dying. But not tonight. I, Katherine Ann Porter Banks, will save my misery for another day. I am brave. I'm so small in the big scheme of things. Life will go on without me.

The door opens slowly and my magazine falls to the floor with a flutter. I look up, studying the face of the woman coming in and . . . and . . .

"Everything looks great, Mrs. Banks. You're free to go. Just be sure to have another one before you turn forty-five. That's what we recommend to everyone."

Really?

"You mean I'm fine? All clear? No problems at all? But what about that pain I've been having? Nothing there?"

"Not a thing. You look fine. It could just be in your head. Stress can do that."

Hmmm. That's exactly what my general practitioner said. It's official then. I'm not dying, just suffering an intense case of hypochondria brought on by acute anxiety. Imagine it sitting latent for years.

"Have a good day now," she says before leaving.

"You too," I mutter, stunned. This Medal of Honor gala could not be coming at a better time, I think. I gather up my hospital gown and rush to get dressed. I'm eager to begin my, er, Daddy's treatment.

CHAPTER TWENTY-THREE

The Ship

Mount Pleasant, South Carolina

Katherine Ann

My father is dressed in a dark gray suit with a pale blue shirt and solemn gray tie. The moon is bright, illuminating the sensual lines of his Jaguar behind him.

"Wow, you look nice," he says, eyes averting. It's as if we are on our first date. In a way, we are.

I'm wearing a crème-colored flowing chiffon dress that shapes my thankfully healthy bust but nothing else. A matching scarf is wrapped loosely around my shoulders. My shoes are the same I wore for my wedding five years ago; I haven't pulled them out since.

"Have fun," says RC, kissing me lightly on the lips. "Have her back before midnight now," he jokes to my father. "She turns into a pumpkin, you know." Bullfrogs laugh from a neighbor's garden.

"Aye, aye, Cap'n," Daddy says.

After removing a clinging Tradd and Cooper from my legs, RC leans down with them. They all wave at me, a tall ship going on her maiden voyage. I smile and wave back. "Be good for

Daddy," I say before I'm helped into the car and the door shuts. My father walks around to the driver's side, slips in, and takes the wheel. My heart is somewhere in the clouds.

Daddy doesn't say a word, but accelerates from zero to forty in a heartbeat. He's always liked going fast, fast enough to be scolded. I don't scold him now. I'm so proud of him for taking this huge step. Facing his demons.

"You ready for this?" I ask him, hoping, pulling out my compact to powder my nose again.

"S'pose we'll find out, won't we."

WE PULL UP to the flying flags and bright lights, and the parking lot threatens to swallow us. In the distance, the *Yorktown* glows in the navy-blue night, bedecked for the affair.

"You ever been here?" I ask Daddy as we roll around, trying to find the perfect parking spot.

"Never. Play golf at the Links all the time, but never been to the ship, no." I can tell he's excited now. "They gonna have an open bar, or what?"

"I think so."

"They better, for all that money," he says.

We sit for a second in silence after the car is shut off, watching the other couples stepping out and making their way to the landing. Most are in their fifties, sixties, and a few appear much older than that. I half expect my father to make some crack about this being a party for old farts, but he stays silent. I know he'd never dare tease about the people here. This event is sacred. I say a silent prayer that Daddy can get through this night with little or few tears.

"You got the tickets?" he asks.

"Got 'em right here."

"Well, let's go then."

DADDY AND I walk arm and arm down a long causeway leading to the USS *Yorktown*. What a magnificent sight. The wind off the water is whipping my chiffon layers around me and I feel other-worldly, like Nike or Helen of Troy. My father, the veteran, keeps hold of my arm with the same care he used walking me down the aisle. This walk is much longer than the one for my wedding, but perhaps there's just as much at stake.

We see patrons leaning over the side of the ship, watching the new guests, us, arrive. The warm salty air blows up my nose and I inhale it greedily, calming my nerves. My sprayed hair, short these days, has not moved a millimeter. Daddy's hair, buzzed to a quarter of an inch, shines silver in the moonlight.

High heels *clink-clank* all around me as we climb up the iron steps. We nod at nicely dressed people we do not know.

We follow the crowd onto the ship and into a large room below the carrier deck with a huge American flag on the wall and curtain partitions that give the austere room a cozier feel. In front of us a man in a wheelchair wears a blue ribbon and Medal of Honor around his neck. His wife in red holds on to the handles of his chair. Seeing a real-life hero catches me off guard somehow and my throat catches. I don't know what I was expecting, but I didn't think it would hit me so hard. I cannot imagine the effect it must be having on my father.

"Want a drink?" he says, clearing his throat when I turn to him. His eyes are darting and he acts as if he never even saw the wheel-chaired hero.

"Sure," I say. He leads the way through a small crowd of evening gowns, suits, and tuxedos to our oasis.

Daddy and I sip our drinks, mine, a white wine spritzer, and his, a Manhattan, in front of a partition, taking it all in. Though the patrons are festive, the steel walls of the aircraft carrier add to my sobriety, and I sip a little faster. To our right, two Medal of Honor recipients are sitting with a teenager and a woman, I imagine a grandson and a wife. They seem to all know each other and are chatting amiably. It's not every day, or ever, really, that one sees true greatness up close and in the flesh. My skin crawls. It's utterly humbling. I nudge my father to look at them as if they are on exhibit in a zoo, and he nods slightly. "Mm hmm."

His face is as gray as the steel rafters above us. I've never seen my father so serious or so quiet. Typically the life of the party, he's become immobilized, and all of a sudden panic nips at my insides. *What was I thinking, bringing him here? What have I done to Daddy?*

CHAPTER TWENTY-FOUR

The Photograph
Georgetown

Lisa

"Ma, *Tet Trung Thu* is coming up in the next few weeks. I thought we'd do it right this year, okay? I'll make *bahn Trung Thu* and we'll tell fairy tales and light star lanterns like we did when I was a child." I used to see so much joy in Ma's eyes during the Mid-Autumn Festival. It's one of those traditions that help take her back to her motherland. I hope to see the same joy on her face now.

In front of her, Dr. Phil berates a young man on the television. The young man takes it quietly, tearfully. Ma doesn't stir. I walk to her and lean down, putting my hand on her shoulder. I move closer to her ear. "Would you like that, Ma? I know Uncle's not here but . . . he would want us to do this. We can honor him and the others."

Ma sniffs and leans her head slightly toward mine, so I can feel the heat of her face, smell her clean hair. She reaches up and touches my hand. It's such a simple gesture, but for a woman whose muteness has become deafening, the feel of her fingers speaks volumes.

"I've got your bath started," I tell her. "Why don't you go on in and I'll finish the dishes." Ma hesitates, then leans forward, holds on to the arms of her chair and struggles up. I walk her to the bathroom and try to help her in, but she turns to me and brushes me away. Such a proud woman.

The door shuts and I stand there, listening to my mother's small movements behind it after the water stops roaring.

I grab the remote control and turn off the television, leaving static in the air. I get so tired of listening to the droning, the mindlessness of that contraption. Then I walk into Ma's room to pull out a clean pair of pajamas just as I do every night.

"Good night, Uncle," I say, before leaning down to pull the drawer open beneath the ancestral altar. I imagine his photo saying, "*Chuc chau,*" back at me as he used to say.

"I miss you."

From the bottom drawer, I pull out the soft worn gray cotton of Ma's favorite pajama bottoms and rub it against my face. I lay the pants neatly on the bed, straightening any wrinkles, just as Ma did for me all those years. Now it is my turn.

I tug on the metal handle of the top drawer, and it snags as it's been doing for the past couple months. I try to wriggle it gently side to side so that it will slide open, but to no avail. If Uncle were here he'd have this fixed in no time. He was our man around the house. He could fix anything, if not conventionally, at least with ingenuity. But he's not here, is he?

The left side of the drawer is stuck and the right side is jutting out like the tip of an iceberg. I push in on the right and pull on the left until the drawer makes a loud *pop!* and lands, corner down, on top of my foot as I'm knocked back to the floor.

The pain is immediate, and I ingest the curse words I want

to scream out. Eyes blurry, I reach down to see the damage I've done to my skin and bone.

That's when I see what I've really done.

The picture of my father has fallen and broken, along with two round candles. Large pieces of glass and wood litter the floor just inches from my bare feet.

My body grows still and quiet. What have I done? Part of me wants to cry, but I don't.

Ma is going to be utterly destroyed. This is the only picture of my father that we have.

I carefully pick up the back of the frame, the part with the little stand that keeps it propped upright, and breathe a sigh of relief. The photograph is still intact and virtually unharmed. Thank God for this miracle. My father's face smiles up at me, unmoved and unperturbed.

Squatting, I lose my balance and reach to the bed to keep from falling into the glass, but when I do, the photo slips off of the wood backing. I catch it before it touches the ground. Holding the photograph in my hand, it feels too thin. My father's image is just a slim piece of paper, not solid and heavy like the frame made it seem all these years. I feel the frailty of the photograph and it sends a flash of fear through me. Then I turn it over gently.

My heart stops altogether.

I am aware only of my foot throbbing faintly in the distance. The gears in my mind come to a grinding halt.

I have never known the true name of my father. Never asked, never been told, never had any inkling of it whatsoever. I even wondered if Ma knew his name. She only called him "your father" or "my American soldier." As to his actual name, I had no idea it was of the slightest importance.

Until now.

There before me, in faded black ink, is my father's name, handwritten on the back of my most cherished photograph. How have I never known? It's been there all along behind glass and frame, and I've known nothing.

In my stupor I don't hear my mother, who has finished her bath and stopped in her bedroom doorway to find me stooped and wallowing in a sea of shattered glass.

MY NERVES SCREAM and tendons stiffen at being caught in this act of secret discovery. Guilt pours over me as if I've stolen something from her.

"Ma! I'm so sorry! The drawer was stuck." I plead for forgiveness with my eyes. Ma remains perfectly still. I think she may be about to speak when she holds her hand up and exits the room. I don't move a muscle, and Ma returns with a plastic trash can and DustBuster. Hair wet and robed in white, she puts on her house slippers and makes her way to me slowly.

I am too afraid to say anything about what I've seen. Too afraid that what I've broken is much more than wood and glass and image.

We pick up shards of glass and bamboo and vacuum without saying a word between us. After I set the photograph up on top of the dresser again, I try to help Ma get into bed, but she'll have none of it. I leave her finally, my mother feverishly lighting candles and incense, trying to appease her ancestors and ward off the bad luck my clumsiness has surely invited into our lives.

LYING IN BED, I toss and turn, feeling something stirring inside, a tsunami swelling in the distance. My mind replays the image of my father's face and the words that have fallen like lead upon my heart.

I know my father's name now. Somehow there is magic in it. His name makes him more than just a flat image; it gives him dimension. It gives me dimension too, makes me slightly more whole. Doesn't it? Another piece of my pie pops into place. He is not just a phantom of my mythology. He was real. He had a name. I had a father. His name was John Porter.

My father's name was John Porter.

CHAPTER TWENTY-FIVE

The Veterans
Mount Pleasant

Katherine Ann

After an introduction by the Medal of Honor Museum director and a "thank you all for coming tonight," each of us, veterans and their wives and children, war heroes, museum patrons, the infirmed and the healthy, hold ourselves tall and put hands over hearts. I try to remember the words to "God Bless America" and catch my father singing softly on my left. His eyes are glassy until they brim over and quiet tears streak to his chest. I move a few inches closer and press my body against his to let him know that I am here and he is not alone. I am trembling now out of nervousness but the heat through his jacket warms me through.

The opening ceremony complete, we make our way up a dungeonlike narrow stairwell in the pit of the ship until we emerge spring flowers from soil into the cool breeze of the open flight deck. To the far left bombers and fighter planes obscure the dance floor and to our right open bars beckon. My father turns toward them and says, "You want another glass of wine?"

"Let's find our table first, okay?"

I snake around the white cloth-covered tables set in china,

silver, and red-and-white flower arrangements, and Daddy follows me dutifully. I'd say there are fifty or so tables and I find ours, number 34. No one is sitting yet, but I set down my purse and claim our spots. Having our bearings, we navigate into the sea of people again to calm Daddy's nerves, and mine, with alcohol.

"There's Mayor Riley," I say, after grabbing a handful of peanuts and shoving them into my mouth.

"Mm hmm."

We pass real estate moguls and media personalities, people we typically only see in the news. All this power in one place seems surreal.

"Oh, and look! Is that Brian Williams?"

"Yeah, how 'bout that," Daddy says, suppressing any hint of awe.

NBC's Brian Williams, our emcee for the night, takes his place behind a podium about a hundred feet away and clears his throat. Lights go bright and the side of the ship converts into a gigantic movie screen showing images of waving American flags and faces of heroism. When the chatter dies down to a murmur, we take our glasses and hurriedly find our way back to our seats.

"Tonight we sit on board the USS *Yorktown* in the beautiful Charleston harbor," begins Williams, "to celebrate the opening of the Congressional Medal of Honor Museum and the lives and service of the recipients of that award. There are 110 Medal of Honor recipients alive today, and sitting among you—look to your right and to your left now—we are privileged to be in the company of forty of those men."

I crane my neck and see one blue ribbon wearer at each table around me.

"I did several local press interviews today," Williams continues, "and I told the various reporters what I'll say here: being around these men is a tonic. Once you know a single recipient, you'll never have a truly bad day again.

"All of these humble men say the act of heroism for which they received the nation's highest decoration was 'nothing anyone else wouldn't have done in the same circumstance.' Later this evening, with the stories you will see and hear about each of them, I must respectfully disagree. What these men did in service to our great country is nothing short of extraordinary."

When the music starts, Brian Williams settles at his table and servers carrying large trays of food begin setting plates down. "Hello," I say, nodding to the folks at table 34. I straighten my dress and shift in my seat.

Daddy goes further, standing and shaking hands with each of the six men and women around us. Then I see him stop. The man beside me is wearing a blue ribbon and Medal of Honor around his neck. He's handsome and regal. "Derek Wray," he says to my father, shaking his hand.

"John Porter," my father says, his eyes lighting. "I know who you are—got a Medal of Honor in Vietnam, right? You're a real hero, man. You gave us hope. I was in Vietnam too."

"That right?" asks Colonel Wray, appearing genuinely interested, although the flight deck is crawling with Vietnam vets.

"The 101st airborne, 1970," my father says proudly. "You were down there, what, in Da Lat, right?" The words flow off his tongue like it's just up the road in Georgetown.

"1968," the colonel confirms.

A shine of familiarity graces Daddy's cheeks as if meeting a fraternity brother.

"Here. Why don't you sit next to him instead," I say, moving my purse and switching my place card with Daddy's to make it official. Daddy doesn't even notice my handiwork. He's engrossed with this war hero. Any hint of alcohol in his system seems to have been steamrolled right out of him now. His speech is clear, deliberate, and thoughtful. My father is a different man all of a sudden. He's a man's man. He seems more at ease talking to Colonel Wray about war and military things than I've ever seen him in his own home with his own family. Ever.

This, Katie-bug, was a very good thing to do. Worth every cent. I smile in spite of myself and sip my spritzer, watching in quiet triumph as the conversation unfolds between the Medal of Honor recipient and my father, owner of a Distinguished Flying Cross and a Purple Heart.

Sitting back and watching the images of soldiers flashing on the screen, I listen to Daddy's conversation as if he's far off. I'm in a dream. I turn my head and see the side of his face, clean-shaven and intelligent, and finally, miraculously, I see it—the whole man—not just the one I've known since I've been alive, but a complete man with past lives that still to this day exist. I picture layers upon layers of transparencies with lines and details, building one on top of the other to create a man who can walk right off the page. By the grace of God, I am privy to another facet of my father tonight—not just the man who drinks too much and makes Mama fume, or the one who screams like a child at my four-year-old, but the brave one who led men into danger and survived. I let the moment linger around me and solidify like my newfound respect for the man who raised me.

DADDY AND I finish our steak and crab cakes and watch, tears trickling, the real-life stories on the huge screen of the heroes around us. We learn the details of what our tablemate, Colonel Derek Wray, did in Vietnam. For two hours on May 6, 1968, he and another man held off the enemy while his platoon assisted in the nighttime evacuation of American dignitaries. Though severely injured, Wray continued his defense even after his partner was killed. The evacuation was successful, and Wray's courage under fire became well-known and helped to boost troop morale in Vietnam.

Each Medal of Honor recipient has an equally heroic and shocking story, and as I watch transfixed, I feel as if I've been asleep my whole life and have only just learned of the sacrifices of men. I am ashamed I have not been more patriotic, have not desired to learn of the history of my country, to learn the history of my own father. I am ashamed to have lived so long in my own little world, and as we rise and end the evening with an angel singing "The Star Spangled Banner," I close my eyes to thank God for finally opening them.

Before leaving, we tour somberly the new Medal of Honor Museum with its interactive exhibits, the sights and sounds of war. I see young faces of the old men around me. There is a young soldier still in each of them.

We walk through World War II and Korea, and when we get to Vietnam, I grab my father's hand, something I haven't done in many years. I feel the heat of his rough fingers in mine and the presence of the soldier within him.

And as I ponder the rarity of clinging to Daddy, I realize I've not felt my heart skip or my ulcer flare, nor have I remembered the worry that nearly consumed me this morning during the mammogram, since Daddy and I first set foot on this beautiful ship, the USS *Yorktown*.

CHAPTER TWENTY-SIX

The Note
Charleston

John

Thoughts of last evening have left his mind unsettled.

John Porter pulls his wallet from his back pocket. The breeze blows cool through the open garage door, the seasons beginning to shift in Charleston. John flips past pictures of Katie-bug—her senior graduation photo, her high school volleyball days, her sixth-grade face in grinning silver, her baby picture faded pink. His fingertips claw clumsily to the very back of the brown leather wallet where credit cards live, the ones he never uses.

He slips out a business card. He reads the name on the front then flips it over, seeing the handwritten words in blue ink. He didn't notice them last night. His heart stops. His eyes water. John remembers Medal of Honor recipient Derek Wray sliding the card into his hand just before they parted on the *Yorktown*.

What a night. He would have to thank Katie-bug for it. She's an amazing girl, and he needs to show her how much she means to him. Honestly, he doesn't really know how. He could buy her something, but he doesn't know what. He'll try hard not to act like a jerk the next time he sees her. That should do it. It's the best he can do.

Dad-gum. The memories she stirred up though. The memories are real, man. It happened. All of it. Stuff he's tried to shove down for so long. John's love for country was stirred last night. It's even bigger than it was in Vietnam. Katie-bug reminded him of it—how much he loves this country. She reminded him of the men who never made it home. She reminded him of his best friend in the world, God rest his soul. Poor pitiful fool. Ernest.

Ernest

In a swift stream of consciousness Ernest Marquette leaves his pond on Marble Mountain and joins John Porter in Charleston. He finds himself in a three-car garage with gleaming race-car floors and a huge train set built for grandsons. Ernest's spirit is invisible just over John's shoulder, but finding himself here is an unexpected blessing. This is what he's been waiting for. No holding back. He's determined to live this experience, brief as it may be, to the fullest.

Spirit fully engaged, Ernest cries out, "John! It's me! I'm here!" But his voice is the wind, and his friend cannot hear him. "John?" He tilts his vision down to John's hands, to the small white card he's studying so intensely. Then, something he's never seen before. Ernest certainly never saw John do this in Nam, no matter how bad it got. Taking John's lead, Ernest joins his friend, breaking down, knees on concrete, crying freely, no holding back. The two men weep, forming one long river that flows to the street thirty-eight years long. There have been tears here and there, yes, but neither man, it seems, has cried properly in all this time.

John

Through a saltwater haze, John looks at the words on the war hero's card and rubs them hard to see if they are temporary like memories that may fade away. He rubs them harder, curling the edges, and the friction burns. He lets the card drop, and it floats to the floor, script side up.

The words on the card are ones John never heard when he returned to New Jersey from Vietnam. *Baby-killer. Murderer.* These were the words that greeted him instead. He touches his left cheek and feels the place he was spat upon in the airport. They'd been told to change into civilian clothes before they de-boarded the plane, but they didn't know why. "You'll see," is all they'd been told. He remembers it just like yesterday. All he could do was just keep walking.

John wipes his eyes now and stares at the card, this gift, on the floor.

"Welcome home, brother," it says.

The words echo off the walls of this garage and out into the cool September air.

"Welcome home, brother." Wray's words echo in the two men's souls, thirty-eight years too late.

Ernest

John Porter is oblivious that the spirit of his best friend, Ernest Marquette, is there with him again, hovering just inches above those blessed words. "Welcome home, brother," he reads. Then he reads the note again.

Ernest is making a new wish.

I want to go home, he thinks, like that little girl who finds herself in Oz. If he could only click his heels and make it happen instantly. But it's not that simple, now is it?

Please let me go home to Georgia, Ernest pleads. *I wish, I wish that I could just go home.*

CHAPTER TWENTY-SEVEN

The Aftermath

Katherine Ann

I dive in headfirst and the water wraps around me, silencing any ailment, any fears. I rise to the air again and feel my shoulders, naked in the cool September breeze. In another month or so, it'll be time to heat this pool, but not yet. The way the sun simmers it so nicely in the afternoons leaves the morning water tepid perfection.

I am on top of the world today.

"So how was your date with John Friday night?" Tillie asks.

"Unbelievable," I say, grinning. Then turning to Mama, "Did Daddy tell you what a good time we had?"

She appears to be constipated, her muscles tight and restrained. "Oh yes," she sings. "Can't stop talking about it, how beautiful you were, how patriotic he feels. And that card the war hero gave him? My goodness. You'd think he was a ten-year-old boy collecting baseball cards again."

I take a deep breath and let my warm feelings permeate the air around me.

"I told Leroy about it and he wishes he'd a-gone now too,"

Connie says, wading up to the shallow end, revealing slowly her wet, dark skin. "I told him, 'Shoot, baby. You come up with that three hundred fifty dollars you'd a-needed for the ticket, and I'll be a happy woman. Yes sir. We can keep the money, say you went and had a good ole time.' Ain't that right?"

"I hear you," I say. "It was a lot of money. Worth it though."

"You should have gone, Betty Jo," says Hilda, pressed against the side of the pool, her elbows resting on the edge. She lifts her feet and flutters them in front of her, sending ripples Mama's way. "Why didn't you go with them?"

"I was not asked."

There it is. The tone in Mama's voice is unmistakable. Passive aggressiveness at its finest. Her plucked blonde eyebrows rise slightly and her head tilts helplessly as if she's an innocent child and the world is out to get her. There is no doubt in my mind now; Mama is hurt I didn't ask her to come with us. Wonderful.

"I really didn't think you'd enjoy it," I blurt out. "Old men, war stories . . . you said you were tired of war talk, remember? You could have come with us though, Mama. I wish you'd said something. It would've been fun having you there."

"Oh, don't be silly, Katie-bug. That ship was the last place on earth I wanted to be," she says, covering up her true feelings with sternness. Then she looks at me and playfully squeezes my chin to make me feel all right. "Anyway, I had a very nice quiet evening, reading my magazines and taking a bath. It was heaven, really, having some peace. You should take your father out more often."

We giggle and get over the whole thing, but there remains a tinge of gray guilt covering my earlier glow.

Tillie says to Hilda, "Hop on up there and turn the music on. I need to work on our choreography." Our synchronized swimming event is going to be on New Year's Eve, we've decided.

The pool will be heated with steam coming up, and we'll come out holding sparklers and wearing top hats in the beginning, only to take them off and reveal our fancy gold swim caps. Tillie's so excited we don't know what to do with her. We've still got three months to go!

Hilda emerges from the water, looking less boxy than I remember. Has she lost weight? I'm not sure if I'm envious or worried. Funny how that is with women. We never say a word when someone's gained a few pounds, for a few reasons. Number one, it would be flat-out rude. Number two, gaining weight is equated with good appetite, which in turn means good health. And number three, watching a friend of yours get heavier just makes you feel better about yourself. No two ways about it. There's no redeeming quality in the whole thing, but it's true. When Connie put on five pounds at Thanksgiving last year, secretly I was jumping up and down because I had only gained two.

On the other hand, when a woman loses weight, other women notice and comment on it immediately like vultures. "Oh, look at you, have you lost weight? Are you eating enough? You're about to wither away." What we're really thinking is, *Shucks, you're looking better than me. Here I was, hefty, and you were keeping my fat self company. Now why'd you have to go and get me thinking about how chubby I am again?*

So I say, "Hilda, have you lost weight? You look good."

And I really do mean it. I think.

"A little," she says, beaming.

"Hilda had a date with Doctor Wildekamft," Mama says. "Tell her, Hilda."

"Yes, tell me, Hilda," I say, intrigued.

Connie and Tillie swim closer so we can all hear over the Beach Boys crooning about a little deuce coupe.

"Oh, nothing to tell," Hilda says, but she's not hiding it very well. Instead, her eyelashes flutter to beat the band. "I just went in to have my lip looked at, you know, and the doctor, well . . ."

"He's single, rich, and German!" Mama squeals.

"Reeeeallyyyy," I say. "Now, would this happen to be the same skin doctor I suggested you go see, Hilda?"

"Yes, yes. Pat on the back for you," Hilda says. "But really, thank you, Katie-bug. Turns out the spot was just a benign growth, *and* I got to meet my doctor. I just cannot believe such a wonderful man, and a German one at that, lives right here in Charleston! We have so much in common. Why, do you know he grew up just a few towns away from me back in Germany?"

I stand there basking in glory, waist deep in water with the women I love around me cooing and the heat of the morning on my cheeks. The happy chatter continues and I close my eyes and fall back, letting the water engulf me. When I rise again, the ladies are silent and staring at something up at the house with wonder. Is it an elephant approaching? It might as well be with their looks of surprise. I follow their gazes and watch my father storming toward us with a paper in his hand. He's got a strange look on his face, excitement, I think, but I'm not sure. It's so rare that he shows himself to the Water Lilies these days, my spine pricks with panic.

"Everything all right?" I ask him as he stands by the music and tries to turn it off. He accidentally turns it up louder and curses, throwing his hands in the air and looking back at me, helpless. He never has been good at anything that runs on batteries or plugs into the wall.

"The red button right there," I direct him. He finally gets it right and turns to us. His blue jeans are held up by an expensive leather belt, and his head, where his hat used to be, is showing age spots beneath the gray stubble of a military cut.

"Look at this!" He points to the bottom half of a folded *Post and Courier*. "You seen this?"

I hop out and hover over the paper, dripping around Daddy's shoes. "Who's that handsome guy?" he says.

"Daddy! Look, everybody. Daddy's in the newspaper with Derek Wray."

Mama moves over slowly and cranes her neck. "He sure is handsome," she says, though I'm not sure if she's talking about my father or the war hero. I'm guessing it's the latter.

"You're a newsmaker, Daddy," I say.

"Yeah, well, don't get used to it. The picture's kind of a funny angle, don't you think? Makes my nose look big."

"Your nose is big, John," Tillie chuckles.

Daddy stares at the picture a little longer and reaches up, touching his proboscis. "Well, at least they spelled my name right. They took pictures of everybody, didn't they, honey? Wonder why they put mine in."

"'Cause Katie-bug paid the cameraman three hundred and fifty dollars," Tillie sasses.

"Yeah, right," I say. But Daddy's not convinced. I can see in his eyes he's processing this information to see if it could be true.

"She's kidding, Daddy. That's Tillie, remember? You got yourself in the paper all by your little self." I lean up and kiss his cheek, leaving a wet mark. "You look very nice too. I bet Derek Wray's proud to be standing next to you."

Daddy doesn't know what to do with my kind comment so his gruffness returns.

"Get back in your pool and do your little dance, ladies." He turns around, wiggling his behind and sticking it out to us. "Some people actually have to work around here." With that, he trudges away and leaves Mama fuming. If her eyes could throw daggers, Daddy'd be laid out flat on the lawn.

CHAPTER TWENTY-EIGHT

THE FESTIVAL
Georgetown

Lisa

Today is Saturday. On weekends, Le's Kitchen is closed. No regulars from the mill means no customers, so we don't even bother. Typically, I'll go in on a day like today and get my bookwork done, prepare the ingredients for Monday, and just sit quietly, being that there is really nowhere else for me to be.

I have no man in my life. And why would I? I don't really look like the folks in this town. There are only a few Vietnamese families—the Dangs, the Hus, and us—and we're not close in proximity or otherwise. I've often wondered how our lives might have turned out differently had we moved to a place like Orange County, California, or Houston, Texas, where "Little Saigons" exist sustained by large populations of Vietnamese immigrants. Perhaps Ma would have married. Perhaps Uncle would have. Perhaps I would have had Amerasian friends who were just like me, half here, half there. We would have been normal around one another. We would have belonged.

Here in Georgetown, I belong to no one. Except Ma.

I'm doing something different today. There is new wind in my sails. I am not going to give up on the one person who is closest to me. I will not let her slip into oblivion forever and leave me.

I walk into the den where Ma is watching the news. I kneel down at the foot of her chair and lay my head on her frail lap. I feel the heat of her thin legs rise in tiny whiffs to my face. After a quiet few seconds, Ma's hand rests on the edge of my head, unmoving. As a child, each night I would crawl in her lap. She'd sit on the couch, and I would lie there for an hour with Ma rubbing, scratching, and petting my back. It was the closest thing to true affection I got from her. Typically, there were few hugs and few *I love you*'s from Ma. But there was always the back rubbing.

Today, I barely get a pat on the head. Of course, I realize I'm thirty-seven years old, and I'm twice as big as she is, but some needs never change, do they? Though we grow older, the child still exists.

I lift my head and lean back on the soles of my feet. "Ma. I have a wonderful idea. Let's prepare the food for *Tet Trung Thu* together. Wouldn't that be fun?" She doesn't move. "You haven't cooked in a very long time. Wouldn't you like to help me make the *bahn trung* like we used to? And the mooncakes?"

Ma keeps her eyes on the television but rubs the knuckles of one hand with her other, her way of reminding me of her arthritis.

"I'll do anything that requires precision, all right? The cutting, the wrapping . . . You can stir and sauté, whatever you like. At least keep me company, okay? What do you say?"

The first Mid-Autumn Festival I remember was when I was six years old. My mother spent it in tears, trying to explain to me that I'd been to five such festivals in Vietnam. "Remember the children in Da Nang?" she'd ask me. "Remember how you would all line up wearing masks and carrying your lanterns for

a procession through the street at dawn? And the unicorn danc-
ers. Remember them? You wanted to learn to dance like that. It
was your favorite time of year, *con gai*. The Mid-Autumn Festival.
The Children's Festival. Remember?"

I would shake my head and my mother would wail. It was
during that particular Mid-Autumn Festival that Ma realized
something—with the journey to America, not only had I forgotten or repressed the tragedies of that trip, but along with it, I had
lost every memory of home. For me, whatever happened in
Vietnam had stayed in Vietnam, and it made her loneliness even
more severe.

It made me a very shallow person.

When you are six years old and you lose five years of yourself,
the result is a thin, flimsy shell, much like the photograph of my
father that sits now behind a new pane of glass.

I still mourn for those lost five years. Ma does too. She
stopped saying, "Remember this" or "remember that." She realized Vietnam was gone for me forever. That my life began here
in America. And what if she pressed? What if I did remember?
Would I remember as well the horrors of the boat people? This
is something she would not chance, so she left it alone.

In the same respect, now that I know my father's name, I will
not tell my mother so. I will not utter the words that she has
never dared utter to me. I have no idea what memories the word
John may unearth for her.

Ma looks at me now, pulling her eyes from the TV screen
and trying to focus on my face. Her mouth opens and her tongue
twitches as if she may speak, and I hold my breath, anticipating,
hoping. She does not speak. She reaches her hand out to me so
that I can help her from her chair, and we walk arm in arm to
the kitchen.

My heart brimming over, I pull up a low-backed stool and help my mother sit on it. I leave her, arm propped on the counter, watching me dance around the kitchen to retrieve the enchanted ingredients that can transport us back to festivals of years past. If, in body alone, Ma and I are together again, I will take it. She has come into the kitchen to cook with me for the first time in over six months. I recognize it for what it is—she is walking baby steps back to me. She is one step closer to coming back to life.

CHAPTER TWENTY-NINE

The Spirit
Marble Mountain, Vietnam

Ernest

Eldest fish is nestled into the crook of a rock, resting. Ernest hesitates a few feet away from him, wondering if he should disturb him when he is so peaceful. Rays of light are beginning to creep into the large cavernous room and illuminate the face of Buddha, the texture of the walls, the top couple inches of the pond. The water is a jade green, murky on the bottom, nearly black, and lighter near the surface. Ernest rises up and opens his mouth, gulping air.

Suddenly, a quick stream of young fish zips by and Eldest fish stirs. Seeing his opportunity, Ernest makes his way to the wisest member of the pond. He is hopeful. Tremulous.

"It has happened again."

Eldest fish stays silent, staring at Ernest.

"I was with my friend again. I was there, in his garage. I could feel what he was feeling. And then—"

"Yes, my son?"

"And then, I allowed myself to feel. They were human emotions. I . . . I cried."

Eldest fish keeps his gaze toward Ernest, but his eyes drift somewhere back behind his head, thinking. He moves his pectoral fins out and in, out and in, and then opens his mouth wide to speak.

"My son. You have been here for thirty-eight years. I have watched you become accustomed to the ways of the water, and you have left nearly every trace of your past life behind. Until now." He swims around Ernest, circling slowly until he comes to a rest at his side. He is close and whispers. Ernest eyes the waterfall in front of him, listening hard for wisdom.

"I will not be here forever," says Eldest fish quietly. "I feel my body growing weaker by the day. It has been my sincere hope that you might be the one to take my place when I am no more."

"But Eldest. I had no idea you—"

"Hush, my child. It is not your fault. I have come to realize that your humanness is not something that can simply leave though your body is changed. No. This mysterious spirit within you is strong and lingers. It is my belief that it is growing again. Soon, you will be unable to remain here. When your humanity returns fully and you are left in this cold-blooded form, it shall be too much for your mind. For your soul."

Ernest waits for Eldest fish to go on. He is trembling now. Terrified.

"My child. It is time for you to leave this place. I do not know how. I do not know when exactly. That is something only you can know . . . when the time is right."

"But how can I leave?" asks Ernest, turning to face his mentor. "I am stuck here. Along with the rest of you!"

"I have told you what I know, my son. The rest, I'm afraid, is up to you. There are things I simply cannot know about your human spirit."

Ernest stills and begins sinking. He allows himself to drop into the darkness until the sediment on the floor of the pond scratches his sensitive underbelly, and he shoots up, wild and furious. "How will I know?!" he yells to no one. He has not felt so trapped or so bewildered since he first entered this body of water so many years ago.

CHAPTER THIRTY

The Living
Georgetown

Lisa

This weekend was amazing—Ma and me in the kitchen again. Well, even though she did nothing. She cut nothing, stirred nothing, lifted not one finger, but she watched *me* cooking, and that is something, right? I tell myself it was something, a step forward. Surely it was. I will not allow my spirit to sink today. I will not look on the dark side.

"We're having something special this morning," I sing to Ma, who's still in her pajamas, watching Matt Lauer on the television.

I reach past the dozen cellophaned mooncakes we made, cooling and waiting to be baked in a few days, and I pull out my crepe batter, made fresh this morning with rice flour, coconut milk, beer, and turmeric. It's been resting for nearly an hour and has these lovely holes from the bubbles that have lifted and thickened it. I toss my sliced onion, pork, carrot, and shrimp into an oiled skillet and cook until the fragrance fills the air.

"We haven't had *Bahn xeo* in a while, have we?"

Ma doesn't answer, of course, but nothing can shake my mood today. I still have the name of my father on my mind. It's been tattooed just behind my eyes. I whistle a happy tune and pour some of the golden yellow crepe batter into another heated skillet.

When the thin crepe is perfect and the edges are getting crispy, I take it off the heat and pour my sautéed meats and vegetables on one half, topping with bean sprouts and green onions. Then I carefully fold it over, forming a perfect half moon.

"Come and get it!" I say, setting Ma's steaming plate on the table and turning back to the stove to pour the batter for my own.

I watch as Ma presses slowly into the kitchen as if a long, flimsy string is pulling her to her seat. She stares down at her half moon.

"Isn't it pretty?" I ask. Ma just stares. "What? What's wrong?" She looks up at me blankly and then I realize what I've done. "The *nouc cham*! So sorry. It's right here."

I pour the sweet and sour dipping sauce into a tiny ramekin and set it on her plate. "Here you go." Ma approves and grabs her chopsticks. It's so good to see her eat, if only to nibble.

I sit there with Ma and we peck at our plates and look out the window at the red birds dancing in the birdbath. One rises up, flapping, and then the other. At times, they appear to be playing, other times, it's more like fighting. Finally, they fly away, one chasing the other, going off to who-knows-where.

Minutes later, Ma pushes her plate forward and leaves a quarter moon intact. She touches my shoulder in appreciation before heading to the bathroom to shower as she does every day at this time. There's a show that comes on at nine o'clock, *Judge Judy*, and she doesn't want to miss a minute.

In her absence, I pull a stack of newspapers toward me—the *Georgetown Times*, the *Myrtle Beach Sun News*, and the *Post and*

Courier. Georgetown just isn't that big of a place, so if you want more substantial news, you have to subscribe to the papers of the larger nearby cities. At least, that's what Uncle used to say. He would spend his early mornings devouring the papers from beginning to end. As a child, I would grab a section and sit next to him at the kitchen table, my eyes flitting back and forth, back and forth, like his. Uncle would nod at me reverently, never letting on that he knew I couldn't read a word.

I smile at the memory of Uncle and skim the tragic headlines of each newspaper, and then I settle on one, skipping to the Arts & Travel section of the *Post and Courier.* By the time I've finished my crepe and am beginning to eat the remainder of Ma's breakfast, I'm deep into the High Profile and Society pages. Searching for some smiling faces to match my mood, I stretch the section out in front of me. I pore over the party pictures, dropping a flurry of bean sprouts on the dark ink. It is then that I see a photograph of two men with the Ravenel Bridge, massive and beautiful, stretched out behind them. One man looks slightly familiar, so I study the caption below his chest.

Then I do something I've never done before. I choke, fully and nearly to my death, on a large piece of pan-fried pork.

BY THE TIME I stumble into the den, it's been at least ten or fifteen seconds since I've had any oxygen, and I collapse, thrashing, outside Ma's bathroom door.

If you have never been the recipient of the Heimlich maneuver, you could not possibly know how it feels to have your life flash before your eyes, the panic of having no air in your lungs compounded by sharp, painful thrusts to your chest by a woman with knuckles that could slice bread.

I am much too large for my mother to lift, so after several failed attempts, she flops me over the arm of a chair and beats the back of me, grunting with every strike.

As God as my witness, the piece of pork that hurls from my mouth is two inches long and not even partially chewed. It pops out and lands in Ma's favorite chair, just as Al Roker is saying, "Here's what the weather looks like in your neck of the woods."

I fall to the ground, clutching my neck and gasping for air. I close my eyes, and when I open them again Ma is kneeling in front of me, moving the hair out of my face gingerly with her fingers. It's been so long since she's actually looked at me, spirit to spirit. I turn away when I remember the reason I choked in the first place.

"Thanks," I tell her. "That was scary, wasn't it?"

Ma stands and hurries to the kitchen. I can hear the water running and her filling up a glass. Then the water stops and I anticipate her coming back to me in . . . three, two, one. But no Ma. There is no sound coming from the kitchen anymore, so I pull myself up and head in, fearing Ma might see the photograph in the paper. But I nearly topple her as she's coming out. She hands me the glass of water and pats my left arm, staring somewhere behind me. I cannot see into her eyes. I cannot tell if Ma has seen the same thing that I did—that my father, John Porter, is not dead as we've always believed, but that he's still very much alive, living in Charleston, just forty-five minutes south of here!

I sip my water and plop down in my chair again. My body is stunned. My head has detached itself, a balloon, rising, escaping my grasp. I study the photo, the nose, the glasses. It's him, isn't it? He looks much older, wider, has less hair than his army days, but goodness, the similarities! It could be him!

I reread the caption.

Charleston builder and Vietnam veteran John Porter shakes hands with Medal of Honor recipient Colonel Derek Wray Friday night on the USS Yorktown *for the opening of the Medal of Honor Museum.*

John Porter. There is no doubt about it. This man is my father. My father! And the love of Ma's life. The dead man we have mourned forever, he wasn't killed in action like Ma always believed. Somehow, he is still *alive.*

PART THREE

WOOD

Dậu đổ, bìm leo.

When the tree is fallen, everyone runs to it with his axe.

—Vietnamese proverb

CHAPTER THIRTY-ONE

The Dragon
Georgetown

Lisa

"Two threes and a number six."

My vision has gone cloudy and I see amber waves in front of me. I am in the middle of a remote golden sea, far away from any other forms of life. I am floating, rocking. In the distance, seagulls cry and call.

"Lisa? You all right?"

I stir and find myself, not in an ocean, but standing in front of the deep fryer in Le's Kitchen. I turn to see the concern on Charlene's face.

"Oh yeah. I'm fine," I say.

"It's been awhile on Donnie's fish, sweetie. Is it ready yet?"

I pull out the basket from the deep fryer and stare at the black, crispy thing that was Donnie's flounder. My heart stills as Charlene's eyes rest on the back of me. She does not say a word about my error, but puts her fingers gently on my shoulder. "I'll just refill his sweet tea for him and take him out some hush puppies."

I spin to her, stunned. I have never burned a customer's food. Ever. "Thanks," I tell her.

Snap out of it, Lisa, I tell myself as I quickly drop another piece of battered flounder into the oil along with several handfuls of popcorn shrimp. It's not like I can share this with anyone. I can't tell Charlene, *Oh, sorry I burned the fish, but I just found out my father is alive and has been living forty-five minutes south of here my entire life.* I can't tell her, *Oh, no big deal. I've never had a father. I've lived in the shadow of his ghost my whole life and it's affected the way I deal with people, with men, with my mother, yet, it's all right. These things happen. Some ghosts do come back to life, you know.*

No. I can't tell her that. She would think I was crazy. I think I might be going crazy.

It is all I can do to get through the lunch rush. I only screw up three orders, and when Charlene leaves to go pick up her son, she says, "You sure you're all right? If you're sick, why don't you call Henry to take over for you tonight? You've been working so hard, you could use the rest. It's all right. You're the boss, remember?"

I tell her I'm fine again, and when the last lunch customer walks out the door, I plop down on the bucket in the corner of the kitchen where my mother used to be. And I cry. I wail and moan as if being ravaged by a storm. I weep for the ghost my mother has become and for the ghost my father used to be.

I don't know how I feel about all of this. I don't know what to do. Things seemed simpler when my father was simply dead. But now. Now there are so many questions. They roll over me, scrambling to be heard, pressing me to the ground. I have no control over the flow of them. They are bacteria multiplying. My mind has trampled me, running rampant, and I am left exhausted.

The savory smell of fried food that I ingest every day, that odor that people go crazy over, the one that draws them into the restaurant like ants to a picnic—that same smell sends me stumbling to the bathroom and makes me retch.

When I come out again, weak-kneed, I go straight to the little black metal desk and pick up the phone.

"Henry? Lisa. Can you fill in for me tonight? Yeah, I'm not feeling well. Thanks. Tomorrow? Well, I'm sure I'll be better by then, but . . . Great. You're a lifesaver. I'll call you first thing in the morning."

I hang up, wipe my swollen face, grab my purse, lock up the doors, and crawl into my car. I sit there, not moving, not starting the ignition. The air is still around me. I have no idea what to do or where to go. I have never felt so foreign in my own skin. I reach into my purse and pull out the folded newspaper clipping, and I stare, unblinking into the face of my father.

If my father is not a ghost anymore, but real, am I the ghost now? I am losing grip on everything I've ever known to be true. With the passing of an eighteen-wheeler, my car shakes and my eyes go wide. The question that has now formed in my head is large and looming and terrifying.

Has my mother known all along that my father is alive? Did she simply not tell me? Is it possible she has known?

No. I won't allow myself to think that. Ma has loved that man her entire life. Every night she would tell me stories of him, how I was like him, how I look like him. And she mourned him. She would tell me what a brave man he was. She would cry that her love never came back to her.

No. There is no way a loving mother would keep that kind of a man from her daughter. Not in a million years.

Yet what kind of man could my father be if he shared Ma's love but abandoned her in Vietnam?

I lean my head on the steering wheel and melt again, teardrops flopping onto my dirty white chef's pants that reek of coleslaw and deep-fried fish.

AFTER A FEW minutes I feel my spirit calm, and I sit straight up, staring through the window at the smoke from the mill billowing into the blue sky. The dragon never sleeps.

Please let me do the right thing, I pray. *For everyone. For Ma, for me. For my father.* "Your will, not mine, Lord," I say out loud, trying to convince myself with the sound of my voice that what I'm resolved to do is right. Then, "But I really need to know, God. Don't you think?"

I open the car door and head back into the restaurant past quiet tables and empty chairs, and I sit down at the desk again, this time determined. I lift the phone from the cradle and spin the dial, 4-1-1. "Charleston, South Carolina. Do you have the number for a John Porter?"

I grab a blue ballpoint pen and scribble nine numbers for the popular Charleston name. When I'm done, I stare, going cross-eyed. The numbers swirl in my vision until I force them to stop. Be still. One of these, I know, will reach my father. But as I go to grab the phone again, the hum of the dial tone whispers warnings. Are you really ready to make these calls? What will you say? One can't simply call up a man from out of the blue and say, "Hi, sir. You don't know me but I'm your long-lost daughter."

CHAPTER THIRTY-TWO

THE SPELL
Marble Mountain, Vietnam

Ernest

It's feeding time. A family of British tourists is on top of Marble Mountain. They *ooh* and *ahh* when Brother Chong fans his feed into the water and the fish rise up like magic. Brother Chong sees a little boy and nods, holding his hand out to him. The boy takes a handful of feed and drops it pellet by pellet into the water, beaming silently when the big ones bite.

Ernest is disgusted by the whole affair. He cannot think of eating. His only thought now is of Eldest fish's last words to him and how he might be able to escape this place. He leaves his fellow fish swirling and bumping like circus clowns into one another and moves directly into the shadow of Brother Chong. Ernest opens his mouth at the water's edge and treads to be still. *Look at me. Look at me!*

Brother Chong does indeed look back at Ernest and they stare for several seconds, man to fish. Fish to man. Then his scarred grimace stretches into a genuine smile, but the gaze is broken when the little boy chirps for more food. When Brother Chong moves toward the child, the spell has been broken and Ernest is empty. What did he expect? That he could just wish to change places with this man? And what does that make him? Who, in their right mind, would ever wish on another being the torture of living in this pond?

What is Ernest becoming? This is not the man he was raised to be. His mother and father taught him better than this. Ernest lowers his eyes in shame. His plans for escaping this place, he vows, cannot involve the harming of another. Otherwise, he would deserve to stay here for all of eternity, wouldn't he? No, Ernest is better than this. He is a good, wholesome boy from Georgia, the way his mama and daddy taught him to be.

Ernest will study the habits of Brother Chong even more closely. Perhaps his chance for escape lies in the pond skimmer and the removal of dead fish and debris.

Perhaps he can play dead. That's it. He will study very closely the mannerisms of the next fish destined to lose its life. Eager for this lesson to begin, Ernest swims to the waterfall and watches the smallest, thinnest fish as it gleefully succumbs to the waterfall's massage. This ignorant youngster has no idea it's feeding time at all. It will only discover it when the others return, bellies full. But by then, it will be too late.

CHAPTER THIRTY-THREE

THE CALL
Charleston

Katherine Ann

There is nothing quite so sad or so disgusting as what the pool skimmer dredges up in autumn. As I'm typically the first one out here, I haul the long pole from the side of the pool house each day and reach across the water, skimming dead leaves, dead frogs, beetles, palmetto bugs, and an assortment of other deceased Lowcountry nastiness. The worst was a baby possum last year that had somehow fallen into the water and not been able to get out. Now that one made me tear up. I even said a prayer for the swollen little thing when I flung him across the river.

This morning it's a turtle about the size of my fist. Poor little guy. My boys love these things. I pull him out of the brown twisted leaves and reverently take him to the marsh, setting him in a pyre of yellow spartina grass.

Amen.

"Mama, what would you do if I weren't here to do the dirty work?" I call to her on my way back.

"I'd get Connie to do it." She smiles. "Or John. No, probably Connie. There'd be less commotion with her."

Connie, Tillie, and Hilda round the corner of the house together, a motley trio of shapes, sizes, and colors emerging from the dappled morning light and into full sun.

"Hey, y'all. Mornin'."

"Hey there!" Hilda looks especially pleased to be here and she opens her arms wide, belting out, "Ri-ise and shi-ine and put on your glory, glory. Ri-ise and shi-ine and put on your glory, glory . . ."

"Enough singing, Hilda," Tillie says. "You ever seen such a chipper woman in your whole life? I don't know if I can get used to you this way. I think I liked your grumpy old self better."

"Go right ahead. Be sour," she says. "Nothing can change my mood today." Hilda wiggles out of her cover-up and shows us a brand-new leaf-green jungle-printed one-piece that ties around her neck, leaving her back open and her bosoms held apart by a plunging v-line, far from each other like positively charged magnets. Never the two shall meet.

I see way too much.

"Whoo-hoo," I catcall. "Look at you, Hilda! Aren't you sexy!" My goodness, this is a first. What has this man done to her? "Another date with the doctor, I presume?"

Mama stands back and surveys Hilda's new body with eyebrows arched. "My goodness," is all she can muster, unable to hide her amusement.

"We had a very nice time. That is all I will say."

"That's all you'll say? Mmm, mm-mm," Connie shakes her head. "Making love after sixty. What's this world coming to?"

"Connie! I did no such thing!" Hilda's cheeks turn crimson and she clears her throat. "Let's just get swimming, all right? I've got some work to do on this figure today. And heaven knows, Connie, so do you."

"Well, you got me there, honey," says Connie, rubbing her hips. "I'll give you that."

"Can you turn on the music?" I ask Hilda. I move slowly into the cool water, one step at a time, letting my body adjust. I don't want my heart to have an attack or anything because of the temperature change. I cringe as Tillie hops off the edge and one-handed, splashes into the pool. "Oh, this is invigorating, girls! Cool weather is coming."

I wipe the dripping water from my face and turn to scold Tillie when we hear a scream.

"Ow! Donderwetter! My foot!" Hilda winces in pain and blood drips onto the white concrete. Drip. Drip. Drip. "You see this?"

"Don't move!" Mama yells, waving her hands, sliding out of the water and slipping on her flip-flops. "Is that glass? I can't believe this!"

We all hop out and hurry over, wet but freshly shoed. My mouth gapes when I see it. There's an entire beer bottle broken into pieces in front of the radio.

"Who in the world would do such thing?" asks Connie, crouching and surveying the bottom of Hilda's foot. "Lord have mercy, she's gonna need some stitches."

"Must have been some kids," says Tillie, looking around as if the culprits might still be here. But Mama doesn't appear convinced. In fact, she's on the verge of tears when I volunteer to go inside and get some bandages and towels.

"In my medicine cabinet," she tells me, clutching her chest from the horror of it all. There's a crescent moon-shaped bloodstain on the ground now, growing. "Oh, and the dustpan!" Mama moves toward me, apparently coming too.

"I got it, just stay put. Look around and see if you see any more glass."

I run across the lawn to the house, and the chill of the air on my wet suit gives me goose bumps when I enter. I go upstairs first, clutching the wrought-iron rail that winds to the second floor. In my parents' bedroom, the bed has been made. There are no clothes in sight. It looks nothing like my own bedroom. This room appears unlived in. How in the world does Mama do it?

I grab the bandages, gauze, scissors, and tape, then haul booty down the steps, feeling my rear end and tummy flop. The enormous Moe's burrito I downed last night flits through my mind along with great remorse, but that's the least of my worries now.

The kitchen leads to the mudroom, and I rifle through the closet for a broom and dustpan. I'll have to come back for the handheld vacuum. Shoot. I just don't have that many hands.

I am halfway across the living room when the scissors fall from my fingers, leaving a gash in the hardwood floor, nearly gouging my toe. I curse beneath my breath and bend down to pick them up. That's when the phone rings.

Trying to hold the dustpan, broom, and bandages, I grab for the gauze that's now rolled a few feet away. More cursing. More stumbling. The phone is ringing. *Ring. Ring.* Ah, forget it. I drop my supplies, completely flustered now, and though it is not my house, I feel perfectly justified in what I'm about to do—taking out my anger on the ignorant soul who is trying to peddle something that my parents do not want or need!

"Hello!" I yell. I hear nothing but silence. I imagine the headset, the computer screen with "chump" written across it, and the telemarketer rehearsing his speech.

"I said, hel-lo." My tone is sharp and cruel and whoever this salesman is on the other end of this line, I can assure you he won't be calling this house again.

More silence.

"Sheesh." I go to hang up. What a waste of time, an invasion of privacy, calling into people's homes like this. It should be against the law. I think I'll write my congressman, I—

I hear a small voice from the receiver. "Uh . . . um. May I speak with Mr. John Porter please?"

Oh, yeah. Telemarketer for sure. Using the full name is a dead giveaway. "He's not in. May I take a message?" Ha. Two can play this game. This always stumps them. When she says, "No message," I'm going to tell her, "Don't call again, take the Porters off your list, and while you're at it, get a new job that doesn't bother innocent people, you creep!"

But she doesn't say "No message." Instead she says, "Oh, well this is . . . uh . . . is this *Missus* Porter by chance?"

"No," I say coolly. "This is his daughter." Then, angry I've given too much personal information, I say, "And just *whom* am I talking to?"

"Oh. Well, it's a little hard to explain but . . . um, my name is Lisa. Is your dad the John Porter who served in Vietnam?"

My breathing halts. Someone from the newspaper? I think of Daddy's photo with Derek Wray and say a little warmer, "Yes, that's him."

The caller hesitates and my nerves fray. Maybe it's not someone from the newspaper.

"Could you please tell your father I'm . . . well, my mother is someone he knew from Vietnam? Like an old friend?"

"An old friend?"

From Vietnam? I cannot fathom what I am hearing. I lean back against the wall, stunned. Out the window, I see the Water Lilies looking my way, annoyed that I'm taking so long. Poor Hilda must be bleeding to death. Connie's holding her foot straight up in the air.

"Yes. And it's really important I speak with him," says the voice. "Could you please give him the message? Oh, and let me give you my phone number."

"Yes," I say, breathless, reaching for a notepad and pen. "Yes, please, go ahead. Give me your number. And your name again?"

"Lisa."

She states her phone number, and I recognize the South Carolina area code, 8-4-3. Then she says, "It's very nice to talk with you. May I ask your name?"

"Katherine Ann," I say without thinking.

"Katherine Ann," the voice repeats.

"Do you have a last name, Lisa?" I ask.

"Yes. Le."

I write down *Lee.* A good Southern name. "Great. Okay . . . I'll be sure to give him the message."

WHEN I WALK back outside, arms full, the women bark at me. "What took you so long?"

"Sorry. I . . . couldn't find some things. Here."

Connie grabs the gauze and tape, and Mama swipes the broom and dustpan. "Did you get a rag?"

"A rag? Oh, no."

"She's bleeding everywhere, Katie! In the laundry room closet. Hurry!" Mama has lost her patience with me. I can see how mortified she is. This daily pool gathering, this hosting of the Water Lilies, is her pride and joy. It's her main contribution to us all. And now this. Hilda is hurt. But worse, I can see Mama's wheels turning. She's wondering, as we all are. Could my father have possibly done this?

I lean down and pick up a large piece of glass with a Dos

Equis label still attached. Daddy loves his Dos Equis. Could he have done this? Was it an accident? Or has Daddy taken to drinking alone at night and smashing things?

Oh, heaven help us. What have I done to him? I've sent him over the edge, haven't I? The *Yorktown*, it was just too much for him!

Oh, good gracious, Daddy's drinking and smashing things. And the woman on the phone? She's tied to Vietnam! There's no avoiding it now, Daddy's past is coming back to haunt him, and it looks as though none of us is out of harm's way.

With furrowed brow, I run back into the house and rummage for rags. Grabbing a handful of white ones, I pass the notepad on the counter and stop. A split-second decision. I rip off the note, fold it, and press it into my bathing suit under my left breast. It pricks me when I face the Water Lilies again, handing over the rags. I make sure they don't need anything else and then flip-flop over to the pool house. Sitting on the bench and breathing heavily, I stuff the moist paper into my purse. I don't know who—if anyone—should see this.

Who is this woman who called? What's going on here? I watch Mama, Connie, and Tillie help poor Hilda to her good foot, and they hold her up as she hops across the lawn. I'm almost glad she's going to the hospital. Not that I want her hurt, but I want all these people out of here! I need to take a deep breath now. I've got to figure this all out.

The past is coming back for my father. It's up to me now to find a way to protect him.

"So let me get this straight . . ." RC paces the kitchen and hands Cooper a sippy cup filled with chocolate milk.

"Go on outside now, honey," I say, patting his little tushie. Cooper runs to the open door to the backyard and hollers for Tradd, who appears to have discovered a bug or frog in the grass. The door clicks behind him.

"So you answered your parent's phone in *their* house, took a message for your father from someone who knew him from Vietnam—the same Vietnam you've been trying to force down his throat for the past month—and now you don't even want to give him the message? A message that the woman said was important? I don't get it, Katie. Can you explain it to me again?"

I hate when he's sanctimonious like this. Doesn't he know that women have a right to change their minds?

"RC, if you've forgotten, Hilda had to go to the hospital. She had to get stitches for goodness sake. Daddy broke a beer bottle by the pool. *Our* pool."

"Do you know it was him for sure?"

"Well, not for sure, but it was a Dos Equis he broke . . ."

"Whoa—" He holds up his hand as if we're in court and he's making an objection. "He allegedly broke a Dos Equis. You can't condemn a man for something he didn't do. What happened to innocent until proven guilty? Hmm?"

I roll my eyes. Way to throw my beloved law back at me.

"And, I might add, it is not your place to withhold phone messages from your father. You were trespassing, in essence."

"Trespassing? It's my father's house!"

"Exactly!" RC points his finger at me. "It's your *father's* house. And it's your father's message. I believe it's your moral duty to pass it along to him. Let him do with it what he will. He's a grown man, Katie. Like it or not, he can handle himself."

"Oh, he cannot," I mumble, barely audible. But I hear it, and I'm surprised at myself. Am I really treating my father like a child? I am. "And anyway, why should you take up for him so much? All he does is give you a hard time."

"Some of us are just bigger people, I guess," he says, winking.

"Fine." I cross my arms in front of my chest. "I'll give him the message. But if he winds up hauling out a sawed-off shotgun at Christmas, it's on your head."

"Gee, I knew you'd see it my way." RC moves toward me, wrapping his arms around my back, and I put my head on his warm chest. I inhale deeply. If I could just stay here all the time and feel this safe and secure. But I can't. The embrace lasts about three seconds when Cooper reenters the house, this time crying and holding the top of his head where his brother, no doubt, has bopped him.

It is in this moment when I kiss away Cooper's tears that I know what I need to do for Daddy. Oh my goodness. It makes perfect sense.

CHAPTER THIRTY-FOUR

The Choice
Georgetown

Lisa

I cannot sleep. My mind is a handful of grenades, a domino trail of explosions. I toss in my sheets, moist from my skin.

I have a sister.

Is it not enough to have found a father—someone who could love me, could make me whole—but to have found a sister? It's simply too much! I've never had a sister. I've always been the only child.

This is a fairy tale. Truly a happy ending, isn't it?

Or is it?

What if he doesn't call? What if my father doesn't want to talk to me?

I pull the sheet up over my head and hide, listening to hot breath escaping my lungs.

Well, I didn't tell her *who* I was, exactly, I just said my name. Will John Porter know the name *Le*? Surely he will, especially since I said *Vietnam*.

So why did he not return to her? If he loved Ma, why did he not return?

I pull the covers back and gasp for fresh, cool air. I rub the hump in my nose.

He's going to have to face Ma if he's going to face me. Is he ready to do that?

I hurl the covers to my feet, jump out of bed, and begin pacing in the dark. A faint shivering glow through the window keeps me from bumping into things until I stub my toe on the corner of the bedpost and curse.

You said too much! Why did you give your name? You should have come up with something more creative like "I'm with the phone company" or "He's won the lottery"! You have no idea what his life is like today. You have no idea what his family is like, whether he has room for someone else in his heart. If he's married, why would he want to have anything to do with your mother?!

I ease my painful toe back under the covers, and fear grips me. *Oh Ma.* What will this do to Ma—or for Ma—if she finds out that the man she has loved her entire life is still living and within driving distance? Is it a miracle? A curse? Will this do her in? Will she crawl over the edge and never return to me, never speaking again? What if her heart can't take it? *What have I done?* I can't let anything happen to Ma. She's all I've got!

I press my hands in on my ears and try to silence the screaming. I feel the pressure, pushing, squeezing. I think my head might explode. I have never carried such a heavy responsibility.

What happens next is all because of me. I initiated the phone call. Now it's out of my control. He'll either call me back, or he won't. And if he doesn't, I will spend my lifetime wondering about this man. Wondering, should I call him back? Should I drive down to see him? Should I introduce myself while he's at a gas station? Follow him? Should we simply pass as strangers and smile at one another, me knowing that he gave me life, and him not knowing that I exist? It might be best for Ma that way. Yes.

But what if he did try to find her? What if he tried to make his way back to her but he got injured and couldn't? Has he grieved his whole life, wondering what happened to the woman he loved so dearly? Isn't it my duty then to tell him that she's still alive? Isn't it my duty to tell him that he has a *child*?

Filial duty. It's of the utmost importance to Vietnamese culture—honoring family, honoring ancestors, honoring the place and the people from which you come. It's been ingrained in my mind from such an early age—so what is the best way for me to honor my family now? Whatever I choose to do will have consequences. I can choose to do nothing, to say nothing, but I will be the one to suffer the void, knowing that I could have fostered a connection with my father and didn't. Ma will continue to suffer in her own silent way, and John Porter may suffer if he's always wondered what happened to Ma. Plus, he'll never get to know me—or maybe that's not such a great thing after all. I'm no great prize.

I sit straight up and swing my legs over the edge of the bed again. Through the darkness I reach for the glass of water that's half-full on my nightstand. I drink it and hold the glass, feeling how solid and fragile it is all at once.

It's settled.

I will tell John Porter who I am and let the cards fall where they may. I will do it without Ma knowing. Let me get my facts right, let me understand the whole picture; let me meet this man who is my father. Then I'll decide whether to subject Ma to this life-altering news.

I crawl back into bed to pray that my mind can erase itself and sleep will find me tonight. Also, that whatever I do regarding my mother and father won't cause irreparable harm—to anyone involved—to me, to Ma, or to John Porter. At this point, praying is all I can do.

CHAPTER THIRTY-FIVE

THE SKIMMER

Marble Mountain, Vietnam

Ernest

The sunlight over Marble Mountain is warm and edifying to the hamlets below. Areca trees and flowers bloom as they do year-round here. The South China Sea in the distance lies calmly, pressed against the white, crisp beach. Mopeds speed through the narrow roads of Da Nang, carrying chickens and ripe fruits to the market. The place is bustling and noisy, but up on top of the mountain, all is perfectly quiet.

Three families of tourists—two Japanese, one American—are climbing the ragged steps of the tunnel in the center of the massive rock. They grunt and wonder if they can make it the full two hundred feet—but there is light at the top. They want to reach that light. After all, they've come this far, haven't they?

The skimmer moves over the cool surface of the water in the little pond at the top, dragging dead bugs and swollen, uneaten pellets of fish food. While the humans make their way closer, Ernest holds himself still, watching the rhythm of the skimmer's dance, back and forth, back and forth, careful of the floating lily pads. Brother Chong is intent on doing his job correctly. His brow is hardened, his eyes focused. His arms strain with the task, and he lifts the mesh up and out and taps it into a waiting bucket.

Beams of light enter the cavern and smoke from incense swirls into them, making the air appear viscous like the water around Ernest's body.

He waits. Watches. The waterfall pushes the debris out toward him and the skimmer comes again. Ernest knows he will only have a few more chances to make it out today. It's coming. Closer. Three, two, one.

In a flash of light and water, Ernest makes himself known a few feet from the skimmer's net. He moves one dorsal fin around in a circular motion and keeps the other perfectly still. The move is unnatural, and his body sways so that he is now lying on his side near the surface of the water. The awkward position makes him feel unbalanced and nauseous, one eye staring straight out of the water at Brother Chong and the other fixed on the dark bottom of the pool.

Brother Chong notices Ernest now and studies the odd behavior. He's seen it so many times in fishes nearing death. Should he lift it out and end its misery or should he give it another day? Ernest knows Brother Chong is compassionate toward the fish. Or is he? Is it more compassionate to allow a fish to suffer in the water with the hopes of revival or to take it out before true misery sets in?

Take me. Take me now! Ernest pleads, holding still, rotating his fin to keep the peculiar position. *I'm dying, can't you see? Just bring the skimmer over and take me from this pond.* It's been days since he's had a glimpse of John Porter's life, days since he felt freedom from this place. Brother Chong moves the skimmer closer, closer. His time is nearing. Ernest spins his fin and his eyes go wild on either side of his head. It's happening. He's going to do it now.

But what then? Ernest stops. What does Brother Chong do with a dying fish once he pulls it from the water? Does he take it somewhere for medical attention? Does he release it in the ocean and set it free? Or does he simply fling the dying thing over the side of the mountain, letting it fly and crash somewhere in the valley?

Ernest stops spinning his one fin, losing his concentration, and the other one begins moving in tandem, involuntarily. Brother Chong sees the fish roll back upright and studies it.

Ernest knows he has blown his chance, and he darts away quickly, heading straight for the waterfall. He is unsure how he feels. What is a worse fate? Long life in a fishpond or no life at all? If he flies through the air and lands on a boulder, will he turn into stone like the Buddha who watches over this place, unmoving, permanently stuck here?

Ernest wishes he was back at home in Georgia. He wishes he was in Sunday school again, paying close attention to Miss Sally's teachings. What did she say about life after death? *All who believe in Him shall not perish but have everlasting life.* But did she ever say anything about animals? About fish? What then, for Ernest?

He is trapped. He has no one to turn to. No one who can open a book and tell him what it says about his situation. His fate. He considers Eldest fish, but he is simply a fish. He's never been a human. Though he did say Ernest's humanity was returning, didn't he? Is it possible to simply turn back into a man? Why not? He simply turned into a fish, didn't he?

Ernest moves to a quiet, empty corner of the pond and meditates on what it is to be human. What is it to be human? What is it? What is so different from being a fish, apart from the body and the surrounding water? There's something else. Something missing. Fish have thoughts. They have desires. He thinks back to his friend John Porter and the way that he felt while in his presence. What was it about John that was so different from Ernest?

The tourist families have entered the cave now, and the room echoes with panting and laughter.

"You all right, Dad?" a teenage girl asks an overweight man. He leans over on his large, wobbly knees and smiles, relieved, amazed he made it. The girl moves to him and wraps her arm around his sweaty back. She squeezes him and in return, he leans his head on her shoulder. His eyes are closed. The girl grins and runs over to the giant statue of Buddha and rubs the belly. "Hey, Daddy, they've got a statue of you up here."

"Had to sit for a whole day, posing for that one," he teases. The man stands straighter and moves to his daughter's side. He takes her hand in his and kisses it. Then he tilts his head back. "Come here, Mother," he says. "Look at this." The three of them stand, glued side by side, marveling at the pitch of the cavern's ceiling.

All three families are here now. They bounce from one place to the next, snapping photographs, more excited or meditative with each new finding. Ernest observes there is an invisible string that seems to connect them all. There is a core in each family, and the individual parts float around the room like planets from the sun, always begging for one or the other to share, to hold, to touch, to laugh. Always coming back to one another.

What is this invisible core? he wonders.

Then it hits him. Ernest's eyes go wide with understanding. Emotions, feelings, caring for someone else. Empathy. It's elementary, but there it is.

Love.

Love is what separates the humans from the fishes. In order to be human again, Ernest must remember what it feels like to truly love again.

To love again.

It seems so foreign to him now. Love. It's exactly what he's tried to forget all these lonely waterlogged years.

CHAPTER THIRTY-SIX

THE STRANGER
Charleston

Katherine Ann

I am waiting for my father to meet me for lunch. Seems simple enough, but I have never had lunch with Daddy alone. Mama is always a soft buffer between us—that cushion of fluid that keeps hip bone from colliding with ball socket and scraping. But today it's better that she's not here. In fact, I wonder if she'll catch wind of our clandestine meeting. I pick up the menu and swivel my head to see if anyone might be in here who knows us. Just in case.

There are three slices of lemon in my un-sweet iced tea to make up for the sugar I'm not putting in. Somehow it feels better this way, less indulgent for once. More wholesome. I push the crumbs away from the smidgeon of buttered bread I've allowed myself and listen to the cacophony of voices and dishes muffling into an unrecognizable drone. As a child, I could sleep in any shopping mall or restaurant, so long as it had this sound. It's soothing for some reason. Makes me forget that my father is still not here.

I look across the table, past the sweetgrass basket of bread and butter to the empty seat. Is he coming? And if he does come, is he ready for this? Am I ready for this?

We've spent a lifetime glossing over my father's oddities and outbursts as if they're nothing more than spilt milk. As Mama would say, "Leave well enough alone." But is it well enough? Is Daddy well enough? Am I?

I read in the paper this morning that there's a new bill going before Congress for veteran suicide prevention, of all things. My mouth runs dry as I remember the daunting figures: over fifty-eight thousand soldiers were killed in the Vietnam War, and since then, over fifty-eight thousand Vietnam veterans have committed suicide. The war that remains in these soldiers' heads is just as bad as the hand-to-hand combat! Good heavens. That couldn't be Daddy, could it? He's no statistic. He wouldn't do that to himself, to us.

Perhaps I'm making too much of this. Daddy's fine. He's had forty years to adjust to life after the war. Life's not fair or easy—no one said it would be.

But he's breaking things now. Someone got hurt. What's next?

I take a sip of tea and look around for my waitress, seriously considering leaving this instant and acting as if I never even brought up the subject of meeting her—this woman, this stranger, this dredger of ghosts from Daddy's past. I see a huge blue marlin, stiff on the wood-plank wall, stuffed and perched forever by the kitchen. Poor fish. Never even had a chance.

Daddy has no idea what's in store for him. And what do I really know about this woman? Nothing. Who is she? Is it just sick curiosity that has me meddling in my father's affairs? Am I sticking my nose where it should not be?

No. No, he needs me. She would have called back anyway, so my calling her first makes perfect sense. Right? Take the offensive position. It's safer this way. He eventually would have talked to her, and I would not have been there. He needs me to be there when he talks with this woman with ties to Vietnam. When he meets his past head-on.

Yes. I am here for you, Daddy.

But what if she does him more harm than good? Oh good gracious, what have I done?

As soon as I've talked myself into calling the whole thing off, my throat catches on a scratchy lump of crust and my father enters the door. I'm anxious, as though he's a perfect stranger. Or maybe I've become the stranger.

I wave and he looks over at me cautiously. Then he heads straight for me, barreling almost, with determination on his brow. He's here now. She's coming. We're actually going to do this.

"Hi, Daddy," I say, standing and kissing him on the cheek as he bends to me, peering at the patrons around us.

"What's good here? Have you ordered yet?" He plunks down and picks up his menu, eyes running rampant over the pages, not seeing a thing. His red cheeks are crinkled as if it's too bright in here, showing his deep crow's-feet from so many years baking in the sun. "Dang painters wouldn't get there on time or I could've been here five minutes ago."

"It's all right," I hear myself say to him, smiling slightly for reassurance. And in the pit of me, I hope everything *will* be all right—once we've heard whatever it is this strange woman wants with my father. Once she's entered our lives, I know there's no turning back.

Daddy looks across the table at the third menu and glass of water next to me and confusion sets in. "Is your mother coming too?" he asks, looking around for her.

"No. Not Mama."

His face scrunches up. "RC?"

"No . . ."

"Well then, who the heck is it?" He's nervous now and agitated. "I thought we were having lunch just the two of us!" Daddy cannot handle last-minute changes. It's like hitting the road with no map to follow. Being forced to take a detour. He simply falls apart.

"Uh, nobody. Just a friend of mine," I play it down. "You haven't met her yet. She might not even come. Probably won't."

Daddy shakes his head and stares at his menu again. Maybe he assumes I never lunch without a friend. What would he know? He's never had lunch with me before.

Then I see her. It's got to be her.

A woman walks in behind Daddy wearing the red blouse she said she'd have on, and my heart stops. She's about my age, a little thicker, slightly more exotic. I take a deep breath and stand up slowly, waving. And Daddy turns his head just in time to see our lunch guest wipe a tear from her otherwise smiling round face.

Oh good heavens. The past has finally arrived. No, wait a minute. The past has turned around and is running out the door as fast as her legs will take her.

CHAPTER THIRTY-SEVEN

THE BOMB

Lisa

I stand in shrubs and bat at the branches as they claw my clothes. I press myself against the building and shake, crying uncontrollably. Was it him? Was that my father and my sister in there?

I'm not ready for this. What was I thinking? I pull my purse up to my face and peer in through hazy wet eyes, searching for my keys. I am so out of here. Seeing that these people are real and not just phantoms anymore has stolen my tongue away. Had I walked in to greet them, I could not have mustered a single word. What could I possibly say?

I grab my keys and step carefully over purple and white pansies, the ones I trampled a minute ago, and a group of restaurant goers eyes me suspiciously. I wipe my face with the back of my hand as my foot hits the gravel walkway.

"Lisa?" The voice is gentle wind chimes over crisp air blowing in from the waterway. I turn and face her. Her brown eyes show concern above parted glossy lips. And there, in between, is that . . . I study her nose to see if it matches mine.

"K-Katherine Ann?" I muster.

She smiles with recognition, and I draw from my toes, up my spine and stand straight and tall. I am a grown woman. I can do this.

Look at my sweet sister, the purely American version of me. She's so pretty.

"I'm so sorry, I just . . . I'm not feeling so well today. Had to get some air."

"Oh, well let's get you some water." She takes my arm gently and pulls me to her as she heads for the door again. An elderly man struggles with the heavy door, and Katherine Ann pulls it open, holding it for him and his wife.

"Thank you," the man says in his Sunday-go-to-meetin' suit.

Katherine Ann says to me politely, "After you." She still has no idea who I am or what kind of bomb I'm here to drop.

I smile thinly and move through the door into the bustle of food and patrons and wait staff. The smell reminds me so much of Le's Kitchen, and for a second I forget I'm so far from home.

There he is.

The back of his head is short gray stubble. His neck is red and lined with deep diagonal creases, and he sits, shoulders hunched over a menu.

As we approach the table, Katherine Ann puts her hand on my back and turns me toward the seated man.

"Daddy?" she says. "I'd like you to meet a friend of mine. This is Lisa."

He turns and lights up. Tears brim again as I look into Mr. Porter's face. My father's face. His eyes behind glasses are round with pronounced lids, his lips, pencil lines, and his nose, long.

With a hump.

He looks much like his photo. He's aged very well and is still handsome. Rugged. This is the man my mother loved.

"Nice to meet you," I say, smiling, about to faint. He pushes up to standing and beckons gentleman-like for me to sit.

"What took you so long? We've been waiting for you," he says.

"Oh, you have?" What a stupid thing to say. "Well, sorry I'm so late, I—"

"Daddy, Lisa lives in Georgetown," Katherine Ann interjects. "Bet you had some traffic coming down here."

"Georgetown, huh?" John Porter says. "Don't get up that way too much. What's your father do up there?"

It's a natural Southern thing to ask. Still . . .

"My father? I—" I swallow hard and my throat clamps shut. I concentrate on not choking. Katherine Ann grabs a glass of cold water and hands it to me. I drink while holding one finger up and stalling for the words that must surely come now.

"Well." I swallow and put my glass down. "I've never met my father, actually. My mother and I, and my uncle before he passed, we run a little restaurant."

"Really? A restaurant. How about that. I built one of those Italian places once. Used to eat there every Friday night till my wife stopped eating carbs. That was a long time ago though." He presses his hands on the table and plays with his paper placemat. He holds the corners and pulls it to him, then pushes it away again, his empty plate and silverware floating with every tug.

Silence engulfs us for a few awkward moments until my father waves at the waitress walking by. He makes a motion toward his mouth likes he's drinking.

"Can I get you something?" The waitress stops at our table, pulling out her pad and pen.

"How about a Drambui on the rocks."

"In the middle of the day, Daddy?" says Katherine Ann.

Then she rethinks and says, "Well, all right. Sounds pretty good. I'll have a glass of white wine then. Your house chardonnay is fine."

"And for you?" The waitress turns to me.

I typically don't drink, but today, well . . . "I'll have what she's having." The waitress scribbles it down.

"Okay, back with those drinks in just a sec."

"No, wait a minute," I catch her after she turns. "Just make mine a sweet tea, all right? No wine for me." She scribbles some more and I take in a deep breath. I've got to keep my wits about me. I picture Ma's empty, sad face sitting quietly in my living room in the glare of the television while I'm sitting here—with him.

More silence.

"So how do you know Katie-bug? You two go to school together or something?" he asks me.

Katherine Ann leans forward on her elbows and clears her throat. "Well, to tell the truth, Lisa and I have just met, Daddy. I . . . well . . . oh, here come our drinks. Goodie."

The waitress delivers my sweet tea, Katherine Ann's glass of wine, and Mr. Porter's cocktail. He swivels the little straw and takes a sip. Katherine Ann picks up her glass and seems to drink it for an awfully long time, and when she sets it down again, it's half-empty.

"Daddy," she says, squaring her shoulders. "After swimming the other day, I happened to answer your phone, and Lisa here . . . she was on the other end." He looks at me with mild attention and picks up his drink again. "So we got to talking, and you'll never believe, but—get this—Lisa is actually the daughter of one of your old army buddies. Isn't that right?" She leans away, looks at me, and gives me the floor.

I smile at each of them, then falter, and then smile again. "Yes, that's . . ."

My father's eyes narrow as he stares, trying to place me. He's very quiet and perfectly still. He's sitting up straighter now. "I knew your dad? Who is he?" he asks.

"Well, like I said, I've never met him . . ."

"Oh yeah, I knew that. You said that."

". . . but my mother is someone you might remember."

He stops and cocks his head, utterly baffled now.

"She said you met her in Vietnam. Near Da Nang? Her name is Margaret Le, but back then you would have known her as Doan Vien Le."

If a word could kill a man, I think I may have done it. Every drop of color seeps from Mr. Porter's skin and drips onto the floor. He coughs. Katherine Ann is looking on, her head shifting between our two faces as if watching a tennis match.

"Y'all 'bout ready to order?" the waitress interrupts. She's back, chipper and busy, looking at her next table that's just been seated.

John Porter's throat catches and he twists his head and grabs for his drink. He sips it dry and jingles the ice, and then he looks over at Katherine Ann as if he wants her to throw him a life preserver.

"Could you give us just a few more minutes? We're not quite ready. Sorry." Katherine Ann sends the waitress away and then turns to face me. "So, your mother met Daddy in Vietnam? Wow. How 'bout that?" Her words are slow and careful. "Daddy, do you remember her? Shwan Veen, is that how you say it?"

His eyes are welling now and tears stripe down his cheek. He can do nothing but nod and cough. He jiggles his empty glass again and turns around looking for the waitress. Seeing her, he holds the glass up indicating he'd like another. Rather desperately, I observe.

"She's still living, my mother," I add, finally. "She . . . well, she's not doing very well at the moment. When my uncle died, she sort of shut down."

John Porter still cannot talk, but tears are no longer forming. Instead, he stares intently at his large rough hands and fiddles with a callous on his thumb. Dark tear spots bleed into his green shirt where his heart is.

"And there's something else." I take a deep breath and close my eyes, saying a little prayer. This is it. *This is it.* "Uh." I glance furtively at Katherine Ann and then at John Porter, who has not moved. "Katherine Ann." I reach over and touch her hand lightly. "I'm so happy to meet you, I just can't say how much. And you, Mr. Porter. My mother doesn't really know that I'm here today but, well, there's just no easy way to say this, so I guess I'll just get it out."

I inhale all the air from the room, and on exhale, before I lose my nerve, I blurt it out.

"Mr. Porter?" His head doesn't move, but his eyes roll slowly beneath his lids to meet my gaze. I attempt a pleasant smile. "Mr. Porter," I whisper. "I'm actually . . . um . . . actually . . ."

My eyes are dams about to burst.

"What." His voice is low and morose. "Doan Vien's dying." He grunts, the act seeming to cause him pain.

"No. No. My mother will be fine," I say quietly. "I just don't know how to say this."

"Say it." The dead man speaks.

"I'm your daughter, Mr. Porter. Sir, I'm your daughter."

CHAPTER THIRTY-EIGHT

THE DEAD MAN

John

Dishes clank, and there is laughter across the room by the bar and all around him. But John Porter is not laughing. He doesn't say a word. And then finally, a sound. It's that sound a child makes when you ask him, has he done something wrong, did he hit his sister, did he empty that bucket of rotting leaves on the living room floor? You ask a child such a question and the face will drop, the eyes will rise slowly, the head will begin to swivel back and forth, then faster, more vigorously. Finally a barely audible sound escapes the throat but is blocked by pressed lips, *Hmm-mm. Hmm-mm.*

John Porter's head is swiveling back and forth shuttering in spasms. Huh-uh. No. *No.* And then before he pushes up from the table to leave this place and this young woman who has stung him so badly, he looks one last time in her eyes. He sees that they are glassy and red, filled with longing for him to be the one, to be her father, to fill whatever it is that needs filling. He looks at her and he sees Doan Vien again, the same way her eyes crinkled when she would cry, that black silken hair, that lovely brown skin. Then he says to her, "You look just like . . ."

He nearly knocks over a waitress carrying an armful of dishes. And with his exit, the two women, daughters aching to love this man with all of his flaws, are left sitting on one side, feeling the emptiness of the opposite booth and the cool, crisp marsh breeze blowing through the open restaurant door.

Katherine Ann

The girl beside me flinches as the door shuts. I am unable to make sense of what just happened. Did she say that Daddy is her father? Did *he* say she looks just like her mother? So it's true! How can this be possible? But then Daddy had said, "No." He shook his head no. Did he mean *no*, she's not his daughter or *no*, he can't believe this is happening, just like I can't believe it?

She is shaking now. My head turns slowly toward Lisa as if mechanically, moving on its own, against my will, and I see her face. It looks nothing like the face she was wearing a few minutes ago. Instead, a dark, grotesque mask has attached itself, to her eyes that now droop down toward the ground, to her brow that is thick and heavy. It is possible that I have never seen a person wearing such sadness. And it is because of this and only this reason that I wrap my arm around this woman and I hold her, this perfect stranger who claims to be my sister. Is she? Is she not? Whatever the truth, I believe that she *believes* she is his daughter. And when it all comes down to it, isn't what we believe all we have to go on? Isn't *what we believe* our reality?

I hold her, crying in the crook of my arm, and I consider crying myself, but I can't. My stomach has formed a tight fist, and I think of my father's face before he shoved out the door. It haunts me. I have seen that face before. Once. Only once.

My parents were chaperones on my sixth-grade trip to Washington DC, that same trip that all sixth graders take. It's the indoctrination into America and what it means to be an American, as if looking at memorials can infuse the young body with patriotism and the understanding of our forefathers and the sacrifices that they made.

It was a cool day in March when our crowd of sixty gawky eleven-year-olds laughed and muddled our way across the Mall. We'd already visited Lincoln's and Washington's memorials, and they'd garnered a few oohs and aahs—but nothing much from me. I had no idea of the power of what we were about to see. I had no idea what it would do to my father. I didn't think of these things back then. I didn't think of them, or I didn't care, or I didn't understand. I'd like to believe it was mostly a lack of understanding.

What I remember of that day in our nation's capital is that as we got closer to the long black v-shaped wall of the Vietnam Memorial, my father walked slower as if wearing lead boots. When I approached the massive wall and looked at all those thousands of names of the perished, I was awestruck. I remembered thinking about the lives of the men who had died in order to be written upon this wall. And it occurred to me that there may have been someone on this wall that my father knew.

The other kids had pieces of white paper and sharpened pencils. They were already making etchings of names to take home with them. I held my piece of paper and pencil and turned to ask Daddy if there was a particular name he wanted to me to etch, but he wasn't there.

My father was half a football field away from me. He was standing motionless, facing us as if he had walked as far as he could and then a glass barrier had simply risen from the ground and held him back. He stood alone. My mother saw me turning back toward him and she grabbed my hand and said, "Come on, let's go." My paper was left white and unmarked, my pencil perfectly sharpened. When we were close enough to see Daddy's face, I saw the tracks of tears and the far-off stare of a man trying desperately to distance himself from his past.

Here, in front of Lisa Le, my father had that same look, quivering jelly over steel. Here she was in front of him, his past, and he simply had to put as much distance between them as possible.

I won't run after him. It would be like trying to tame a wild animal if I approached him now. Who knows where my father has gone—physically or mentally? Will he ever be able to return?

What have I done?

I've destroyed him by bringing this woman into his life. I've destroyed him and possibly his marriage.

I know my mother, Betty Jo Porter, and I can only imagine what this news is going to do to her. Her relationship with my father is tenuous enough as it is. Is it true? Does Daddy have another daughter from another woman? Truth or not, if my mother finds out about this, I honestly don't know if she has patience enough or love enough for him to stick around and see Daddy through.

May God help us all.

Lisa

It's easier to mourn a dead man than a coward.

I am dangling on a rope high above the rocks. Just cut the rope. I cannot do this anymore. I cannot be strong anymore. I have lost all hope. Any glimmer that I had to meet my father, to be accepted, to fill that other half of me, is gone. My mother is sifting away from me. She barely exists. My sperm donor of a father doesn't want to have anything to do with me. I have never felt such utter rejection in my life. I never knew that it was possible to feel this way. At least when I thought my father was dead, I had hope of a heavenly reunion some day. I would run into his outstretched arms and he would know me and love me and say he'd waited forever to finally touch me.

But this man detested me. He could not stand the sight of me. Who is this woman holding me upright? My sister? Does she not feel the same revulsion that her father does at the mere sight of me?

My stomach curdles and there is no time to move. I retch over this poor woman's legs. She squeals and pushes away from me. It's fitting. I don't know if I apologize to her or not. People stare at me as I wipe my face and swagger to the door. I have to leave this place. I want to leave this world. I do not fit in. I have nothing to offer. My own blood wants nothing to do with me.

I am done. Done longing, done hoping, done trying to help Ma, done trying to pretend I'm American, to pretend I am Vietnamese, to pretend I am happy being all alone. I look out over the water at the boats, rocking in the growing unrest. I want to step onto that boat again, the dreaded one that brought me here, and go back to wherever I came from. I want to drift out to sea, away from everything and everyone. I am drifting. Sinking. I can't do this anymore, pretending to live.

I suppose I am John Porter's daughter after all. I am as much a coward in this world as he is—that man who gave me life and then left me with no life at all.

Ernest

Ernest is dying.

If this is living, I don't want it anymore, he thinks. He feels his body growing weaker, his spirit wavering like vapor, in and out, in and out. The water around him is cold at times, other times he doesn't feel it. He doesn't dream of escaping anymore. He simply wants to cease to exist, in this form anyway. Perhaps there's something better on the other side. What was he afraid of? Dying is not the end of the world. It could be the beginning of a new one, another one, a better one.

It is nighttime on Marble Mountain. The monks at the bottom of the hill are all asleep in their bunks. It's dark in the cavern. There is a faint sliver of pale light coming in from the moon. Ernest knows it won't be long now before Brother Chong makes his way through the tunnel with his lantern and sits beside this pond and pulls out his Bible. He does it when the other monks are not watching. Ernest wonders, do they know? These men and women are contemplative. Isn't that what living in a monastery is all about? The contemplative life? Contemplating what is real, what is true, what is noble, what is worth fighting for, dying for, living for? Brother Chong is searching. What's the harm in searching the Bible for truth? What if he finds it? Ernest feels his gills fill in anticipation. If only there were some way to get him to read aloud so he could hear the words of God again.

Ernest can hear them now. The words of God are in the voice of his mother, how she would read him a chapter each night before bed. *Just one more,* he would say to his mother with eyes closing. *Read to me*, he thinks now. He stares intently at Brother Chong. Comes right up to the surface, lifts his eyes, opens his mouth, and says, *Please begin.*

There is a chill in the air tonight. Brother Chong assembles his tunic around him and from the folds he pulls out a small brown book. The lantern casts ghostly shadows over the cavern. The walls dance. The face of Buddha is no longer smiling, but instead, Ernest doesn't know—something else, something less jovial, less benign. Brother Chong's face glows orange like a jack-o-lantern. His eyes gleam with the risk he is taking, with the forbiddance of it. There is passion in his eyes tonight. *Read to me, Ernest* pleads. *Please. Let me hear God speak.*

He has nothing left to go on. He is dying and all alone.

Won't you read to me now and fill my soul?

PART FOUR
FIRE

Ông ta mà đấu tranh lửa với lửa đốt cháy cái nhà
(của) anh ấy hai lần nhanh hơn.

He who fights fire with fire burns his house down twice as fast.

—Vietnamese proverb

CHAPTER THIRTY-NINE

THE MONSTER
Georgetown

Lisa

I don't remember the drive back to Georgetown from Charleston. I don't remember the long straight highway or the yellow blinking lights through sleepy towns. I don't remember crossing the Georgetown Bridge or going past the mill or the restaurant. It's frightening, but somehow I'm here.

That's all I can say. I'm here.

Ma has not changed. She is still her silent self, barely alive, propped up in her cozy chair where I left her. I wonder, who is more alive at this point? Ma or me?

I have no one to share this with. I have no one to cry to, to tell that my own father, my blood, has rejected me. Oh, why did I have to contact him? Why did I have to see the newspaper or learn his name or break Ma's picture frame in the first place? What I wouldn't give to be able to go back in time and never set foot in Ma's room. None of this would have happened.

I thought I was nothing before. But what is less than nothing? I am less than nothing.

I am torn between anger at my mother and compassion for

her. No, anger. How dare she choose this man for my father! How dare she . . . oh, it's not her fault. She has no idea he is even alive. She still mourns him as she always has. Is it better to mourn a dead man than a coward? Yes. It is. I should at least let her have that.

But I am a seething monster at this moment. I am not myself. I am tired of tiptoeing around this old woman in my own house. *So you lost your brother. Well, I lost my uncle. I loved him too. He was the only man in my life. And he's gone. Big deal, Ma. Get over it! I am still talking, functioning, cooking at the restaurant, paying all the bills, and taking care of you, Ma! I am continuing on in this life, this wretched life. My own father hates me. Life is not fair!*

I jump from my seat at the kitchen table. My eyes peel away from the birdbath outside, dark and murky with old water and brown decaying leaves. There are streaks across the otherwise clean window. I do not feel my feet hit the ground on my way to the living room, but they must have because I am here now. I grab the back of Ma's chair and swivel it around so she is facing me.

"He's not dead, Ma. No, he's very much alive." My voice seems to be coming from some far-off place. It's cold and cruel and shrill. My mother blinks at me, her eyes grown large and frightened. Her body stiffens. She doesn't recognize this warrior in me. "Not Uncle, Ma. He's still dead. But John Porter? Yes. You know that name? Remember him?"

Ma's left eye twitches as if I've struck her with the back of my hand.

"John Porter, Ma. My father. He's alive!"

MA CLUTCHES AT her heart, and I watch her brow form deep creases. Her face goes pale, but she doesn't move. Cannot move.

Oh, what have I done?

I collapse to my knees, hugging the lap of this woman I love more than life itself. I cry and moan and the whole earth moves painfully out of my chest and into the air.

My mother's thin legs are stiff, and I wonder if I have killed her. I try to catch my breath and steal a glance at her face. I watch her inhale suddenly as if she stopped breathing moments ago. Her eyes are closed tight and her hand falls from her chest and onto the back of my head. Her fingers rub gently behind my ear, barely noticeable, and then stop when a low, guttural groan engulfs her. Then she's silent again. And I am silent. All I hear is audience laughter, hollow and fake, from the television.

I sit back on my feet, but Ma avoids my gaze. Then she stands shakily from her chair and moves around me. She feels her way, leaning on the couch, touching the side table, reaching for the wall as if she may topple.

"Ma? I'm sorry. Wait . . ."

While I sniffle and whine, Ma trails to her bedroom, opens the door, and then closes it softly behind her. The last thing I hear before my own guilt-ridden wail is the quiet click of Ma's door shutting me out again.

CHAPTER FORTY

THE SCORPION

John

What if, in the midst of chaos and destruction, you saw an angel? You clung to her, she saved you. She helped you remain human in the midst of monstrosity.

What if that same angel walked back into your life nearly four decades later when everything was smooth and calm and the mere thought of her could evoke the danger, the death and despair from so long ago? This is the scenario that faced John Porter when Lisa Le told him her mother was Doan Vien—that she was the daughter of his angel who could now destroy everything he'd worked so hard to build.

When faced with this scenario—past and present wrapping around and touching each other, a scorpion's tail to its prey— you can choose one of two paths: to face head-on the impending collision, or simply—

To run.

John Porter chose the latter. He ran as fast as was humanly possible away from the girl and into the waiting, comfortable arms of Silence.

Some scars are just too deep.

To a young man, there's only one thing that leaves scars deeper than war, and that's the love and loss of a woman. John Porter's scars are about as deep as a man can get, for his were formed by the love and loss of a woman in the midst of the hell of war. There's no separating the two for him. One is as the other. There is no war without memory of the woman. There is no memory of the woman without hearing gunfire and fearing for his life. Or fearing that he would have to take another's life.

Is it ever truly possible to love again when there's been an association made between destruction and love? Or perhaps there are only different kinds of love, less passion, for instance, more sensible, less danger.

"Marry me when we get out of here," he had told her all those years ago, bended on one knee and exposing his heart. The rain had ended and condensation clung to his skin. He could hear raindrops dripping through the leaves of the surrounding jungle. With a tentative smile he said again, "Marry me."

But looking in her eyes he knew it would not happen. Could not happen. Her head was shaking slightly, side to side, and she pulled her trembling hand from his and held it to her heart.

"*Chuc ahn chi tram nam hahn phuc*," the young woman whispered, tears rolling down her velvet cheeks. "I wish you hundred year of happiness."

He'd wanted nothing to do with a hundred years of happiness if they didn't include Doan Vien.

CHAPTER FORTY-ONE

THE REFLECTION

Katherine Ann

Oh, no, not now. I can't handle this today. My boys are fighting again, this time over a G.I. Joe figure. Why'd I have to buy that thing? I just couldn't resist the little soldier dressed in army fatigues like they're wearing in Iraq these days. I just wanted to support our troops and give my boys a real hero. But seeing them go at it, flesh of my flesh, pieces of me, born from my own body, fighting like that—it's too much to handle! Blood should not battle against blood.

"Enough! Stop it this instant or I'll . . . Tradd, go to your room. Right now. Cooper, go to your room too."

They pull apart and Cooper is left holding Iraq Joe. He's crying.

"I had it first!" says Tradd, scowling and stomping his foot.

"Noooo, I hadddiiitt!"

"That's enough! I mean it, Tradd, go to your room right now or Mama's head's going to explode. Do you hear me? Do you want Mama's head to explode?"

They've been at it for the past forty-five minutes, for a toy or a book or a coveted spot on the sofa. Apparently he hears me this time. Maybe it's the way my eyes are crossing or the vein bulging in my head, but whatever it is, it works. Tradd skulks up the stairs, heavy footed. I hear him mumble, "Had it first . . ." before his bedroom door shuts.

"And you, mister. Give me that." I hold my hand out and Cooper sniffles, his blue eyes red and sullen. He turns away and hides his toy from me. "Mine," he says.

"Cooper Richard . . ."

My little boy frowns and whimpers. He knows hearing his middle name means I'm serious, so he resigns himself to losing this battle and regretfully holds the figure within reach.

I go for his hand and grab it, pulling him into my neck, hugging him tight. I smell his no-more-tears shampoo. "I love you, sweetie. I love you so much. I just don't want you fighting with your brother like that. Do you hear me? It's not right. You're supposed to love each other. That's what brothers do." He sniffs and wipes his nose on my shoulder. "I'm going to hold on to this for now, but I want you to go on up and tell your brother you're sorry."

"But he—"

"Aack—I don't care who started it. You go on up there and you and Tradd play in his room for a while. Don't come down until I get you, okay? Mommy really needs a little quiet to think."

He doesn't budge. I take a needed deep breath.

"Go on now."

Cooper frowns and thinks of crying again, but he nods and turns, trudging up the stairs. I watch his ears that stick out from his short haircut and his baggy toddler jeans. He's so little. So very little. Oh God, how I love that child. Oh, how I love them both. They're all I have.

My head is down in my hands and I'm thinking of crying when I hear the door open. RC steps in, carrying plastic grocery bags. He might as well be riding on a white horse.

"Oh, thank God you're here," I say. I flop back on the couch, tears finally stinging my eyes.

"What's going on?" he asks.

"The boys! What happened to our sweet little boys? They used to play, get along, take care of each other, but now . . ."

RC approaches me carefully and sits on the arm of the sofa. "Where are they, upstairs?"

I nod and pinch my eyes shut. RC rubs my right shoulder. "Sam and I used to fight like that all the time. You know how children are."

"But not our children. They're just . . . out of control lately."

"Well, kids can sense things." He stops rubbing my shoulder. "You've been pretty distracted lately. They're probably just trying to get your attention."

"You think this is my fault? You think I caused this?"

"Honey, I'm not saying . . . Look, I'm worried about you. I can almost *see* the tension surrounding you. It's like a black cloud."

I look up at him mortified. Then I take a deep breath. "My children are the most important things in my life."

"I know they are, honey. Listen, I'll go up and have a talk with them. You just try and relax. Okay?"

He brushes a strand of hair from my eyes, and I squeeze his hand. "Okay," I say.

I watch as RC climbs the stairs to go be with our children. My two children. Two extensions of me. Who would I be without Tradd and Cooper in this world? Who in the world was I before them? A lawyer? A woman only concerned with her own ambitions, her own desires? I did not truly live until I loved RC and gave birth to our boys. I never felt at peace in my own soul before I saw their smiles. Have I forgotten all that? Where is that peace now?

I think of my father. He has another daughter. Another *child*. I'm so sad he can't face her. What would I do if it were my child? What if Lisa's a wonderful person? What if he's missing out on having her in his life too? For that matter, what if I'm missing out on her? She seemed very nice. So very nice.

Good heavens, I have a sister. There is someone else on this planet who shares my genetics, my desires perhaps. What if my kidney fails someday? What if I need a new one? I have a sibling! We have shared blood! Is it possible she could be an aunt to my children—one who keeps them for sleepovers and spoils them behind my back? Maybe she could share cooking responsibilities with me for holidays, Thanksgiving, Christmas? And we could commiserate on having a father like Daddy.

I stand up and walk to the window, staring into the backyard. Two squirrels play chase up the trunk of a large oak tree, tails flitting. My God, what am I missing? I feel a void now, one I never knew I had. Or maybe I did always feel it, but didn't know what it was. I know what it is now. There is another part of me, floating around just north of here in Georgetown. How can I have peace now that I know she's out there?

I see a faint reflection of myself in the window. I am wispy and pale and halfway here. *Like it or not, Daddy, you're going to have to own up to this one. I don't care if it is hard for you to face.* The past is the past. There are people, real people living in the here and now, who will benefit from getting to know Lisa. There!

I would like to know Lisa. I would like to know my sister, thank you very much. I just have to figure out a way to bring us all together. If ever there has been an impossible challenge, it's this one. But if ever there has been a more worthy cause to fight for than family, I simply don't know what it is.

John

John sits on his Boston Whaler, watching birds fly up from the marsh grass and circle, searching for food. He takes the last swig of his Dos Equis and then clumsily fits it back in the six-pack container. He grabs another one and thinks of her, the girl's teary eyes, her skin like her mother's. He closes his eyes and presses his lids tight until the inside of his head goes black and he can't remember her face anymore.

He takes a long swig and swirls it on his tongue like fine wine.

Dad-gum Katie, he thinks. *What did she do? Why would she bring that girl to see me?*

His eyes become slits, and he watches a boat go by in the distant waterway just south of his inlet. He thinks back to those days in Vietnam. It was a long time ago. He hates to remember, but he has to now. He didn't touch her, did he? No! Hell no, he didn't touch her! Or did he? Shoot, it's been forty years since the war. He was a different man then, just a kid. How the heck can he remember that far back? How can he know for sure?

But he does remember. He remembers how he longed to touch Doan Vien to the point of feeling physical pain in his chest, in his gut. He remembers dreaming of being able to finally touch her on their wedding night. After she'd agreed to marry him. Which she had not.

Heck, no. He never touched her at all.

But that *face.* That young girl's face, Lisa. It was him, wasn't it?

It was Ernest. Lucky dog, he'd been sleeping with her behind John's back. What a chump! What a sucker he'd been! There John was, thinking she'd been so virginal and pure while his best friend, Ernest, was making boom-boom with Mamasan.

You had a little girl, buddy. You had a little girl! And she's almost as pretty as her mother except she looks just like *you*.

John rubs his whiskers and feels his sandpaper face. It snaps him back to the here and now.

This child thinks I'm her father. Is that what Doan Vien told her? It has to be. Doan Vien told her daughter that I am her father.

For an instant, John imagines what life would have been like with Doan Vien at his side and little Lisa between them. He shakes his head. It doesn't fit. Doesn't feel right. His life is with Betty Jo, always has been. She's his wife, the mother of his child. He was there when little Katie-bug was born. Katie is the one. She's the only one for him. Lisa is simply delusional.

He does wonder about her though—about Doan Vien, what her life has been like all these years. Thank God she's alive. He's amazed she's still alive. What would it be like to see her again? What would she think of him? Of who he'd turned into? Belly too big, not much hair left, but this house! He's done all right, right? But when he tries to imagine Doan Vien as a sixty-year-old woman, he can't do it. She will always be young and beautiful and flawless like an angel in his mind.

John grabs the beer and stands up, rocking his boat. Enough of this. He leans over and sticks one leg on the dock, sets his beer down next to it, then pushes with all he has up to standing. He stumbles, almost falling back into the boat, but he holds it together. He takes a final swig and the last beer is empty. He pitches it into the boat, aiming for the six-pack, and misses. The bottle rolls until it comes to a stop under the driver's seat.

John walks straight for his house. He's walking, walking. It's the middle of the day. If Betty Jo sees him home at this hour and in this condition, she'll never speak to him again. She'll kick him to the curb. And how would he explain himself? How would he explain he just really needed a drink after this girl shook his world? God knows, she puts up with a lot from him as it is.

John veers to the left and ducks into the pool house. He closes the door behind him, sits down on the wooden bench, and puts his face in his hands. He rubs his eyes behind his glasses then takes them off. The bleached white starfish on the walls peer over him as he considers crying, but nothing will come out. He's completely dry. John leans back and swivels his feet up, shoes still on, then lies down on the bench, one arm draped over his eyes to keep the light out.

He'll just lie here for a few minutes to clear his head. That's all. Just a few minutes. Right now, he can't think of Doan Vien or Lisa or Ernest anymore. He can't think about all that. It's too much for one man. He's only one man.

But the girl. She looked just like him. There's no mistaking, that's Ernest's baby. *Oh, dear God, Ernest. What did I do?* Just the thought of him makes the tears finally stream into his ears. *I'm so sorry. So sorry, buddy!*

For an instant, just before he drifts off to sleep, John Porter wants nothing more in this world than to be able to touch Ernest's sweet child, to stare at her face. Just to have a piece of his little brother back again. Just a piece of him. That's all he wants.

With the weight of it all, John's arm slides slowly and then falls off his face with a plunk to the floor. He doesn't feel it though. John Porter is already fast asleep and dreaming of the mountain again.

CHAPTER FORTY-TWO

The Chill

Katherine Ann

There's a chill in the air. October leaves are beginning to turn gold, but only a little. A Lowcountry autumn is green for the most part, only fringes of colors popping up here and there. I watch a blackbird land in the top of a large magnolia tree and disappear in the foliage. Then I open the pool house door and step in.

I nearly trip over him.

My father is lying on the floor, flattened by some invisible force.

"Daddy?"

I leap to his side and grab his hand. "Daddy?" His head turns toward me and he opens his eyes. He feels around the floor for his glasses and I hand them to him.

"What the—?" he says, confused at seeing me and being in here on the ground. Then he groans. "What time is it?"

"Eight thirty."

"In the morning?"

"Yes, in the morning."

"Dang!" He sits up quickly and hits his head under the bench. He grabs his forehead and scrambles to stand. "Aw man . . ."

With the other hand he grabs his aching back, and then he looks up as if he's seen a ghost.

My mother, the apparition, appears in the doorway wearing a long printed cover-up tied at her waist. Her hair is showered and blonde and coifed. She's completely put together. Her arms are folded tight at her chest and she stares at Daddy.

"I must have fallen asleep in here, honey. Dang it. Why didn't you come get me? My back is killing me!"

Mama's eyes rise and become apostrophes on her forehead. This is just like Daddy. He knows he's in deep trouble so his first response is to turn it around and put Mama on the defensive.

She's not buying it today though. She twists her mouth and appears to be sucking on a top tooth. Her head moves ever so slightly from side to side.

"Go take a shower," she says. "Get some coffee."

Thankfully, this is one time Daddy knows to keep his mouth shut. He moves swiftly past us and, with arms pumping at his sides, hauls off into the house. I look at Mama as if she's on exhibit. I'm waiting for her next move. She turns and shuts the door quietly behind her.

"What's going on," she says. It's not a question. It's a command.

"I don't know. I just opened the door and there he was." I try to sound convincing.

"Don't give me that. You know something. Tell me what's going on. I mean it."

She's absolutely right. She does need to know, especially since her husband has taken to sleeping on the floor in the pool house. She's going to blame me. Oh, that's all right, I guess. I'll take the blame. Better me than him. I mean, if she doesn't kick Daddy out after not coming home last night, surely she can stomach this long-lost daughter mess. Right?

However. I'm not quite sure *now* is the time to tell her.

"Sorry, Mama. I truly don't know what you're talking about. You tell me. Why was Daddy in here?"

"I found him in here last night passed out cold! When he didn't come home for dinner, I knew something was wrong. Makes me so mad. I looked everywhere for him. Do you know, he even parked his car down the street? Serves him right, sleeping on the floor. I tell you what, Katie-bug, I just don't know anymore. I just do not know if I can handle that man."

Maybe he's going through something terrible, I want to say, but I don't. I know when to keep my mouth shut too. So I turn from Mama and begin stripping off shoes, shirt, and sweatpants. I put my things away nicely in my cubby and slip outside. I'm not sure whether my goose bumps are from the crisp autumn air or from the chill of my mother.

Connie and Tillie stroll across the yellowing grass and say good morning. I smile, and when Mama comes out from the pool house, she doesn't look at me. She only glances at them and nods. I watch her pull her stomach in tight and walk to the edge of the pool. She sticks her toes in and then settles on one foot. Then the other. She reminds me of a queen, proud and stiff, staring off toward the marsh. It's awfully quiet out here. The normal chatter of the Water Lilies is absent.

I turn on the radio and relax a bit with the music on. It seems less awful out here somehow, diffuses the tension surrounding Mama like a cloud. I sit on the edge of the pool and dangle my legs in.

"Whoo, it's cold," I say. "I hate when it's cold."

"Is it cold this mornin'?" asks Connie, setting hers and Tillie's towel on a lounge chair. "Maybe it's gettin' time to heat this thing up."

Nobody responds to her, me nor Mama, and Connie looks over at us, wondering what's going in. She gives us each a look of suspicion, but stays mum.

Mama clears her throat. By now she's made it waist-deep into the water. She scrunches down by the wall and then pushes off in a graceful breaststroke. She's begun without us. Her ripples lap up around my ankles.

Connie slides in next to me and we sit, kicking our feet. She whispers, "Everything all right with your mama?"

"Mm hmm." But she knows I'm lying. So I utter it again slower. "Mmmm hmm."

"Hello, ladies. Sorry I'm late." Hilda hobbles toward us. She's favoring her right foot, the one with three stitches, but only slightly.

"How's the foot?" I call to her.

She knows it's a sensitive subject for Mama so she plays it down. "Almost good as new. Can barely feel it."

Good girl, Hilda. Don't get Mama upset. If there was any doubt about who broke that beer bottle, today there's no doubt in my mind or Mama's that it was Daddy. He must've gotten drunk and . . . oh, Daddy, what to do with you?

I watch Hilda sit on a chaise and take her shoes off. She peers around cautiously for glass but sees none. Then she disrobes. Hilda's a wonderful distraction for me this morning. Lord knows I need it. My, my, I believe Hilda's lost more weight. She actually looks really good except the wrinkles on her face are becoming more pronounced with the weight loss. At least that place on her lip has almost completely healed up.

"What are we going to learn today, Tillie?" Hilda claps her hands together as if this is just the most fun. It's amazing to see the change in a person when she's feeling good and in love. She's oblivious to our misery.

"I thought we'd go over that one sequence again," says Tillie. "You know, diving in without killing each other and then moving into the leg flutter."

Mama is on her third lap now. She slides by us stealthily like a shark, barely making a wave. On a normal day, she'd protest and complain about having to get her hair wet, but not today. Her lips are tight.

I turn toward the house when I hear Daddy's truck pulling away and the garage door closing. It's faint, but I imagine Mama hears it too. I shiver and dread getting fully submerged.

I think of Lisa. Of her face. Of her getting sick at the table, poor girl. It makes me want to vomit myself. I think of how destroyed she must be right now. What is she doing? I need to see her. Need to talk to her. Daddy needs to deal with her. Mama, well, Mama's either going to be able to stomach this or not, but she's a grown woman. I cannot worry about everybody.

"I can't do it," I say to nobody. Then it dawns on me. It's perfect. I say it to everybody, "Nope, I can't do it. I've changed my mind."

"'Bout what?" asks Connie, now in the water and floating on her back toward the shallow end.

"I don't want to do our big event on New Year's."

"What?" asks Hilda, horrified as if I'm committing treason.

"Just the thought of it makes me want to crawl outta my skin," I say. "It's too cold on New Year's. Even if the water *is* heated."

The ladies all turn and stare at me.

I put my finger in the air. "I propose . . . well, we already know these moves. I mean, come on. Last week we nailed that whole snowflake sequence. I think we're hot right now. I say we move it up. I say we do our big event this month."

"This month?" says Tillie, brow furrowed.

"I thought we had it all planned? I already told my doctor friend about it," Hilda whines. "He's coming to see us." She breaks out in a grin with the thought of him. She can't help it. "We were going to kiss on midnight."

"I know, I know, but Tillie, we're almost ready, right? And personally, I'd rather do it before the holidays. I don't want anyone to see me in my suit after Thanksgiving."

With this, everyone is silent, thinking about holiday bodily transformations. Score, Katie-bug. They know I have a point. Everyone except Tillie and Mama, that is. They never gain an ounce.

"I say we just do what we did last year. The beginning of November was nice, but we could really do something cute if we did a Halloween theme. The boys would love it."

"No," says Mama, speaking up for the first time. "No Halloween. I am not dressing up as a witch." She said *no Halloween*. I realize I'm making headway. She could have insisted on keeping it New Year's.

"All right then, let's just do it the same time we did last year. First week in November?"

Tillie scratches her head and runs her fingers through her hair. I can see she's thinking about it.

"Well, that's all right with me, I reckon. Heck, at my age, my motto is 'why put off what you can do today when you might be dead tomorrow?'"

"Tillie!" I squeal. She grins. Loves to get my goat. I clap my hands. "Terrific! Why don't we just keep everything the same? We can keep the sparklers and all."

"Hey, we could give it a Veterans Day theme!" Connie's getting into this now. Mama shoots her an evil glare.

"She's just being patriotic, Mama."

"It's the eleventh this year. Yeah, yeah, I like that," says Connie. "Leroy would like that. We never do much for him. It'd be good to make a party out of it. And we could do red, white, and blue caps instead of gold!"

"Is it settled then?" I look around and put my hand up. "All in favor of moving to Veterans Day weekend?"

"Aye."

"Sounds good to me."

"All right, ladies." Tillie steps into the water, taking over, her eyes beaming. "We only have a few weeks to get this right. No more piddlin' around now. We got work to do."

Except for her Halloween protest, Mama hasn't said one word since she got out here this morning. I know I'm not the only one who's noticed, but there's nothing I can do. My stomach churns with excitement about the show coming up. I can see it all now. This is destiny. What better way to let Daddy know we love and support him no matter what than by doing the Water Lilies event on Veterans Day weekend?

It'll be perfect. He'll be so happy with all of his friends here. Drinking champagne, laughing, cutting up . . . He'll be taken off guard, yes, but seeing Lisa under festive circumstances and not just one-on-one will be good for him, right? Good for us all. And Mama still doesn't need to know a thing about her. Not one thing. Lisa can just be someone I invited. Just a friend. No big deal.

I breaststroke over to the other side of the pool and realize the chill has left my system now. Connie, Tillie, and Hilda are laughing and having a good ole time just as usual. If I didn't know better, it might seem like any other morning with the Water Lilies, practicing our moves. Nothing unusual. Nothing going on behind the scenes.

Yes, this will work. It *will* work. I just knew there'd be some way to make this right.

CHAPTER FORTY-THREE

The Well
Georgetown

Lisa

I had no idea that frying fish was such an empty existence. As a child, I remember Uncle and Ma in here, in Le's Kitchen, cooking away. The looks on their faces, especially Ma's, was always so serious, so determined. To me, it appeared they were doing something very important with their lives. Keeping the customers happy. Providing a needed service to the community.

But today, now that I have taken their place, it seems empty, futile. My customers might just as well go grab a burger across the street. They would fill their bellies just the same.

Charlene has been annoyingly chipper all morning, but she comes to me, dirty dishes in hand and says, "Mr. Donnie hasn't come in today. Word is he's sick."

"Oh." I dip another basketful of popcorn shrimp into the hot oil. It bubbles and hisses and fuels my dreary mood.

"No, I mean, he's really sick, Lisa."

I look up from the fryer and see Charlene's face. Damp curls spring from her temples, escapees from her pulled-back ponytail.

She'd be such a pretty girl if she weren't carrying all those dirty dishes.

Her brown eyes are severe and tender at the same time. Then it hits me. Donnie. She knows I care about Donnie. I've been praying for that sweet man for years, every time he goes into that godforsaken mill. He's watched me grow up. In a way, I used to imagine my American father to be something like Donnie, kind, polite, hardworking.

My father is nothing like Donnie.

"Thanks for letting me know, Charlene. I'll pray for him."

It's the answer she wanted so she strolls back out front to take more orders.

I close my eyes. *Dear God, please take care of Mr. Donnie. He's a good man. Don't let anything happen to him. He needs to come back here and see us. He needs to work to take care of his wife. Please let Mr. Donnie get well, God. Amen.*

Saying my prayer is dry and unemotional, but it's all I can muster. As soon as I'm done, a tear streaks from my right eye. Donnie. How I wish Donnie had been my real father.

Not John Porter. I wouldn't care if I never saw that man again in my life.

ON MY WAY home at the end of the night, it's dark and I'm exhausted. I park my car on a little road in Old Georgetown, the quaintest part of town right near the Baptist church, and I grab two to-go containers of food sitting in the front seat.

The lights are on. I follow the narrow walkway to his modest ranch-style home and knock quietly on the front door. I knock again, the heat from the containers seeping through the Styrofoam and toasting my hand. The curtains ruffle and his wife peeks out the window and sees it's me.

"Hey, Mrs. Ferguson." I hold up my food when she opens the door. "I heard Mr. Donnie's under the weather. Thought you might could use some late supper."

"Come on in, Lisa. It's always good to see you."

"No, no. It's late. I can't stay."

"Oh, but . . ." She looks over her shoulder at the television news. "Donnie would love to see you."

"I don't know," I say. "Well, okay. But just a minute."

I walk the containers to the kitchen. I know the way, having been here about ten years ago when Donnie slipped a disc. Nothing much has changed in here since then. I set the food down on the counter and Mrs. Ferguson takes my arm.

She whispers, "The doctors don't really know what's causing the bleeding yet. They'll be going in on Wednesday to do surgery and find out for sure. He's on pain medication now, so he might not seem quite right."

My stomach stiffens. I don't do well around sick people. I never know what to say. Right before I step through his bedroom door I wish I'd just stayed on the doorstep.

Then I see him.

His old cap is not on his head; instead a slurry of gray hair sits on top like a nest. His eyes are closed and the room smells like Old. Smells like Sick. Mrs. Ferguson nudges her husband.

"Donnie? Look who come to see you. Miss Lisa from the diner is here. She brought us some food."

He opens his faded blue eyes and I think I've woken him.

"Hey, Mr. Donnie," I say.

"Hey-hey, little Lisa, what a nice surprise. Sorry you got to see this old man looking so bad." He tries to scoot himself up a bit but it's obviously hurting.

"You look fine."

"Well, I feel like you-know-what," he says. Then he smiles, yellow teeth. "You must have missed me today."

"I did. *We* did. You're one of those folks that shows up no matter what, you know?"

"I know, I know, but what you gonna do." The fact that his hind side is bleeding is like an elephant in the room with us, but we don't acknowledge it. I'll avoid that topic at all costs.

"You hurry up and get well now. Okay?" I squeeze his calloused hand and then let it go.

"Will do," he says.

I turn away from him to leave and he calls, "Miss Lisa?"

"Yes?" I face him again.

"You feelin' all right? You don't look so good yourself."

"Doing fine, Donnie," I lie. "Just tired."

"That's 'cause you work too hard. And your mother?" he asks.

"Oh, you know. 'Bout the same."

"I'll keep her in my prayers," he says.

"And I'll keep you in mine." I force a grin. "Now get you some rest. I expect to see you soon." Turning to Mrs. Ferguson, I say, "Keep me posted on our patient. I need him back in the restaurant as soon as possible. The mayor and Stevie Wilkes are already causing trouble for me."

"Oh, no," says Donnie. "You tell Stevie I'll tear his hide when I get back, he steps outta line in your restaurant."

"Will do," I say.

Donnie smiles sadly and watches me leave. I say good-bye to Mrs. Ferguson with a hug, and then I'm on my way home. To see Ma. I'm dreading it, so I drive around and around the neighborhood until my eyes are so heavy, there's just no avoiding it.

I haven't spoken to Ma since I told her John Porter was alive. I left before she was even out of bed this morning. Just couldn't face her. I can only imagine what she's thinking or doing. I realize this might have done her in for good. I park the car, turn off the ignition, and press my forehead into the steering wheel. Me and my Pandora's Box. There's no way to shut that lid again.

I stick my key in the door to our small house and the wind blows. I get a strong whiff of the fried food odors embedded in my chef's clothes, and I breathe in deep. I turn the knob and open the door quietly, imagining Ma is already in bed.

But she's not.

Ma is standing just feet away from me with her arms outstretched. She is silent. I hesitate, numb from the long day of work, spent from the sadness of seeing Mr. Donnie. I drop my purse and walk to her, stunned that she's reaching for me at all. She touches my shoulders softly and then I bury my head against her cheek. She's so warm, so familiar. It's been such a long time.

I wrap my arms around my mother and hold her, and then tenderly she holds me too. I cry like a baby—for me and for her and for Uncle and Donnie. And Ma weeps also, a serious, desperate cry that leaves her gasping for air and me, holding her up. My sadness is one thing. I can touch it. Feel it. But Ma's. I can only imagine how deep the well is that fills my mother's eyes with grief.

CHAPTER FORTY-FOUR

THE PLEA

Marble Mountain, Vietnam

Ernest

He remembers now. Her face, the honey smell of her skin, the way her long straight hair fell across his eyes as she kissed him.

Oh, how he loved her.

As memories of Doan Vien roll over his cold body, he shivers. At first, he is soothed and floating—then something like pain. It's physically painful to remember her, how he could not go back to her and keep his promise.

For decades Ernest has tried desperately not to think of her—for exactly this reason. He is stuck. Time has passed. How long did it take for her heart to break? A week? Two weeks?—for her to realize Ernest wasn't coming back? Or did John go to her and tell her that Ernest was missing? If he'd thought about it all these years, he never could have lived, knowing he did that to her, abandoned her.

But now, remembering Doan Vien and the way he loved her may be the only thing that can bring him back. He knows it. He hears her staccato voice, her single syllable words that conveyed so much emotion. He thinks of her hands pressed to his cheeks and the smell of her sweet breath as she told him she loved him too. That she would marry him. He was honored to be able to give her hope. She'd suffered so much already. And Ernest, he'd never been so happy in his entire life.

Ernest remembers how he pressed a photograph in her lovely hand before he left her. In it his buddy, a proud John Porter, posed and smiled while Ernest ran blurred into the picture after setting up the camera and clicking the timer. It was a crappy photo, but the only one he had of himself. If anything happened to him, he wanted her to have it—to remember him by. He thinks of that 1969 Minolta SR2 101. Funny how he can remember the name of it exactly. He'd bought it at the commissary and developed the first roll just weeks before he . . .

He imagines his poor parents opening the box of his belongings. Surely one was sent back to the States. He imagines their wails and tears, how that camera was probably never used again, the film inside left intact and undeveloped. He imagines his parents' torture of being told their son was missing, that there was no body, no closure for them.

Think harder. Think harder how you loved these people! It's the only way!

Mama, sweet Mama. He doubts her heart would have survived the pain of losing him. Daddy would have silently gone on, kept the store going, and buried his grief in chores and yard work. But what about his brothers? What did they do with their lives? Did they get married and have families? Are there nieces and nephews he'll never meet? Did they run their own farms and lead the life that Ernest always dreamed of living with Doan Vien?

The unfairness of it all! Why did this have to happen to him? Why is he stuck here? *Oh please, let me turn human again so I can walk out of this place. I'll grow my legs back. I'll climb down this mountain, crawl through the tunnel that brought me here. I'll kill any VC soldier who gets in my way with my bare hands. I am not afraid anymore. If the war is still going on, to hell with it! I will make it home. I'll get there by boat or by plane, however I have to do it. I will make it home to Georgia. I will see my family again.*

I will.

ERNEST DIDN'T NOTICE Brother Chong when he entered the cavern, but he sees him now, hears him. It's not feeding time, is it? No, the moon is rising. Brother Chong has tears in his eyes. He is praying, rocking forward and back on his haunches. His head is down and he bobs, he bobs. Ernest stops and sees the pain on Brother Chong's face. His scar has stretched tighter and twisted.

I feel for you, brother, he thinks. *It'll be all right, buddy. Everything's going to be all right.*

Brother Chong is pleading with his Maker. He is still rocking, bobbing, pleading more fervently. Ernest calms himself down and forgets his pain for the moment. He cares more for Brother Chong. He feels sympathy. He'd like to make it all right for him. He is becoming more human. He feels it. He knows it. His humanness is growing. *Oh God,* Ernest pleads, *whatever Your will be done, but please won't You make me human again? What good am I to anyone else, here in this fish bowl?*

What good am I? What use am I?

Use me, oh Lord!

HE HEARS IT first, a noise like a low moan, then shuddering, spasms of pain. Fish have highly sensitive auditory systems. For

Ernest, the sound is felt with his entire body. Then, in a blurry haze, Ernest sees a man crying. Brother Chong? He looks closer.

It's his father before him.

He looks old, spent. His shock of dark hair is now white and thin, combed over to one side. His once-broad shoulders are now hunched over. There is a carved walking stick propped next to him and resting against a bed. *Where am I? Daddy?* Ernest can't believe this is happening.

He'd been praying to go home to Georgia when, it appears, it's happened. He doesn't recognize this place. This is not his childhood home. He looks around. The walls are supposed to be white, but they're blue-gray. Metal bars surround a white-sheeted bed. The confusion subsides, and when Ernest gets his bearings he realizes he's seeing his father for the first time since he left for war.

"Daddy!" He wants so badly to hug him, to tell him that he's here with him, that everything is okay. He wants to tell him how sorry he is that he had to go through all that worry. "I'm home, Daddy!" he cries. "I'm right here! I didn't die, I'm here!"

His father does not seem to hear him. Instead, Ernest feels his total despair. He's an indigo hole with hardly a sliver of light inside. The more his father cries, the dimmer the light becomes.

"Oh, Daddy," says Ernest. "Can't you hear me? I love you. Tell Mama I love her. Tell Caleb and Martin and Randy and everybody."

Ernest can feel himself slipping away and he fights it, claws with everything in him.

"I'll come back, Daddy. I'll come back to you! I promise! Just hold on . . ."

And then, before he can finish his words, Ernest is no longer in Georgia but back in the water in Vietnam with an Asian tourist dropping bits of bread on his head.

Ernest flees and hides in a dark corner. He's not sure he can keep doing this. He had wanted to go home, to see his family—and he *did* see him, his father anyway. But seeing him made it harder to leave. Seeing him and not being able to communicate hurt worse than anything he's been through in his entire life, hands down. He is torn now between wanting desperately to go back to his father and wanting never to see his face again . . . not if he can't hold him or touch him or speak to him, console him in any way. Watching his father suffer is, by far, his worst experience yet.

Be careful what you wish for, he thinks. It's true. He'd wished to go there. Right? He was there. Now he's unsure he knows what to wish for at all. Perhaps he's better off not hoping, not feeling, just swimming aimlessly, with no thoughts at all. Perhaps he was better off living the uneventful life of a fish. Perhaps being human is not all it's cracked up to be.

Oh, dear God.

Ernest is questioning everything now.

CHAPTER FORTY-FIVE

The Blur

Georgetown

Lisa

"*Đó là . . . thời gian.*"

It is time.

My mother's voice is scratchy and faint from lack of use. We are resting on the sofa now, arms around each other. We have spent the past few minutes crying, and we are both sick and swollen from our tears.

I cannot believe she's spoken, and I think perhaps I'm hearing things. Then she speaks again, Vietnamese words dripping from her mouth like lava, her eyes searching my own.

"It's time you knew the truth."

She takes her arms back from me and holds her hands in front of her, balling them up and rubbing her knuckles on one hand then the other.

"It was a long time ago. You know the story, how our family was killed. How your father came and helped rebuild the village."

I take in a deep breath. I feel as if I'm in the middle of an accident. I cannot get up and walk away or close my ears. Though my feelings for John Porter are destitute, I suppose I still need to hear the truth of him once and for all. Don't I? And the fact that Ma is speaking, well, I imagine I'd listen to her reading the phone book aloud just to hear her voice. The sound of it after all this time makes me feel not so alone. And her words in Vietnamese seem as if my own soul is speaking.

"Your father, he was a very good man."

"But—" I want to tell her how awful he was to me, but she clamps down on my arm and stops me.

"Your father was kind and good. He was honorable. Brave." Ma's swollen eyes crinkle up to nothing as she remembers him. "I told you already about the day your father first came to my village. What I have not told you is that he was with someone. There was another soldier with him that day."

Ma clears her throat, and I shift in my seat and pull my legs up Indian-style, trying to relax.

"John Porter was this soldier's name. He was with your father. *With* your father. John Porter is not your father."

I am stunned and let loose a little chirp. "He's not my father?"

Ma shifts her gaze and nods. "I have something to show you." I help Ma up and keep my place, worried that if I stand I'll tumble. I watch as she moves slowly to her bedroom as if every step hurts. When she returns, she is carrying the red-framed photograph.

Sitting next to me she holds the picture up and points. "You see? This is John Porter. And this man?" She points to the blur of a figure running to his side. "This man . . . is your father. Your father's name was Ernest. Ernest Marquette."

I gasp and hold my chest and tears form again, spilling onto my smelly work clothes. My father is not John Porter. My father's name is Ernest. "Who is he? My goodness, Ma. Why didn't you tell me? Who is Ernest Marquette?"

It takes a moment for my mother to speak again. Then she says quietly, "Ernest and John, they were very close. They were the best of friends." Ma sets the photo on my lap and pulls her hands to her face. She closes her eyes and whispers, *"Tôi yêu họ Cả hai." I loved them both.*

My eyes level, and I look at Ma. She is suffering. I put my right arm around her and pull her close. "Shhh. It's okay. You've said enough for now. You don't have to go on."

"I ashame."

The words pierce the air, an off note in her symphony. Ma's use of English catches me off guard, so I stay silent.

"In Vietnam, girl cannot lie with man before she marry but . . . I tell him, I marry you. I want to marry you. I want war over. I want my life back. I worry 'bout my soldier, if they not come back to me. Every time they leave the village I think I might not see again."

"It's okay, Ma, you don't have to explain. It was war. I know how things were."

"The look in John eye when I say I cannot marry him . . ."

"They both asked you to marry them?" Ma nods slowly, and I search her face for the beautiful girl she must have been. "Oh, my—so what happened?"

Ma stares at the blank television screen for answers. Then she says, "They going to China Beach for few day. That what they say. They never come back."

"Neither one?"

She shakes her head and sadness brushes her cheeks crimson.

"I think they been kill. I mourn. I mourn for you, *con gai*, when my belly get big—"

"Oh, Ma." I hang my head. "So you had no idea John Porter was still alive until I told you last night?"

Ma coughs and rests her head on the back of the sofa, exhausted. "No."

"I'm so sorry! I had no idea. I saw John Porter's name on the back of that photo and assumed *he* was my father. You never told me, Ma. Remember, you would point to him? I thought the man in the photo was my father. Why did you let me think it was him all these years? Why?"

"I want you see strong, kind man was your father. Not blurry mist, not ghost. John was different from Ernest, yes, but he was very good. Very caring."

"Oh, Ma."

"Your uncle know the truth. One year later he come home. I was so happy see his face, and you been born already. I ask him, find out what happen to American soldier, but they were gone. Dead or missing. Maybe back in America, he say. Probably dead."

I exhale. I need a break and from the looks of her, Ma does too, so I stand and walk to the kitchen to put on some tea. I wait for the kettle to whistle and then pour two cups. Ma's eyes are still closed when I come back in. I hand Ma's cup to her and she takes it, holding the warmth to her legs.

"I suppose I really messed things up then," I say. "I just didn't know." I sit on the sofa again next to her and square my shoulders, realizing the weight of my error. "Ma, the other day . . . I met him. I went to see John Porter."

Ma lifts her face and steam crosses it, turning her eyes ghostly white.

"I told him. I mean, I told him I was his child."

Ma closes her eyes tight and she wavers as if she may fall over.

I set my cup down on the coffee table and grab hers so it won't spill. "I'm sorry. I just didn't know. I wanted to know my father. That's all."

Tears roll down Ma's cheeks again. Then her shoulders shake to some internal rhythm. After a minute I hear a faint, "How you find him?"

I'm not sure what to do. Should I show her the photo? I'm tempted to lie, but she's been so open to me. Now is not the time for lies. I get up and walk to the door where my purse was dropped. Squatting down, I pull out the newspaper clipping. I pad back slowly and then kneel down in front of her, setting it with quivering hands on her knees.

Ma stops crying and looks down. I watch as her eyes fix on John Porter's face, then she reads and rereads his name below. Finally, she traces her forefinger along his nose and she is still. Calm. She is a million miles away, decades from me.

"Ma? Ma." I take her hand, but she keeps her eyes fixed on the newspaper. "What I did to him was terrible," I say. "Thinking back, how he reacted—goodness, it all makes sense now. Ma, there's no way around it. I'm going to have to see John Porter again."

She looks up at me now. I hear a clunk and then a flutter against the window as if a bird has hit it headfirst.

"Somehow I have to make this right," I tell her.

"No." Ma's eyes turn dark and clear, and she grabs my hand. "No, *con gai. Tôi Cấm nó.*"

I forbid it.

CHAPTER FORTY-SIX

The Secret
Charleston, three weeks later . . .

Katherine Ann

Mist rises from the wet yellow grass this morning. The Wando River looks frigid from here, a dark blue icicle. I shiver just thinking about it. I pull my jacket closed in the front and hope the pool is heated by now. Stepping around the back of the house I see the cloud hovering just inches above the warmed water and smile and thank goodness for it.

When I go to push the pool house door open, I realize it's ajar. I step inside and shut it behind me, looking for Daddy. I pray he's not passed out on the floor again. But he's not here, so I relax, sit down, and begin disrobing.

That's when I hear a little mewing sound. A cat? Is there a cat in here? I can't imagine, but there *is* an orange tomcat that roams this neighborhood. We see him every now and again. I stand and survey the curtained shower stall from where the sound is coming. I pull back the curtain and don't see a cat. Instead I see Mama, crinkled up in the corner.

"Mama! What's wrong?!"

I bend down and touch her. She just shakes her head. Her

pretty face is marred with red splotches and tear tracks. Her painted lips are contorted into a pink trapezoid.

"Mama? Tell me."

"He's . . ." She just shakes her head again, unable to speak.

"What! What is it?"

"There's . . . another woman."

"Another woman?" I take in my mother's crumpled frame. "No. There can't be. He wouldn't do that."

"There *is* another woman, Katie-bug. You just . . . there always *has* been. Another woman."

Well, now that stops me. I straighten up and tighten my brow. "What do you mean?" Keeping my eyes on Mama, I reach out of the shower stall and grab a wad of toilet tissue. She takes it from me and blots her eyes.

"This whole war mess," she says, sniffling. "I told you nothing good would come of it."

"What? You think he's having an affair because I brought up the war? Because I wanted him to deal with his past?"

Mama shakes her head again. "No, Katie-bug. He's not having an affair."

"Okaaaay . . . well, what's the problem then?"

Mama stops crying and sets her arms on her knees. She pulls the tissue apart and then wads it together again, studying it.

"Your father . . . was in love once with another woman. He told me so. It was during the war."

I fall on my rear and press my back against the stall wall. I am sensing what's happening here, and my mind struggles to keep up.

"And so you think my bringing up the war is bringing this woman back for him?"

Mama nods like a sad child. "I hear him calling her name

when he's sleeping. He used to do that when we were first married. It's been years since I've heard that name."

We are quiet for what seems like an eternity and then I say, "Mama?"

"What."

"Is the name . . . is it something like . . . *Shwan Veen*?"

Mama's intake of air is swift and loud. She clutches her tissue to her chest and glares at me. "You *knew*? How could you know?"

"Oh, Mama." I know it's time to tell her. I just wasn't prepared for this today. Oh, great heavens, give me strength. "The other—"

"Yoo-hoo, anybody home? Somebody having a party in here and we ain't been invited?" It's Tillie's voice. Mama and I look at each other in alarm as if we've been caught. I motion for Mama to blot her eyes, which appear covered in soot.

"Be there in a minute," I yell. I tell Mama to strip while I go flush the toilet. When we come out together, Tillie and Connie are changing, and Hilda is standing in the open door.

"Shut the door!" Connie yells, covering her bare arms. "It's cold out there!" Hilda closes the door but keeps her eyes on Mama. In fact, everyone's eyes are on her; then they turn to me.

"Something going on? Something wrong?" Hilda asks.

"No," I say.

"Yes," Mama says, and I turn bug-eyed to her.

"This is silly," Mama tells me. "I know how bad I look right now. There's no hiding it. And these . . . y'all are my friends. My closest friends. If I can't tell you, well, I might as well send you on home and tell you to stop taking up my time."

The pool house is so quiet, I swear, I can hear a moth beating its wings against the window. Or maybe it's my heart.

"Sit down, honey," says Connie, scooting over on the bench

and patting the place beside her. Mama goes and sits there, pulling her pink cover-up tight around her. Hilda takes the spot on her other side, and I just stand here, watching, waiting, figuring out what I'm going to say.

"I've never told you any of this." Mama sets her hand on Hilda's pants leg. "I don't know why. I try to seem like I'm all together, and most of the time I am. But not always."

Connie glances up and catches my eye.

"When John and I first got married, it was rocky. I won't lie. Well, not that it isn't now . . ." Her eyes drift toward the window. "And then we had Katie-bug," she smiles up at me sadly, "but John was still having a hard time after the war. It had only been a couple years and . . . well, I figured he just needed time. He'd just adjust, go back to normal. But he didn't.

"When I met your father," she says, directing her words to me now, "he had just come back from Vietnam. I was serving malteds and root beer floats at this little place over on King Street—Feldman's—it's not there any more. Anyway, John came in looking handsome one day. He was confident and funny. He was different from the other boys. He'd been to war. My father, your grandfather, had been in World War II and had never come back. I fell in love with John because he was a survivor."

I slide down the wall and sit, knees up, watching my mother's lips move. I've never heard her talk this way. I've never heard her say she loved my father at any time in her life. I've never realized the pain she felt, losing her own father to war. She simply doesn't do this, open up like this. All of us are mouth-dropped stunned.

"When John asked me to marry him, he told me I was the prettiest girl he'd ever seen. Well, he lied.

"When I was pregnant with you, Katie, I'd wake up at all

hours of the night. Your father, I learned, talks in his sleep. He would have nightmares from war sometimes, I could tell. I remember being so frightened for him. Sometimes I would wake him up just to keep him from going back to that place. To keep whatever was happening to him from happening. So one night, it was so strange. He was saying these Vietnamese words over and over in his sleep. And he did it for the next few nights and then—"

Hilda keeps her eyes glued to the ground but reaches over and grabs Mama's hand. She squeezes it tight and Mama starts crying. "Then one night I heard him say, 'I love you.' I thought he was awake and talking to me, but he wasn't. He just kept saying, 'I love you, Doan Vien. I love you, Doan Vien.' Just like that."

Tillie coughs uncomfortably and walks to the bathroom. When she returns, she hands my mother some more tissue.

"Thank you, dear," Mama says. She pulls herself together and sniffs hard, sitting up nice and tall. "Anyway, I asked him about Doan Vien and he told me. She was a girl he met in Vietnam. He was *in love* with her. He wanted to marry her."

"Oh, goodness, John," says Connie. "But that was in Vietnam, right? It was over. It's been forty years, Betty Jo."

"Don't you get it?" Mama blinks her eyes as if synapses are misfiring. "He loved her *first*. I was second choice. I was his consolation prize."

"Mama!" I say. "Daddy loves you!"

"Yes, he does," Connie says. "I've never seen a man so whipped by a woman in all my life. And John? Great God in heaven. He ain't an easy one to tame, neither."

Tillie walks tall and lanky like a praying mantis over to Mama and touches her cheek. "That was years ago, Betty Jo. Just let it go. Let it all go now. Life's too short."

Mama looks at me then for answers. I take a deep breath and say, "Okay. I suppose it's time."

The chatter stops and they look my way. I breathe in deep and exhale. "Here's the thing. When is the past . . . not really the past?" What an idiot. This is not the time for jokes or riddles. "No. I'm sorry. I mean, all right. Here goes. Mama's upset because—because Daddy's been saying her name again in his sleep. That woman's name."

"Oh, honey, that doesn't mean anythin'," says Connie. "It's just subconscious. Why, sometimes I dream I'm in a hammock in Bermuda with Denzel . . ."

"Wait," I say. "There's more." Mama's blue eyes glisten and search my face for truth. "There's something you should know, Mama." I pause, wishing I could vanish from here and just be home, watching soap operas, drowning in a large bowl of macaroni and cheese.

"Well, go ahead and say it." Mama grabs Connie's and Hilda's hands for support. "Go ahead. These are my friends."

"She's still alive," I say softly. And then my eyes go blurry. "She's still alive, Mama, and she has a daughter. Daddy—"

There is a chorus of collective "ohs" and Tillie, Connie, and Hilda surround Mama like she might fall over. Like she might tumble into a hole in the earth. "Shhh, dear. It's all right. Shhh," they say.

Mama holds her chest and makes not one sound. Her eyes are still fixed on mine.

"I'm sorry I didn't tell you, Mama. I just . . . well, she's very nice . . ."

"You *met* her?" Mama's sense of betrayal flies at me from feet away and smacks me hard.

"Not *her*, just her daughter."

Mama grows quiet. "So, it's true? Is she John's—"

I nod and cover my mouth with my hands. Mama groans and random arms hold her up. Then she stiffens and her eyes ping-pong from me to Tillie and back again. "Don't tell me she's from Geor—"

I nod again more vigorously. Just get this over with.

Tillie says, "Wait. How do you know where she's from, Betty Jo?"

Mama is silent, rocking slightly back and forth. We Water Lilies are all afraid to move a muscle. Finally, she takes in a deep breath and lets it out, a deflating balloon squeak. "There were letters. John's gotten some letters over the years, and I just never . . ."

"Oh, dear God," says Tillie.

"And the money. At times there's been money missing . . ."

Tillie cocks her hands on her bony hips and says, "You mean to tell me, he's been supporting that child behind your back?"

"That sneaky *schwein*," Hilda says, seething. Her fists are balling up.

"Hold on, hold on," says Connie. "We don't know anything for sure yet. Give him the benefit of the doubt at least. All right? Till we know for sure." But even Connie doesn't sound convinced. Mama looks up at her with hope in her eyes, and then it dawns on her that this situation feels hopeless. Mama crumples and sinks to the floor and we Water Lilies are left shivering, waiting for the crackling ground to settle.

"It's the only way," Hilda is saying. We are in the house now and making Mama some iced tea. She's sitting at the kitchen table with her hands folded in her lap, a faraway look in her eye.

"Why can't she just ask him about it?" says Connie, sipping her drink. Her ice clinks together and rattles me even more.

"Because, Connie, that does not work. Trust me." Hilda rubs Mama's back. "When I confronted *my* husband, he said, 'What are you talking about? Of course I'm not seeing another woman. I love you, wah, wah, wah.' Men are liars. That's why it has to be this way."

"Hold on now, speak for your own man," says Connie, setting her drink down on the table. "My Leroy is a good one."

"My Fred was too, Connie," says Tillie. She sits down next to me and folds her arms. "But maybe Hilda's got something here."

"I do! Tillie, thank you. Betty Jo?" Hilda turns Mama's face toward her and holds her chin. "Look at me. Would I steer you wrong? The only way you'll ever know the truth is if you see them together. Mark my words. He might be able to lie when she's not around, but with her there? A man's eyes can't lie at a time like that. You'll finally know for sure, and you'll be able to move on one way or the other."

"The question is, how do we get them together?" asks Tillie.

"Wait a minute here," I pipe up. "I am going on the record as opposing this vehemently. This is my father! Mama, you can't do this. It's a private matter. Just ask him about it."

"All these years, Katie-bug," Mama pleads, tears in her eyes. "We know he's kept something from me for all these years. Why would he tell me the truth now?"

I don't have an immediate answer that will hold any weight with this crowd. "Oh, Mama." I sigh and press my fingers into my eyes. "Okay. Uggg. I'm going to regret this, but . . . I guess I better clear the air. Before all this happened, I had thought about inviting Lisa down here. You know . . . to get to know her better."

"You what?" squeals Hilda.

"She's my sister!"

"Ohhhh . . ." Mama moans and puts her head down flat on the table.

"Look what you've done!" Hilda snips.

"I'm sorry! I just . . . well, I was thinking of having her down here for the Water Lilies show. You know, so there'd be more people around. I thought it would be less pressure on her."

"Yes . . . yes." Hilda's eyes are bouncing wildly back and forth. "So . . . you invite her *and* her mother."

I slam back in my seat. "You've got to be kidding!"

"No, no, it's perfect! That way, Betty Jo can see for herself if there's anything between John and this woman, and we'll all be there to support her no matter what happens."

"Now wait a minute, I didn't say . . ."

"You know what? I like it," says Tillie.

"Tillie!" I whine.

Connie shushes me with her eyes. "What do you say, dear?" she says gently to Mama. "Is this really something you want to do?" Then to the rest of us she asks, "How in heaven's name will we be able to perform, knowing all this is going on?"

"We'll make do." Hilda seems to have made up her mind. "Betty Jo?"

Everyone is deathly silent, waiting for Mama to lift her head and give her decision. When she finally does, there's a strange new look on her face, as if someone else has inhabited her brain. She looks tired. "Oh, let's just do it and get it over with. Katie, just do whatever they tell you to do, honey. I can't think right now. I'm going to lie down."

CHAPTER FORTY-SEVEN

THE MIRAGE

John

He's had another one of those godforsaken dreams, and he's awake now. He's sweating and breathless. John gets up to go to the bathroom and then crawls back into bed, far away from sleep.

It doesn't go away. Those feelings John had, he still has them. Feelings of worthlessness, of desperation to be somebody, of being unworthy of the woman you love.

John still feels unworthy of Betty Jo's love. Look at her there, sleeping like an angel beside him. How does she keep her breath so sweet, even in the morning? She works so hard to take care of herself, and it only makes him feel worse about how he's aging. How is it possible that Betty Jo can be even prettier today than she was when he first met her?

He remembers her hair was pulled back in a ponytail with a white ribbon that day in 1971. He'd come into the diner, wondering what in the world he was going to do, being back in the States. He'd already escaped from New Jersey. He couldn't take anymore of his messed up family. Couldn't take anymore antiwar crap. The folks in the South, they were still cruel but in a more polite way. Less yelling, less spitting. There he was, a Yankee in Charleston, not knowing a soul.

Just walking the streets had been enough to make his skin crawl. He could still picture gooks everywhere, behind trees, behind buildings and cars. He would reach for the gun that was no longer at his side. He kept his hand perched on his belt loop just to keep it still. He had started to let his hair grow. In those days, long hair made a young man invisible. It was his close military cut that caused him to stick out, that made even polite Southerners stare and glare and scowl.

But Betty Jo had nothing to do with hippies. She was clean and crisp, and her sweet smile was absolutely the brightest John had ever seen. She was the epitome of innocence—easy life, stateside, no thoughts or images of war to have to wash away. Looking at her bright blue eyes and milky-white skin, John saw a new beginning. A clean start.

Betty Jo was the very opposite of the girl he'd left in Vietnam. John had loved Doan Vien for the sadness that emanated from her. He'd wanted to take care of her, to help her heal. But Betty Jo. Betty Jo was unspoiled, untarnished. And John had sensed she had the ability to help *him* heal. To make John a better man.

Sometimes he feels like a better man. Right now he does not. Betty Jo spent most of the evening giving him the cold shoulder. His pork tenderloin came with a side of the silent treatment. It's by far her scariest move. John never knows what she's thinking when she's quiet. He imagines, as always, the worst.

John sits still and watches the covers move up and down, up and down, slowly in the moonlight. He wants to pet her, his wife of thirty-seven years, but he doesn't. He doesn't know why she's stayed with him for so long, simply cannot fathom it. She is the best thing to ever happen to him. And he knows without a doubt that she'll finally have had enough if he doesn't straighten up. And quick.

Tomorrow is a new day. He'll only have one drink, maybe two at dinner, tops. Nothing more. He wants to make Betty Jo proud of him. He doesn't want to say anything stupid or mean or outrageous. He just wants to lead a normal life. He's a builder and a darn good one. He's got a nice house, a pool, a beautiful river flowing in his backyard. He has the prettiest wife in the world. And a daughter who loves him. And two sweet grandsons.

You got it all, man. Just straighten up, Porter. Forget about that girl. Forget about Doan Vien. She's not the woman you were supposed to end up with. You know that. Get off your sad, pitiful rear and get back to work. Be a man. Be a good man now for Betty Jo. Just one more slip, Porter, and you know it—she'll be gone. This whole life you've created for yourself? It's like a mirage. Poof!

It can be gone before you blink your eyes.

Ernest

Ernest is alone now. He doesn't see the other fish. He doesn't see Brother Chong or the tourists. His eyes are growing milky and opaque. He is aware that he is aging quickly. His heart, his human heart seems to beat larger and louder, his physical body is withering. The body is dying, the spirit is growing. It's not an altogether unpleasant experience. At least something is happening. Something. Not the day-to-day fluid nothingness he's existed in for so long.

His father must be dying.

He remembers his face so clearly, how old he's become. His tears. He remembers the bed and the sterile-looking place he was in. It seemed colder than water. Ernest doesn't want to go back, he's decided. No more wishes to go here or there. He's in this body of water, on this mountain, in this war zone. Somehow it feels safer here now. There's less heartache, less confusion. He's a fish. It's easier. It's so much easier.

In a moment of clear vision, Ernest focuses on Brother Chong as he comes and sits beside the pond. Is it feeding time? No. Ernest can't remember the last time he ate. He has no appetite. It is dusk and blue light fills the cavern, that pale, hopeful blue that exists before black comes and swallows all the colors of the world.

Ernest hears movement. There are others here. He watches Brother Chong but sees no stirrings in him, only his eyes closed and a lantern unlit, resting on his thigh.

After a few minutes, Ernest notices something about Brother Chong. He seems more at peace this evening. There is less fire, less strife in his eyes. Something more like acceptance has taken over. Surety, confidence. After the others have left, Brother Chong looks around him and makes sure the room is empty. Then he strikes a match and lights his lantern. It fills the room with warm gold. He pulls his Bible from the folds of his tunic and begins to read. Aloud.

At first, the words are foreign, Vietnamese. Ernest settles himself in the crook of the pond lining and lets his eyes rest. Then something magical happens. Ernest begins to understand. He cannot fathom how he can decipher these foreign words, but they're as clear to him now as when he was a child, listening to his mother read passages to him. No. It's clearer than that. It actually makes sense now.

Keep reading. His thoughts are tinged with excitement. *Those who have ears.* Ernest has ears now. He can hear.

"That all shall not perish but have everlasting life."

I'll not perish. He hears. He understands. He believes. He knows it now, deep in that large beating human heart. He'll not perish. There is something after this. There is life after all, after this godforsaken mountain.

PART FIVE
METAL

Cầm dao bằng lưỡi

Holding a knife by the blade

—Vietnamese saying

CHAPTER FORTY-EIGHT

THE YANG
Georgetown

Lisa

My mother used to tell me about *yin* and *yang*. They are the two forces of the universe, working in tandem, complementing one another. One does not cancel the other. Rather, where one descends, the other ascends. Good, bad. Heaven, Earth. Mother, Father. *Yin* without *yang* is impossible. My mother still believes this way. If good luck would come our way she would say, "Bad luck only around the corner," not because she's a pessimist—which in my opinion, she is—but for her, it's simply the fact that life is a delicate balance. Never too good, never too bad. She used to say I was her *yang* in the *yin* of war.

I am at the restaurant, playing in my batter with a wooden spoon. I am drawing the *yin* and *yang* symbol, two tear drop shapes with dots in them that when fitted together, make one complete circle. I am trying to think which side I am in right now. *Yin* or *yang*? I finally know who my father is, yet he is dead. Knowledge, *yang*, death, *yin*. Yes, that seems about right. I am completely balanced now. Nothing too good, nothing too bad.

I am contemplating my state of evenness when the phone rings. The lunch crowd will not be here for another hour, so it wouldn't be a customer. I imagine its Ma on the other end of the line, asking me to run by the grocery store on the way home to pick up tissues or noodles or green tea like she used to when Uncle was alive. But part of me doesn't believe it. Part of me worries her talking is only temporary. That she will revert back to mum at the slightest provocation. I don't allow my hopes to rise and carefully pick up the receiver.

Ma is on the other end, shrieking.

"What's wrong? What is it?"

"Come home now! I answer the phone!"

"You answered the phone?"

"I don't know why! I answer it! For months, no talk, no answer phone, now I answer! Why?"

"Well, who was it, Ma? Calm down now. Just take a deep breath and tell me what happened."

"The girl, she call here."

"What girl?"

"The girl! The girl, you know? John Porter daughter! She call for you and I answer. *Choi oi!* What I done!"

"Ma, what happened? Are you all right?"

"She ask us go to John house. I not know what to say. I'm surprise. I tell her yes! Yes! Why? I can't go! You have to call and say we not coming. Oh, what I done?"

I walk the phone across the kitchen and grab the wooden spoon. I begin stirring slowly to balance my *yin* and *yang* again. "You're telling me, we're going to John Porter's house?" I ask, dumbfounded. "She invited us to his house?"

"Yes! Yes!"

"I thought you forbid me from contacting him."

"I did! But she so nice. Now what I'm going do? I can't go! Look at me! Why she call? Why I answer?"

"Oh, goodness. Ma? Okay, I want you to calm down. I want you to please just calm down. Now, listen. When did she invite us to John's house?"

"One week. Saturday. One week! Look at me! I can't go. I'm old lady now. You go. You go and say I'm sick. You say you not his daughter and come home and it's all over then. Okay? You good girl, *con gai*. All right. You just say I'm sick and this all be over."

"Ma." I watch the bubbles forming in my batter and realize I'm practically whipping it now. I set the spoon down and lean on the counter with my elbows, my head resting in my hand. "Now, don't get upset, okay? But . . . I can't do that. I'm not going to lie for you."

Ma is silent on the other end for several seconds, and I wonder if she's still there. Then she says in a growling whisper, "You not lie for your mother? For the one who give you life? Who was shame for so many year having child with no father?"

"Ma . . . Ma, listen. It's not that. It's just . . . there have been too many secrets in my lifetime. Don't you think? In your lifetime. I'm done with all that. You're a big girl, Ma. You have nothing to worry about. You can meet Katherine Ann. You'll like her, she's very nice. You can see John Porter and have real closure in your life. Wouldn't that be good? *I* would like to have some closure in my life. Can't you do this for me? Can't you face things once and for all?"

"You think I don't face things?"

"No, Ma. Not very well."

"You think I'm coward?"

"I didn't say that."

"I'm no coward, Lisa. I'm been through war, I suffer great loss, my family, my village—"

"You're not a coward, Ma. I didn't say that."

I can hear her thin breath entering her lungs then exiting with a sigh.

"My hair need fix. My nail need fix. I'm not look old."

I feel a grin forming like a balloon in my belly and stretching my insides on the way up. "I'll make you an appointment. We'll make sure you're as beautiful as ever."

"And need new outfit."

"We'll get you some new clothes too, Ma. It'll be fine. We'll do this together."

"Lisa?"

"Yes?"

"Why this girl want me to come to Charleston? Why not only you?"

"I don't know, Ma. Maybe because she knows how her father felt about you. Maybe she thinks he needs closure too. Finding each other after all this time, it's a big deal."

My mother seems to let that settle in her mind. Then she says, "Bring home some tissue, okay? We out."

"Okay, Ma. I will. Hey, you know what?"

"What."

"It's so nice to have you talking again. I'm proud of you . . . for all this."

"Okay then. Bring home noodle too. We running low."

Before I can say good-bye, Ma hangs up. I am left with the receiver dangling on my fingertips and happiness brimming over my soul.

Ma is back.

CHAPTER FORTY-NINE

The Invitation
Charleston

Katherine Ann

"So what did she say?"

We are all in Mama's laundry room with the telephone cord pulled under the door like sneaky teenagers. We're hiding in case Daddy comes home and hears what we're doing. Tillie is about to wet her pants with excitement. It's taken them three weeks to convince me to do this. I am simply worn down.

I lay the phone back on the hook and close my eyes when it's done.

"Well, is she coming?" asks Tillie.

I nod my head. Eyes still closed, I can hear Mama covering her mouth with her hands, her breathing muffled.

"Can y'all back up a minute?" I open my eyes and stand up. "I feel like I'm going to suffocate." I open the door, letting fresh air in, and then I exit, breezing by my accomplices. I wait for Mama to emerge from the tiny room that smells of clean towels and dirty laundry. Tillie, Connie, and Hilda come out after her, stunned at what we all just did.

"It was her, wasn't it?" Mama asks me. "It was Doan Vien."

"Yep."

"How did she sound?"

"How does any home wrecker sound," Hilda snips. "Sounds like your heart is breaking in two. Like you can't live anymore. Like you want to kill her with your own bare hands!"

We all glare at Hilda, who has balled her fists up tight and has tears threatening to fall. Apparently her wounds are still just beneath the surface.

"Sorry," Hilda says. "Got carried away."

"She sounded genuinely shocked to hear from me," I mutter, "and I could tell she did *not* want to come."

"Yet she *is* coming." Mama's words rumble, a thunderstorm.

"She's coming," I say, looking into Mama's swollen eyes. "They both are. She and her daughter, Lisa. They just have no idea . . . I feel like this is all a setup." I sit down at the breakfast table and ponder what I've done. "I think I'm going to throw up. I know I'm going to regret this. How did y'all talk me into this? Lisa is such a sweet woman—my *sister,* even. I am jeopardizing my whole future relationship with my sister so that we can use this poor old woman to confront Daddy. Luring her into a snake pit like that . . . y'all ought to be ashamed."

"You're the one who invited her," says Tillie.

I glare up at her. "Y'all made me do it!"

"It's not a snake pit," Hilda says. "It's not like we're waiting in the bushes to bash her over the head or anything."

"Gee, I feel so much better," I say.

"Heck, Katie-bug, it'll serve her right!" Tillie squeals back at me. "She can't be sending John letters for all these years, keeping secrets about their illegitimate daughter behind your mama's back. I, for one, cannot wait to see this woman's face—and John's—when you confront them both."

Mama tears up and grabs Tillie's hand now resting on her shoulder. "Don't worry, dear," says Tillie. "We'll be right here with you."

"It's not like that, Katie-bug," assures Hilda. "It's simply a means to an end. If there's nothing there between them, then this will have been a meaningless little exercise. Harmless, really."

"I just hope you know what you're doing, Mama. This does not sound like the loving, rational way to deal with all of this. You'll probably give Daddy a heart attack or worse." I stand and go to the window. I can see that big dog again, loose and sniffing my parents' shrubs for a good place to pee.

"I just know this is a mistake. Mark my words," I say. "I want nothing to do with this anymore. I have a good mind to go tell Daddy what's going on."

"You know you can't do that," says Tillie. "This is your mama's life too."

Mama doesn't speak. No one does. Then she gets up from her chair and trails out of the kitchen like a pink wisp of smoke up the stairwell. When I call after her, she puts her hand up slightly to let me know she wants no one to follow her. Arms folded, I stare from Tillie to Hilda then Connie. "Connie, you, of all people, can't be supporting this. Can you?"

"Oh, honey," she says, taking my lead and folding her arms across her chest. "In love and war, baby, a woman's got to do what a woman's got to do. This is your mama's call now. I'll stand behind her no matter what. But I understand you got an allegiance to both your parents. I just pray this whole thing don't blow up in Betty Jo's face. I just pray it don't blow up. I just pray it. It's all I can do."

"Makes me sick just thinking about it," I say. "Oh, we'd just *love* for you and your daughter to be our guests at our annual

Water Lilies' event." I hold my hand to my ear like a telephone and mimic myself in a falsetto voice. "Daddy will be *so* pleased to see you again and Mama just can't wait to meet Lisa. Oh, and while you're at it, why don't you bring a dish? We're all about potluck down here. Oh, and don't forget to tie it up nice and tight with a noose now—*so we can hang you with it the second you set foot on our lawn.*"

I can't breathe so I dart through the kitchen past our so-called friends. I am disgusted at myself, disgusted at the Water Lilies. I feel wholly responsible now for the damage that just keeps mole-holing its way through our lives.

Katherine Ann, you are a no-good busybody. My shame bangs like cymbals in my head.

I barrel my way out of the house, open my car door, and plop inside. Then I shut the door tight, rest my forehead on the steering wheel, and solemnly swear to keep my filthy nose in nobody's business but my own from here on out.

CHAPTER FIFTY

<hr />

THE METAMORPHOSIS
Georgetown

Lisa

"What do you think about this?" I hold up a celebrity magazine and show Ma a picture of that famous actress who played Queen Elizabeth. She's so refined. A little curl would do Ma good.

Ma just stares at her. Then she cocks her head a little and looks at herself in the mirror. She's propped up on this barber's chair and her legs stick out like a child. We're waiting for the hairdresser, Monica, to finish up with another customer. I rarely get my hair done, but when I do, Monica's the only one I'll let touch my hair.

"What about her?" Ma whispers, nodding toward a woman three chairs down from us.

"But her hair is red, Ma," I whisper back. "And she's, like, my age. I'm not sure that would work for you."

"You say I'm old?"

"No, I didn't say that."

"I'm not old. You old."

"Oh, Ma."

I hand her the magazine and she flips through the pages like she's read all this before. She stops on a picture of a waif-thin actress with long black hair. She folds the paper back and holds it farther from her eyes, squinting. "There. I like that."

"Ma, you can't dye your hair black again. It's too white. It would never hold the color."

"It's what I look like in Vietnam."

"I know, but that was a long time ago."

"He'll see me and don't know who I am. Won't recognize me." I know she's talking about John Porter and I want to alleviate her fears. I want to tell her that *he* looks older too, you know, not just her. Everybody ages. But the hairdresser comes over, wiping her hands on her apron, and stands behind Ma. She smiles and takes Ma's chopsticks out of her tightly wound dirty gray bun. Her hair spirals, a snake down her back.

"My goodness, what a lot of hair you have. What are we going to do for you today?"

"My mother hasn't had her hair done in a long time," I say.

"Yes, I can see that."

"I'm not vain," says Ma.

"Oh, well, you don't have to be vain to feel beautiful," says Monica. "Are you wanting to go short? Color? Is there a big occasion coming up?"

"Yes," I say.

"No," Ma says at the same time. We catch each other's eyes in the mirror. With nervous laughter I say, "Well, we're getting ready to see a very old friend and we would like to look our best. Right, Ma?"

Ma just clucks her tongue.

"Okay then," says Monica. "Well, do you have any ideas of what you'd like?"

"Ma, show her what you saw in the magazine." Ma holds up the picture of the waif-thin black-haired girl.

"Here, let me show you another look I was thinking . . ." I take the magazine from her and hold up the picture of the more mature actress.

"I see," says Monica, winking at me. "I think I have just the compromise. Do you trust me?"

THREE HOURS LATER, Ma and I emerge from the House of Beauty with our nails bright red and manicured and jittery smiles tic-tac-toeing on our faces.

"Ma, you look gorgeous! Oh my goodness. Wow, wow, wow."

"You think?" She takes her hair in her fingers, still straight but now bleached whiter and cleaner and cut in a dramatic longer-in-the-front layered bob. She tucks a strand behind her ear like a schoolchild. It's amazing, but that woman just took twenty years off my mother.

"Now, we just need some clothes to match your new look," I say. "You like it? It's really different. You look like a soap star."

"Mm hmm. Like *Bold and Beautiful*. It's nice."

TWO HOURS LATER, I'm exhausted. We've gone to five stores, tried on everything in her size, and settled on a very nice couple of pants outfits. They're sleek and sophisticated, but also a little exotic. Like Ma. I cannot remember doing this with Ma before. It was always about me, taking care of me, making sure I had what I needed. I have never seen her treat herself.

"I look like American. You think?" she says on our drive home, eying herself in the pull-down mirror.

I don't respond, unsure if looking American is a good thing or not.

"Funny how I look." She closes the mirror again and leans back against the seat. "I always think in my head that someday I go back to Vietnam. I think coming to America just temporary. When we make it to Philippines after boat ride, *con gai*, I see the American soldiers. I see them and glad we alive but I know I'm not return to Vietnam no more. I have no family left behind. No father, no mother, no sisters. They all pass away. I'm cry, I'm cry, I'm cry so hard."

The wheels bounce over a pothole and out of the corner of my eyes I see Ma's hair swing around her ears. It's so strange seeing movement around her face. Seeing hair move, lips move, listening to sound come out. I feel as if I've been sleeping for the past several months. Or Ma has.

"When *Ahn* Dien die, I not want to live in this temporary place without him. But is permanent now. I know it. We in America now."

"It's been more than thirty years, Ma."

"Thirty year and now I look like American."

"You look beautiful, Ma. I just can't get over it. She really did a great job."

We are silent as we lift over the Georgetown Bridge. I see the mill and watch the smoke hover out over the river. A pelican swoops over us. We're almost home.

"Lisa?"

"Mm hmm?" My ears perk. The tone of Ma's voice hints at more secrets.

"I think . . ."

I wait for more and then prompt, "What is it?" I glance over at her and then put my eyes back on the road.

"I think we make spring roll for Saturday. Wrap them up. Keep them moist?"

"That's a great idea, Ma." I exhale, relieved. "Fresh spring rolls sounds perfect. I'll get everything we need tomorrow."

I press my hands on the wheel and watch the glare on my cherry red nails. Then I look over at Ma's painted hands. She's still holding her fingers out in a fan across her legs, scared to mess up the enamel. A smile I cannot resist wraps itself around my cheeks, hanging from ear to ear. I think of Ma's transformation in the past few days. It's as if she entered a cocoon and has now metamorphosed into something . . . vibrant.

I just pray Saturday brings her the peace and resolve that she needs. And doesn't crack her altogether. I remember how destroyed I was when I met John Porter. I imagine though, now that he knows we're coming, the surprise will have worn off, and he'll be able to deal a little better with his past. Especially when he finds out I'm not his daughter. He'll be able to deal a little better, a little kinder with us. Won't he?

Oh, God only knows what will happen.

The smile drips off my lips as I bite the lower one nearly clean through, and the metal taste of blood singes my short-lived burst of joy. All I feel now is unabashed worry as Ma checks her hairdo in the mirror again.

CHAPTER FIFTY-ONE

THE FLAME
Charleston

Katherine Ann

The water is warm, but not warm enough to shake this chill that has permeated my bones. There is steam rising in little whiffs here and there over the surface of the water. The cool night air has settled in on us, and the sun is an orange ice chip melting into the marsh grass.

I look over at Mama who is decked out in a stunning navy blue one-piece with white stars up the bodice and red piping along the fringe. She never has been bothered by the cold like I am. Her feet are dangling over the edge of the pool, and her hair is tucked neatly up into a swim cap just like mine, sparkling red sequins covering her crown. She's as pretty as one of those mermaids must have been back in Weeki Wachee. She doesn't look a day older than thirty, her cap pulling back on her face in all the right places.

I look down at my own body in a red, white, and blue striped one-piece. You might as well hang me up on a flag post and let me flutter in the breeze. I feel big as a tent. All this worry about tonight has added a few pounds, though I don't know the exact amount. I've not been in the mood to weigh myself.

Every year at this time I get nervous about our big performance. Will I remember the moves? Will I hit my head on the bottom and have an aneurism? Will I lift from the water and lose my suit, exposing parts that should never see the light of day? But tonight I'm not nervous about any of those things. Instead, I am sick—sick to my stomach, sick in the head, sick of spirit that I am luring a couple of unsuspecting women to a trap.

I am picturing a bloodbath.

I suppose I should look at things from Mama's point of view. If RC had been in love with another woman before me and had a child with her, then kept it from me, I, well, okay—maybe I'd be out for blood too.

I am resigned to watch this macabre event unfold. I have no idea whom to feel sorriest for—Mama, Daddy, or these women from Georgetown.

And then there's me. I suppose I'll just feel sorry for me that I played any part in this family tragedy. No good deed goes unpunished, right? All I wanted to do was help Daddy . . .

"Is that them?" Tillie moves close to me and whispers.

"No, not yet," I tell her. "That's Mrs. Meyers and her granddaughter. Remember, they come every year?"

"Oh yeah. Wonder who invited them in the first place?"

"Who knows," I say, "but somehow they made it on the address list. Once you're on it, you know, it's hard to get off. It's like the black list."

"Well, you tell me when you see 'em, Katie-bug. My eyes ain't what they used to be, and I wanna make sure I get a front-row seat."

"I'll do no such thing," I snip. "And they won't be here until after our swimming. I made sure of that." Tillie slips off to greet

Connie, and I murmur to nobody, "I hope, anyway. Told them not to come till six . . .

"Cooper, Tradd, I need y'all to sit still now." I turn to my boys who are dressed in these matching baby doll sailor suits. Mama went out of her way to buy them for me at one of those frilly children's clothiers that act as if it's a sin to let your child set foot in the store. I mean, there have only been a couple incidents, the piggy bank and the snow globe, but other than that . . . well, they *are* little boys after all. And just look at that. They're already dirty. Imagine, dressing a boy in white.

"Sit right here on this chair, baby. Now scoot back. All right, I want y'all to stay right here until Mommy's done with swimming, okay? Can you do that?" They nod. "Good. Now, if y'all stay real still, I'll give you an extra big piece of cake when we're done."

"I don't want cake," says Tradd.

"Okay, then you can have ice cream instead."

"I want ice cream," Cooper chimes in. "I don't want cake. I want ice cream."

"Okay . . ."

"Chocolate for me," says Tradd.

"And chocolate for me," Cooper chimes in.

"Chocolate ice cream for both of you," I say. "Now be quiet, please, and be still. We're starting in just a minute."

"I wanna swim too," Cooper whines.

"We can't swim now," Tradd tells him. "It's only grown-ups. Right?" Tradd smiles up at me angelically as if he's no problem at all, only Cooper.

"That's right, honey. Okay. Here we go. Now watch Mommy and Nana dance in just a minute. Okay? Love you."

I blow kisses to my boys and head for the pool house when my mother beckons. Connie's husband, Leroy, is poised over the boom box to press the play button when we emerge. We knew not to give the job to Daddy again after last year when our big event was preceded with a barrage of curse words as he couldn't find the right button to press.

Before I enter the doorway, I see our annual mass of party-goers, stretched in a semicircle on the lawn around the pool. All the neighbors are here, even Miss Shelley who's in a wheelchair now after falling and breaking her hip. She has a red throw covering her lap, and her husband, a dear, sweet man who fought in World War II, is standing right behind her. And I'm pretty sure I see Hilda's doctor friend, a tall, white-haired man standing a little separated from the others and talking to RC. Then there's Daddy, swigging a bourbon and coke with his other hand resting on the back of my boys' chair. I try to smile at him, though it's weak. He's happy tonight, excited about us holding this thing in honor of him, in honor of veterans. He has no idea what's in store. I cringe and point my hypocritical finger at my fidgety babies. I mouth the words *Be good*, one last time.

The door closes, and then we, Water Lilies, look at each other, teammates, friends, accomplices.

"Girls, this is it." Tillie stretches her hands straight over her head, and then bends one down behind her, grabbing her elbow. We each follow suit and do our warm-up arm and leg stretches, absolutely mandatory before every event. "I don't want you to be thinking about anything but what your next move is, all right? You and you, especially." She gives me and Mama stern looks, then winks. "We've worked hard for this all year. You know how to work together, you know your stuff. Now. Let's go out there and show these folks that we don't just lollygag every morning, but that we work hard to be the best mermaids, I mean swimmers, that we can be." Tillie breaks out into a girlish grin and clasps her hands together. "Connie? How 'bout a prayer?"

Connie closes her eyes and reaches her arms out. Mama takes one of her hands and I take the other. My left hand grabs for Hilda, and Tillie steps in between her and Mama and fills the circle. We are all joined together, an unending ring of estrogen or lack thereof. God help us all.

"Father God," says Connie, "we come to honor You today with our bodies, with our souls, with our joy in movement. Lord Jesus, we ask that You bless each and every one of us Water Lilies and every single person who comes today to watch us."

Hilda squeezes my hand obnoxiously to remind me of Lisa and her mother, and I squeeze hers back harder so she'll leave me alone.

"Father God, we know that You are the only reason we're here today with breath in our lungs and the strength to use our bodies to celebrate Veterans Day. We know that You alone, Great God in heaven, are the one who brought these men we love so much home from the wars, home from the battles. But lo, the battles, they never end. You, alone, sweet Jesus, are the only one who can win the battle for us. Oh, Lord . . ."

"Amen," says Mama, cutting Connie off, just as she was finding her rhythm.

We all open our eyes, and I see a slight scowl in Mama's pulled back brow. Then she smiles a devilish grin and says, "Well, if we're gonna do this, we certainly can't take all night."

"Okay then, ladies," says Connie, shaking her head at Mama. "God be with you. Especially *you*, Betty Jo. Now let's go do it to it."

Tillie hands out the sparklers, one by one, and then flicks the lighter, igniting our flames. I try not to squeal but I can't help feeling like a kid again on the Fourth of July. Tillie reaches for the doorknob and my stomach lurches. I grab on to Mama's hand and squeeze it tight, sparks flying all around us. She looks back at me with wide eyes, and I smile. "I love you, Mama. I'm right here. Now let's go have some fun."

CHAPTER FIFTY-TWO

<hr>

THE FOG

John

John hates this annual Water Lilies event. Not the party part, but the part where his beautiful wife shows everybody they know just how beautiful she is. That's for John to know and others to wonder, he thinks, but she doesn't see it that way. Has a mind of her own. He's jealous over Betty Jo even though she truly never gives him a reason to be jealous. She's not the flirty type that starts fights or anything. No, John's wife just happens to have aged better than anyone he's ever known, him included. And she started out prettier than anyone to begin with.

John swirls his bourbon and coke and looks down at his grandson's heads. He rubs Cooper's hair and the little boy looks up at him and grins with tiny teeth. John's heart melts every time one of these boys looks at him this way. Like they love him. Like he's a good guy. He just doesn't deserve it. Buys them everything they could ever want, but still. There is no other way to feel. He figures all men walk around fearing the rug might get slipped out from under them at any time, without warning.

If he thought about it, he might realize it has something to do with his upbringing, with his family being split apart, adding foster home frailty to an already insecure young boy's heart. He doesn't think how going from no home to a home among men in the army—only to watch them die and get maimed and disappear off the earth—added to his feeling that nothing is forever. If he thought about all this he might be able to rationalize it, realize that his mind is malleable, that he doesn't always have to feel so all alone and afraid. That we are not chained to the habits and mechanisms we once used to protect ourselves. That we can break free at any time of our choosing by accepting God's simple grace.

But he doesn't think about it, and that's that.

John watches a sparkler slip from the pool house door, and he takes a sip of his drink nervously when Leroy punches the music. Tillie leads the formation of women who are all marching like soldiers to the edge of the pool and finding their places. Sparks are flying everywhere as the sound of "Stars and Stripes Forever" fills his ears with nostalgia, and he chokes back tears.

John takes another, longer sip and then jiggles the ice. Dang it, he should have filled up before this thing started.

Would you look at that, his wife is beautiful. He only has eyes for her. He watches her slip down to sitting with her feet in the water and Hilda at her side a few feet away. They kick their legs to the beat and wave their sparklers across from Katie-bug and Connie who grin at them from the other side. Tillie splashes at the head of the pool, a long spindly mess of pick-up sticks.

John wonders if the women are cold and hopes the heater has warmed the water enough. He sees the thin fog hovering over the surface, but still. He should have stuck his hand in and tested it. He wishes he could catch Betty Jo's eye. He would smile at her. Encourage her. Let her know he supports her no matter what he might have said in the past about this whole charade. But she doesn't look over at him. In fact, if he thinks back on it, Betty Jo hasn't looked him in the eyes for a very long time. Not even to fuss at him. That just makes him even more nervous, and he peers around the group to see—just to see—if there's a good-looking man who has his eyes on her. There *is* that new guy standing next to RC, but . . . she couldn't be . . . no. Betty Jo wouldn't do that to him. Would she? She'd never see another man.

The thought of Betty Jo leaving him dumps barrels of hot sand all over John Porter and leaves him sweating, immobile, barely able to breathe.

MARBLE MOUNTAIN, VIETNAM
Ernest

Ernest rests. There is a new peace that has enveloped him, suspending him in more than just water. If he could close his eyes he would. He would not see the green-blackness that is over him, under him. He would not see the ripples moving overhead from the waterfall, stretching its tentacles to him, calling him. He needs no pleasure now.

It is very early in the morning at the top of Marble Mountain. Still dark. On certain days, there is a mist, a cloud that forms just outside this cavern, and sometimes it spills inside. Today is such a morning. The bright moon highlights swirls of clouds like ghosts, spirits, coming alive.

Ernest is not afraid. He welcomes them.

Brother Chong is up earlier than usual. Or perhaps he never left for sleep. Ernest is unsure. He had stopped studying him, stopped wondering what passages he was reading sometime in the night. He never noticed the lantern had gone out. Brother

Chong is now kneeling at the edge of the koi pond. His head is down with his hands clasped to the back of it, and he is still. *Is he sleeping?* Ernest wonders.

If only I could close my eyes and sleep.

A look of alarm and of resignation all at once brims in Brother Chong's eyes. He lifts his head and seems to be staring at Ernest.

Not today, my friend, thinks Ernest. *You have your life. It's not so bad. You'll not change places with* me *today. Go back to your work. No matter how menial, in your heart, you are serving your Lord.*

Did I *say that?* The maturity with which Ernest is handling his fate shocks him for just an instant. *Oh, how I've grown.* He feels old, brittle. His tail barely moves him through the water. Perhaps he is still able to move swiftly like he used to. He doesn't know. Doesn't care. Moving swiftly is for the young, for the hopeful. Ernest is a tired old fish. Tired. At peace. Wishing only that his eyes would close.

In a short while, the fog will lift, gongs will sound, and life will begin to bustle on the streets below and quietly in the monastery. Quiet, but nonetheless alive. Ernest wonders for a second what kind of tourists might visit his pond today. What strange person will point and throw him bits of bread. But it doesn't interest him, not really. The tourists may come and go for all he cares. This life is but a passing fancy anyway.

CHAPTER FIFTY-THREE

THE SPECTACLE

Lisa

My mother has not spoken since we woke this morning other than grunts and minimal hand language. I found her kneeling in front of her ancestral shrine with a photograph of her parents in her hand and head bowed. Her new haircut had slipped into white sheets to the floor, hiding her face from me, but she wasn't crying. She's too scared for that.

I walked in quietly and touched her back, and then we lit candles together. Ma was lighting candles in honor of our family members who have gone on to the afterlife. She was asking them for their good favor. And I lit two myself—one for my father, whom I'll never meet, and another for Ma. As the stick nearly burned out, I touched it to the wick and it smoldered, sending a thin line of smoke into the air, then the fire erupted. I prayed for Ma that the light of Jesus would come into her life, that whatever comes her way today she'll be able to handle.

I should have lit a candle for myself.

As I drive south down Highway 17, the long stretch of nothingness between Georgetown and Awendaw, I listen to the silence between us. In my peripheral vision, I see Ma in her new outfit, a green tea-colored linen pantsuit. She is holding a white platter of fresh spring rolls we made this morning. I suggested we put the platter on the backseat, but Ma insisted on holding it. She is clutching the edges as if the delicate spring rolls wrapped in cellophane are her nerves, her heart, her soul on the platter. She will offer this food to these strangers, this man from her past, his family, his friends, and say *Here, take, eat of me. I offer you everything I am.*

A communion of sorts. I pray that Ma's spring rolls are consumed with delight by all and not shunned, ignored, left sitting and hardening on the platter.

This is completely out of my control now. My fingertips are moist on the steering wheel. What if Ma sees John Porter and she still loves him? What if he sees *her* and still loves her? What if my bringing Ma to his home tears his family apart? What if they see each other, form a passionate embrace, and then run off together, trying to make up for the past forty years?

Oh, sure, that'll be the day. I am becoming delusional. My mother is so frail. She is simply trying to survive.

"You okay?" I ask her. I wait for her response. She grunts, which I take to mean *Yes, as good as can be expected.* "Just think, Ma. In a few hours, we'll be on this road again, heading home, and all of this will be over with. Just another memory."

I turn on the radio and try to find something cheery, but I don't really hear the music. My beating heart seems to be running a race. The more I try to calm down, the more it fills my head, pounding out a desperate S.O.S.

Katherine Ann

The audience is putty in our hands. We creep into the water, the five Water Lilies, careful not to put out our sparklers, and breaststroke with one arm to the middle of the pool, except for Hilda, who clutches a red noodle and kicks with her feet. Then we turn, facing the edge, and fall in back layouts with our heads nearly touching. Being so close, I can hear the breathing of my fellow Lilies over the music. We lift our right legs straight up in the air and stick our still-lit sparklers in between our toes. Then, as Neil Diamond's "Coming to America" comes to a close we sink down under the water and do handstands, never letting our sparklers extinguish until we fully submerge at the same time. I catch Mama's eye under the water and smile at her, bubbles rising from my nose.

I know our final song is going to be a tearjerker, but we thought about it and decided it was the necessary sentiment to end upon. As Lee Greenwood sings about how proud he is to be an American in "God Bless the USA," we all lie back, heads together again, and clasp arms. We point our toes and stretch our legs parallel with the water, doing alternating frog kicks out and in, out and in, and form a large human star, pulsating, alive. I look up at my father then and see him wiping his face with a white handkerchief. I am so proud to be an American at this moment, to have honored him in this way.

"I love you, Daddy," I say, barely audible.

When our routine is finished and we are thoroughly out of breath, we Water Lilies stand chest deep in the pool and listen to the clapping and cheering around us. Then Connie cues Leroy to turn the music off.

"We hope you have enjoyed this year's Water Lilies Veterans Day Event," Tillie says. "In all my years, even at Weeki Wachee, I don't believe I've performed in a more meaningful routine. I imagine the girls would all agree with me. Wouldn't you, girls? Especially since we have our own young men and women battling overseas this very minute." Tillie pauses a few seconds for effect. "And now, we'd like you all to join us in singing 'The Star-Spangled Banner.'" I watch as the audience moves closer together, stands straighter, and puts hands over hearts. My little boys observe the goings-on and slip out of their designated chair, copying the grown-ups. Sweet Cooper is using his left hand to cover his heart, and Tradd is holding his stomach, but that's all right. It's the thought that counts.

Our voices rise up from out of the marsh grass and into the sky. I picture fallen soldiers up in the clouds, wearing their Purple Hearts and pleased at our homage. The look on my father's face, and Leroy's face, and neighbor Mister Charles who flew bombers in World War II, is worth every second of preparation for today. I can honestly say, no matter what evil things we Water Lilies may have up our sleeves for later on, our synchronized swimming event was touched by the hand of God Himself.

Secretly, I pray He'll extend a little mercy and leniency for the rest of the evening. I shiver, waiting for the real fireworks to begin.

CHAPTER FIFTY-FOUR

The Hero

Katherine Ann

We have dressed, fixed our hair, reapplied our makeup, and I'm quite warm now. This being November, night has fallen early, and though it's only six o'clock, the stars have come out in full force, dotting the indigo sky. A crescent moon looks over the drooping live oaks and this backyard celebration, which has really begun to get underway. I help Mama carry trays of food to the banquet table outside covered in a white tablecloth and flanked by two tiki torches, keeping the no-see-ums away.

Leroy took it upon himself to create music for the rest of the evening, so at this moment we're listening to the best of Motown. It's perked us up considerably after our sentimental water performance.

Hilda strolls over to me, her thick frame not quite so thick these days. She chose to keep the red, white, and blue theme going. She's wearing a white dress, which, knowing Hilda, is a subconscious way to make her doctor friend picture her in a wedding gown, with touches of blue jewelry and a red corsage to throw him off track just enough.

She leans in my ear. "What do you think?"

"Of your outfit?"

"No! Of my man . . ." she whispers.

"I think he's handsome! Very nice too." She glows. "I'm so happy for you, Hilda. You deserve to be in love."

"Shhhh." She puts her finger to her mouth. "Don't let him hear you. You'll scare him away." We hug and she sneaks back to her doctor's side. He seems more than happy to be interrupted from his conversation with Tillie. I can only imagine the things she's been saying to that poor man.

I scoot back inside the house and grab some more ice from the freezer. The cold hits my face and I breathe it in deep, eyes closed. Warm hands slip around my waist, and my husband's scratchy cheek nuzzles my neck. "You were wonderful," he whispers.

"You think?"

I fill the ice bucket and set it on the counter, leaning back on the closed freezer door. I look up into RC's eyes and see he means it. "I have never been so proud of you. I know it meant a lot to the veterans out there. I watched your dad tearing up."

I kiss him full on the lips and say, "Thank you." I lean up and kiss him one more time. "Now, can you help me with this? We need some more ice."

There is a bucket of beer, soft drinks, and water bottles next to the food, which happens to be all-American fare—mini hamburgers, shoestring fried potatoes, macaroni and cheese, and my favorite, stuffed mushrooms, which I made myself this morning. It's all I can do to keep my boys from eating all the brownies. They're swarming like flies.

"That's enough." RC removes Cooper's little hand from the plate. His mouth is stuffed and he has brown goo on his lips and a long brown streak down the front of his pinafore. "Where's your brother?"

Cooper points behind me and I turn and see Tradd stealthily stacking two brownies on a napkin. "No sir," I tell him. "Any more sugar and we'll have to tie y'all down. Now here, I'm gonna make you some plates and I want you to eat real food first, okay?"

I busy myself, making the boys' plates and trying to keep my mind off the secret guests who are about to arrive. After RC and the boys teeter off to a table balancing paper plates, I pour the ice into the drinks bucket and do not hear Daddy over the clatter.

He puts his arm around me, scaring me to death.

"Hey! Oh, hey." I reach my arms around his waist and squeeze into him. "Did you like it? Are you having fun?"

"It was . . . it was real good." He coughs, choking up on genuine emotion. "How 'bout reach in there and grab me a beer."

I do and hand it to him.

"Got an opener?"

I look around for one.

"Sheesh. Some party planner you are . . ."

"Hold on, I'll get it. I don't drink beer, Daddy, remember? It's the furthest thing from my mind."

I open the sliding glass door and go to Daddy's bar to rifle though his drawers. Finding a bottle opener with some sort of claw on the end of it, I race back to hand it to Daddy. "Here you go, I—"

But Daddy's face has gone white, and he's dangling his beer at his thigh. He's looking around the house at his persimmon tree. At least it seems. When I shut the door behind me, I realize it's happening—this thing I've been dreading for weeks. It's happening now.

I see them. I recognize Lisa. She's wearing a blue sweater over black slacks. And beside her is a petite woman with stylish white hair, wearing green linen from head to toe. She is carrying a tray of food, and her eyes are fixed on my father.

I look at Daddy, my heart in my throat. He's watching her, his old love, a ghost walking. Daddy's eyes glass over and I take the beer from him before it drops.

"Oh look, Daddy. More company," I say stupidly. I've betrayed him. I've betrayed my sister. I feel so much like Judas that it occurs to me, I could just jump right into that swimming pool now and never come back up.

Lisa

Ma stops in the grass when she sees him. How she knows it's him out of all these people, I don't know, but there he is, John Porter, watching us approach.

I put my arm behind Ma's stalled back, take the tray from her, and say softly, "It's okay. Come on. We're almost there."

He begins to move toward us, a step and then another. Before I know it he is standing before us, saying weakly, "Doan Vien? Is it you? I can't believe this."

"I believe you know my mother," I say.

Ma bows her head, a sign of respect, and then looks at him. Her lips are trembling. She is about to cry.

"John?" I'm thankful she still has words left in her.

Ma reaches a shaky hand toward him, never taking her eyes off his, and he looks over his shoulder then back at Ma. His face is red and swelling. He's crying behind his glasses, shoulders rising and falling with every breath. Ma leans closer and puts her head on his chest and closes her eyes. "John. So many year," she whispers. But John doesn't move. Perhaps he cannot move, paralyzed.

"I can't believe this," he keeps saying. "I can't believe it."

It seems the world has stopped spinning and all that exists is their embrace. I am crying now too, watching these two souls touching again after all these years. It is a miracle of sorts, watching Ma connecting with another human being, other than me, other than Uncle. I feel as if her ancestors, like the Goddess of Mercy, are hovering just overhead and cheering her on, saying, "Now you are getting what you have always deserved."

A tall old woman wearing a periwinkle skirt and blouse appears at John's side. Her hair is back in a loose bun and it wiggles when she looks over her shoulder. "Betty Jo?" she calls. And more ladies come over to join her.

Finally, a beautiful woman in a pink tailored suit walks up, her mouth gaping, a look of terror on her face. This must be Betty Jo. Through her mask of pain I can see the resemblance to Katherine Ann.

"John?" she squeaks, covering her mouth at the sight of her husband in another woman's arms.

Out of nowhere comes a large boxy woman in a white dress and red corsage. She hauls off and smacks John across his back with her purse as hard as she can. "Home wrecker!"

John reels around and then looks back at my mother and then at his pretty wife who's so distraught. Finally, he looks at me.

Then as fast as it all happens, it's over. John Porter slips out of Ma's grasp and moves slowly at first, unsteady across the grass, then gaining momentum. He reminds me of one of those wildebeests on the nature shows, dazed and desperate to escape the jaws of the lion.

Katherine Ann

"Daddy! Daddy, wait!" I kick my heels off and run barefoot through the grass around the house toward the garage. I can hear RC calling after me, "Katie! Ka-tie!" But I keep going until I reach Daddy's truck. The garage door is opening behind him, and he's cursing up a storm.

"Go on!" he yells. "Leave me alone. Move!"

He pushes me away and opens the truck door, pouncing inside.

"Daddy, listen, please wait. You don't understand!" I run to the other door and open it.

"Get out of the way! I'm serious! I'm backing up!"

I don't think I've ever seen Daddy so destroyed in all my life. I cannot let him drive like this.

"Please, Daddy! Please! I invited them."

"You what?"

"Mama *knows*, Daddy. She knows everything. She knows Lisa is your daughter."

The wheels have been rolling slowly, me having to walk backward to keep up. Suddenly, Daddy stomps on the brakes and the truck jolts.

"She is NOT my daughter!" he bellows, slamming his hand on the steering wheel and crying all over again.

"No," says a small voice behind me. I turn and see Lisa standing in a crowd on the edge of the driveway. "No. I am not his daughter," she says.

The crowd around Lisa breathes a collective, "Ohhhh . . ."

Lisa says it one more time. "Katherine Ann, he is not my father. I was wrong. This whole thing was a terrible mistake."

I look over at Daddy, who is shaking violently now.

What? What have I done? "Oh, Daddy." I crawl into the cab, and he doesn't try to stop me. With the rest of the partygoers behind us and silent, I reach over, grab Daddy's hand, and lay my head on his shoulder. "I love you. I'm so sorry I did this. It's okay. Shhhh. It's going to be okay."

Lisa

As soon as the truck is silent, a scream pierces the night air. Not a yell, but a bloodcurdling sound. I look to my side and see Ma is not there. Something inside me stiffens. We all run, a mob, to the back of the house by the pool. The woman in pink, Betty Jo, zips by me yelling, "Tradd? Cooper! Where are you?"

"Nana!" a tiny voice calls out by the marsh, and she runs to it. A little boy wraps his arms around her, and she lifts him, holding him tight.

"Where's your brother!" He simply cries, unable to speak. "Where is he?" She shakes him, and he points to the waterway.

"Cooper? Cooper's in the water?"

In seconds, we're all on the dock, peering frantically into the black river with only a single dock light shining overhead.

"Where is he? Cooper! Oh, God, look for Cooper!"

I look everywhere, but it's too dark out here. Then I realize, I still don't see Ma.

"Ma? Ma! My mother is missing!"

I am terrified for the little boy, and now a new panic grips me, and I start wailing.

John Porter and Katherine Ann appear after hearing the commotion, and men are throwing off clothing and jumping into the river, splashing and turmoil all around.

Then my mind clouds with images and sounds. They are not from this place and time in Charleston, but from deep within my own soul.

I HEAR SCREAMING and see my mother, young again, begging to jump overboard. There are bodies floating in the water, some dead, some struggling to survive. My uncle holds my mother's arms and says, "They're gone."

"But we have no food! We'll starve to death!"

"We can make it, Doan Vien. We've come this far."

"Please, I can't do this anymore." Ma falls against him.

"You *will* do this. You hear me?" Uncle shakes her until she stands upright. Then he turns her and forces her to look at me. "You have a child. You will do this for your child."

Ma crumbles and grabs my tiny body, telling me she's sorry for having such little faith. I sense that she'll never let me go.

THE EXPERIENCE IS quick, intense, and then gone. My knees buckle and I fall on the dock just as a man's voice calls, "There he is!"

Time seems to have stopped altogether and I cannot feel myself moving to the end of the dock, but I'm here now and Ma's aged head is slick and just above the water. She is sputtering and holding a little boy on the surface. He is not moving. Ma grits her teeth and struggles to keep him up.

Katherine Ann

"Cooper!" I hear the sound of my own voice from far off and I reach for him, but Daddy grabs Cooper like a baby doll. He lays him on the dock. In an instant, Hilda's doctor friend is kneeling over Cooper, doing mouth-to-mouth to my child. *My* child.

I have left my body. I am watching all of this unfold from behind a thick window. I have never been so sick in all my life. If something happens to my baby, I will die. Absolutely die. Fear grips me and I search around for Tradd. I see Tillie on the lawn, holding him firmly in front of her, pressing him into her legs. RC is on all fours beside me with his head on the wood planks. He is moaning and writhing, saying, "Oh, God, please, please . . ."

I don't know how long this takes, but at some point I hear my son cough, and I scream. I lurch to his side and hold him in my arms, rocking him, rocking him, my sweet baby boy. He is wet. He's crying.

My baby is alive.

Lisa

A black man reaches his hand toward Ma and helps me grab her. We pull her from the river, and I thank God for saving her. For saving that little boy.

"Ma, are you all right? Here, sit down." I hug her and press the cold wetness of her into my body. "Can we get a blanket, please?" I yell out. Ma is shivering.

"No," she says. "We go now."

"But you're soaking wet! And you saved him, Ma! He's going to be okay. You hear that? You're a hero."

"I'm no hero," she says through chattering teeth.

Betty Jo, John's wife, comes running down the dock in her *clickety-clack* heels. She hands a blanket to Katherine Ann for the little boy and another to me for Ma. I wrap it around Ma's shoulders and watch as the two women finally meet eye to eye.

"Thank you," says Betty Jo. "I just can't thank you enough." John Porter, whose face is wet with tears, sees the two women he's loved his whole lifetime in the same glance, puts his arms around his lovely wife, and sobs to Ma, "Thank you for saving him."

Katherine Ann

I turn and see Daddy twisted over Mama, a large weeping willow. He's murmuring in her ear, "She's not my daughter, I promise, she's not," as if forty years of anguish are seeping from his skin. Mama's arms are stretched around him. She is patting him softly on the back saying, "I know, honey. I know."

Mama smiles at me a weary, grateful smile over Daddy's shoulder. I swaddle my sweet baby Cooper in his blanket and nestle him against my chest. He has stopped crying and is looking up at me. He's shivering. "I'm cold," he whimpers. I must be in shock because I cannot feel my body, only his. RC is breathing heavy in my ear, thanking God, stroking our little boy's head. And just before we stand to walk Cooper into the house, I see Mama kneel in front of Doan Vien and take her hands. She rubs them and says, "I owe you an apology. I had you all wrong."

Doan Vien is silent at first, but her lips move. Finally the woman who saved my son's life grunts, *"Chuc ahn chi tram nam hahn phuc."*

"Oh, I'm sorry, I . . ." Mama looks over at Lisa for help. "What did she say?"

Lisa, who's now cradling her shaking mother in her arms, translates. "She says . . ." Lisa pauses to touch my father's hand as if she knows the effect the words coming next will have on him. She holds him steady and whispers, "Ma says, 'I wish you a hundred years of happiness.'"

CHAPTER FIFTY-FIVE

THE TRUTH

John

Everyone is gone. The guests are gone. Connie and Hilda stayed to clean up the mess, but they're gone now too. Katie and RC took Cooper to the hospital to be sure he's all right. He is, thank God, but they're keeping him overnight. John's throat catches when he thinks about his grandson nearly drowning in his own river.

It's all he can handle. He pours his third scotch and waits for Betty Jo to protest, but she doesn't. Instead she stands from her seat and climbs the stairs quietly. Turning to him she says, "Come on up, John. It's time to go to bed."

He barely moves. Twitches. He doesn't know how to feel at this moment. Doan Vien showing up from nowhere like that. Seeing her again. And Betty Jo knew all along. She brought her here to confront him. But then she saved Cooper's life. What if she hadn't been here? Would he have fallen in the river anyway?

It's all too much for him. His mind is blurry, rain on a windshield, wipers barely working. And Betty Jo is speaking to him again. It's what he's been longing for. He stands slowly and then balances his drink while his body lumbers up the stairs.

The door to the guest room is open. John stands there and waits for his wife to come out. She emerges from the darkness, shuts the door behind her, and says, "He's asleep."

John nods. He's glad Tradd is staying for the night. He wishes he could go crawl into bed with him and hold him, but he doesn't. Instead, Betty Jo takes his hand and leads him to their bedroom. She takes him to the bed and he sits on the edge. She bends to her knees and unlaces his shoes, pulling them off gently. John stares down at his beautiful wife.

"I love you," he says.

"I know you do. I love you too."

John can't remember the last time they've had this exchange. Betty Jo pauses and then, "You feel like talking about any of this?"

John shakes his head.

"Okay then. Tomorrow."

John lies back on the bed, rests his head on his pillow, and says, "Tomorrow," before slipping into a long, dreamless sleep.

MARBLE MOUNTAIN, VIETNAM
Ernest

Feeding time is over. The young fish have all gone on their ways, resting with full bellies. Brother Chong has returned to his monastery, and only a couple of tourists linger in the cavern, staring in awe at the statue of Buddha. He is still there, unmoved after all this time.

"You did not eat."

Ernest turns toward the voice and sees Eldest fish beside him. His eyes are so cloudy, hardly any pupil shows.

"I see no need for food these days," Ernest replies.

"You have resigned to die?"

"Not to die, but to leave this place. This body is useless to me now. My spirit has grown larger. It longs to be free. Bodily death is just a means to an end."

"You have gone mad then," says Eldest fish.

"No. I'm not mad. I am not in anguish. Not anymore. There is something after this. I'm sure of it now."

Eldest fish stops moving his dorsal fins and sinks down for a moment. Then he rises again, moves to the other side of Ernest, and says with urgency, "How can you be sure? Tell me what you've seen. Tell me what you know."

Ernest, once the student, now is teacher, and Eldest fish, though he is but a fish, listens intently to this place that Ernest calls heaven.

"You must open your mind and forget what you think you know," he says. "Heaven can only be understood by the heart."

Night comes, then morning, then day. Then night again. Eldest fish still listens to his voice. Ernest continues to teach, his spirit growing stronger as his body diminishes. Cycles of life flow all around them and heaven's light comes into the cavern reflecting off the water in a shimmering glow.

"I believe you, my son," says Eldest fish to Ernest, his first words in days. "This Jesus of yours. Keep talking, child. I want to hear more."

CHARLESTON, SC
John

John scratches his head and stares out the window. His wife's figure has become a black spot in the glowing sunlight. "So you had no idea Doan Vien was even alive?" she asks.

"Not until her daughter told me."

Betty Jo looks sternly at Katherine Ann, who has come here first thing this morning to get Tradd. He's watching cartoons upstairs with his hair sticking up. John's own hair does that in the morning too. Poor little kid, looks just like his granddad.

Cooper is already home from the hospital and RC is watching him. John hopes to be able to go see him sometime today, but at this point, his wife and daughter have cornered him at the kitchen table. It feels like an interrogation, and John's fingers turn slippery with sweat.

"Oh, Daddy," says Katherine Ann. "I cannot imagine how that must have felt, seeing her after all those years."

"I just knew she was dead," John says, his voice cracking. "There was no way she could have made it out of there after Saigon fell. Not by herself."

"So did you ever tell her good-bye?" asks Katie.

"No!" John shakes his head. "I'd just found out about her and Ernest, and then . . . I just couldn't handle seeing her again."

"But I don't get it," says Betty Jo, eying him and twisting her lips. "Then who were the letters from?"

"What letters?"

"I know you've gotten letters from someone over the years, John. I also know"—Betty Jo pauses until he looks at her again—"I also know about the money you have sent. Somewhere." Katherine Ann reaches under the table and grabs her mother's hand for support. Betty Jo speaks slower and quieter. "If the money did not go to support Doan Vien and her daughter, then where did it go? I had always assumed it was to someone in your family until recently. Was it?"

"I told you I haven't talked to my family in years." John takes off his glasses and wipes his face gruffly with his hand, holding his fingers tight over his eyes. "I need a drink." He stands and goes to his bar. Betty Jo and Katherine Ann look at one another, but neither stops him. John clanks his bottles, pours a bourbon and coke, and takes a swig. Then sets it on the bar again and walks away, heading for the stairs.

"John?" Betty Jo calls after him, but there is no reply.

In a couple of minutes, John's feet are heavy lead down the stairway again. He grabs his drink, slurps it, then comes to the kitchen table and sits, cradling the glass in his hand. In his other he holds a folded piece of paper.

Head down, John Porter takes a deep breath, then with eyes still closed he starts at the beginning—he talks for the first time about that fateful night on Marble Mountain.

CHAPTER FIFTY-SIX

The Mountain
Vietnam, 1970

John

They had left their M-14s in the jeep, grabbing smaller, more portable pistols. They knew climbing inside the mountain would present spatial challenges. But they were ready for a change.

It was John's idea. Ernest had sat gloomily on China Beach, the prettiest one John had ever seen, long enough. "C'mon, man," he told him. "Let's get outta here."

Ernest trusted his buddy. He'd always taken care of him, since the first time they'd met in boot camp and Ernest had missed a spot, shining his shoes. The inspection was imminent when John reached down and wiped it away. He could have caught hell had the sergeant seen him, but it was just natural for some reason. John always had Ernest's back.

In Vietnam, you never knew who the enemy was. That was the hardest thing. Not knowing. The only man you could trust was the man beside you. You'd have Mamasan in the hooch doing the laundry and Papasan bringing supplies. All the Babysans would play ball and giggle and wait outside the camp—but look out on the day you didn't see them. You knew there was going to be an attack that day. Next day, here comes Mamasan and Papasan back to work. Babysans back at the gate again. No, you never knew who the enemy was in Nam.

That's what made true friendship even stronger.

Of the two men, John Porter had more street smarts. He was a New Jersey city kid. He was less sensitive, didn't cry in his bed at night like farmer-in-the-dell Ernest did sometimes. Having seven younger sisters, John had taken Ernest under his wing like a man might do a younger brother. He was his charge. His unspoken responsibility. John couldn't stand seeing him so forlorn on their short liberty from hell. After all, they'd only be in Nam for two more weeks. Their tour of duty was almost over. They'd made it. Shoot, Ernest was going to have fun if it killed him.

There was a marine base at the north side of a group of mountains just south of Da Nang. John had heard the legend. Everyone had. But it was a rumor, a ghost story. That's all. The legend was that an entire platoon had entered Marble Mountain and never come out again. Ooooh, spooky. It was pure superstition, the one thing that didn't scare John out of this whole Vietnam experience—these people with their myths and legends. It was quaint, really. He could dig it.

John had also heard there was something like Nirvana at the top of Marble Mountain. A man could see from here to Kingdom Come—the gorgeous sea off one side, the mountains, fields off the other. John could imagine it. Looking down, there'd be nothing but beauty to take back home with him to the States. He wanted to fill his eyes with the unbelievable beauty of this place, beauty other than Doan Vien's. He wanted to wipe away the images of death. He could do it, he thought. He just needed a different vantage point.

John led the way past the pagoda at the bottom of the mountain and into the cave. Ernest followed. Chiseled walls surrounded them, and there were moments when the tunnel grew so dark and so tight that John second-guessed himself. Should they have come up here? What the heck had he gotten them into? But Ernest had a blind trust in John; he'd follow him anywhere. And John had promised him a diversion, an adventure, and that's exactly what they were going to have. The two men continued climbing until a band of light illuminated the end of it all.

For nearly two hundred feet they'd said nothing, listening to their grunts and heavy breathing, stumbling boots on rock. The sound of sweat.

"Hey, man," said Ernest, catching his breath. He was a few feet behind.

"Yep," answered John.

They continued climbing, and then Ernest spoke again. "Listen, there's something I gotta talk to you about."

"Speak up, boy."

They climbed a little more and the opening began to widen. The tunnel gave way to flat marble stairs, and the men got their footing and stood up straight.

"It's Doan Vien," Ernest said, his voice hardly a whisper.

John stopped and panted, keeping his eyes fixed on the shards of light above them. His legs trembled from the climb. Bending down, he put his hands on his knees and breathed in deeply, preparing himself. *Ernest knows I've fallen for her. Somehow he knows I asked her to marry me. Did Doan Vien tell him? They're friends, right? Maybe she told Ernest she does love me. Maybe she sent Ernest to relay the message, that she'll marry me after all.*

The thought was more than he could handle. John's heart skipped and though he'd stopped climbing, he wrestled for his breath again.

Then Ernest said, "I'm in love with her."

It pierced him. John turned to face Ernest and saw this silly, scared grin on his face. He was serious. "I'm so gone, man. She's amazing. I wanna marry her. I swear I do." Ernest leaned up against the tunnel wall and closed his eyes. "I can see her back home, on a farm, raising children. I can totally see it. Is that crazy? You think it's nuts to fall in love in a war? It's nuts, right? I mean, how am I gonna get her outta here?"

Everything was clear in that instant. John remembered Doan Vien's face, her tears, her head shaking no. Her *hundred years of crap* she'd wished him. Ernest was in love with her too. Doan Vien loved Ernest, not him.

How could John not have seen this coming? Was he so blinded that he didn't even realize what was going on behind his back? The weight of his foolishness crushed him, and he grabbed Ernest around the neck, pulling him from the wall. He hugged him violently, nearly choking him. He fought back tears. His lip quivered. John spit on the wall. Then he loosened his grip and patted Ernest hard on the back. He shoved his face back toward the wall and felt his moist, soft features—that squirrelly chin, that humpbacked nose.

He loved this guy. He was more like family to him than his own family had ever been. This was his little brother, right? It wasn't his fault. He'd never told Ernest about his feelings for Doan Vien. Shoot, he never showed his feelings for anything, anyone. How could Ernest possibly have known? And who in their right mind could not fall for a woman like Doan Vien? She was so helpless, so gorgeous.

It crossed his mind then to choke him. John thought about killing Ernest right there in that tunnel and racing back to tell Doan Vien he was gone. He'd console her and tell her, "But I'm still here, and I love you. Tell me you'll marry me when this crap war is over."

But he couldn't do it.

"Lucky dog," he told him instead. John smacked Ernest hard on the side of the head. Ernest's face was red, searching John for approval. "She's a great girl," John added. "Yeah, I can see her on a farm in Georgia. Fit right in. Gotta make it outta this war though first, right?"

It was all John could do. Step aside. He was a man. A real man. He was tougher than steel. He'd been through hell and back so many times. Foster homes, abuse, drill sergeants, VC booby traps, guns in his face. She was only a woman. John knew he'd survive this too.

THE TWO MEN emerged at the top in a huge cavern and were startled, pleased with what they discovered. Remnants of incense filled the air and Buddha surveyed his kingdom. Ernest walked directly to a dirty pond in the middle of the room with overgrown lotus leaves reaching out for light. "Wow," he said. "Amazing."

John watched his friend staring into the water. She loves *him*. Son of a gun. Scrawny little thing. His eyes grew hazy. He shook his head and walked around the edge of the cavern until he found a small opening about chest level. Sticking his head in, he adjusted his eyes to the dim light. He climbed through the opening and found himself stooping in a smaller cave, a hovel of some sort. There were half-burned candles and rolls of blankets on the ground. Metal cups and bowls sat strewn on the edge of a mat.

"Hey! Ernest! Come here, man. You gotta check this out!" John's pulse was quickening. Thoughts of Doan Vien were fleeing and being replaced with something else—something like panic, alarm. Someone was staying here, in this cave. Living here. Was it a monk or the enemy?

John turned in a flash and stuck his head out the opening just in time to see the small man grab Ernest from behind.

John burst from the hole and rushed to save his friend. He shot the guy in the face when he turned his way, the bloody knife still held out in front of him. John twitched to shoot him again, but the man was gone, lying unrecognizable in a pool of black blood mingling with Ernest's. The echo of gunfire still filled the cavern around them, bouncing off the walls like bats.

Ernest was hanging head down in the little pool, and John grabbed his back and pulled him out. He held Ernest's wet body and rocked him against his chest, too afraid to cry or scream. Then he laid him down and pressed his mouth to his lips, blowing with everything he had in him. He saw the wound on Ernest's neck and was desperate to stop the bleeding. He ripped his undershirt off and pressed it tight into his neck.

John was going into shock. He'd never been so scared in his life.

He looked around but no more guerillas came. John kept his gun poised and cocked just in case. Then he grabbed Ernest's limp body and began their clumsy descent to the bottom of the mountain. "I gotcha, buddy," John would say over and over as his grip would slip from the blood of Ernest's neck. He couldn't let him die. He just couldn't.

"I gotcha. Just hang on." It was John's mantra that focused him and kept him going even as tears fell. "We're almost there, man. You hear me? Oh God, just hang on, we're almost there. Almost there . . ."

CHAPTER FIFTY-SEVEN

The Road

Katherine Ann

Charleston sleeps. The night thinks of slipping into morning. The sky glows red beneath a blanket of fog swaddling the full moon. We are leaving this place to chase a ghost. It's the only way we'll ever be free.

I am driving my minivan with Daddy snoring in the passenger seat. Mama says he hasn't been able to sleep for days, worrying about this trip, so I suppose it all just caught up with him. I'm glad he can rest.

Mama is in the seat behind me. She's so quiet, I can't tell if she's awake or not. I'm glad she's coming with us today, supporting her husband. Loving him unconditionally. Beside her, Lisa Le peers out the window, flashes of yellow highlighting her nose. I still can't get over how much she looks like Daddy, but I believe him when he says his buddy Ernest could have been mistaken for his brother.

Doan Vien declined our invitation and stayed in Georgetown. From what I understand, she has not been doing well these past couple weeks since she saved Cooper from the river. Came down with a cold or something. Hopefully it goes away soon and doesn't turn into anything serious. I am praying this trip helps her in some way—that by allowing her daughter to meet Ernest's family, her very own family, it will do her some good. It's all I can do. It's the least I can do. Doan Vien saved my son's life, and I'll always be indebted to her.

There's hardly anyone on the road this time of morning except for eighteen-wheelers. I sip my coffee, still hot in the thermos, and think of Cooper and Tradd still sleeping in their little beds, and RC, the love of my life—he'll be having his first cup of coffee in another hour or so. I smile, thinking about my boys at home.

Then the smile melts away as I relive the morning after the Veterans Day party a couple weeks ago. What a long, long way we've come.

There we were, Daddy looking terrified, and Mama and I soaked in guilt—so much it seeped from our pores. My mother allowed Daddy to have a drink before noon with no complaint. Then she asked him a pointed question about money and letters. That's when he finally opened up.

My father told us about a place called Marble Mountain. He told us that after his friend Ernest was attacked, he'd brought him down to safety instead of leaving him for dead.

"Biggest mistake I ever made," he said.

They had told my father his actions were heroic and that he'd saved his friend's life. "I was no hero," Daddy whispered, holding back tears. "His family deserved to have him come home in a box like all the others. Honorably. They could grieve and move on. But no. Ernest went home a vegetable. A burden. No soldier would want that."

"But you saved his life, Daddy."

"Saved his life? What life? What kind of life did he have? He would have been better off if I'd left him there. Or if they'd killed me too."

"Oh hush, now, honey. Don't say that."

Mama had moved to Daddy's side, and he buried his face in her chest. I'll never forget how he couldn't get enough air, how he couldn't hold on to Mama any tighter than he was that very moment. I kept running to the bathroom for more tissues, for water, to give them privacy.

But I came back, and I did see the letter Mama was asking about. It wasn't from Doan Vien, it was from Ernest's family in Georgia. Daddy showed us a crumpled paper he'd been hiding all these years in an army boot. It was the last letter of the sort he'd ever received.

Apparently Daddy felt so guilty about Ernest's condition that he'd sent money secretly year after year to his family to help with long-term care. Unfortunately, Ernest never woke from his coma, and the letter Daddy showed us was from Ernest's father, dated July 6, 1985. He told Daddy that Ernest had finally passed away and not to send any more money. He said he was grateful for all that Daddy had done and thanked him again for saving his son's life.

Daddy never heard from Georgia again.

My father's healing began in those moments when Mama was holding him at the kitchen table and I was looking on. We're his family now. He was shedding his burdens like a second skin, tissues like secrets were scattered all over the table and floor.

That's when it struck me that Lisa Le was Ernest's daughter and there's family in Georgia she's never met. I struggled with the idea that I was meddling again, but I knew this was the right thing to do. Everybody in this whole tangled mess needs closure,

Daddy, Mama, me, Doan Vien, Lisa—even my sweet, patient RC. With Daddy's permission, I made the call to Ernest's family, explained who I was, and his brother invited us all up.

It feels good to be doing something right for a change.

The highway hums beneath us. I look over at my father. He's awake now, staring off in the distance. I imagine taking his hand in mine and holding it like we did that night on the USS *Yorktown*, but then think better of it. I know the warmth of my fingers will only make him cry again. For Daddy, this road to Georgia has been forty years in the making. Never once did he visit his best friend. Never once did he forget.

Lisa

We'll be there in just a couple of hours. It's my first trip out of state. My life in Georgetown has been a sheltered one. Except for my attending college in Conway, Uncle, Ma, and I rarely left town due to running the restaurant. I know Henry will do a good job there today. He's always reliable. And Charlene will help him. No, I'm not worried about Le's Kitchen. In fact, I'm not worried about anything. Just anxious.

I'm not hungry, which is unusual. In fact, I wonder at this moment how I ever had an appetite in the first place. Oh, what this trip means to me, and what it means to Ma. I am going to meet *my family*. There are people who carry my genes, share my blood.

I smile and watch my dim reflection in the window. I cross my legs under me and settle in. Just when I'm closing my eyes I hear my name.

"Lisa?"

Mrs. Porter is sitting next to me. I turn to face her.

"Yes?"

She fidgets with her hands and says, "I hope you can forgive me for my behavior . . . that night . . . a couple weeks ago. It was wrong. Even if you had been John's—"

"It's okay," I say. "It was unusual circumstances. You couldn't possibly have known."

"Would you please tell your mother how very sorry I am? And tell her . . . tell her again how thankful I am for what she did, saving Cooper like that. I've never seen anything so courageous in all my life."

"I'll tell her, but I know what she'll say: it was nothing that someone else wouldn't have done."

"I know but—"

"Mrs. Porter, my mother has been through so much. I've come to realize that I will never fully know the depths of her suffering. What I do know is this: Ma feels that by saving your grandson, she has finally been able to restore honor to our family. This is something I don't expect you to understand. Things are so different in this country. In Vietnam, honor is all that one has. When it's gone, there is nothing else. Ma feels that her ancestors finally looked favorably upon her and allowed her to redeem herself by placing her in the right place at the right time. I have not seen her so at peace in all my life. For that, I suppose I should be thanking you."

"Oh, no. Well, in that case . . ." she says. Then she's quiet and watching the cars go by. And I feel in my soul that my father in heaven is pleased with me, and with Ma, and with John Porter, with all of us. I know that someday I will see my father again. And he'll know who I am. Because he's part of me.

CHAPTER FIFTY-EIGHT

THE MONK
Georgia

Lisa

"Daddy's awake," the man says. "Your grandfather, he's awake. We better go in now before he goes to sleep again."

My uncle, I can't believe I'm saying this, *my uncle* holds me again in a warm embrace. He has my nose. I think it looks better on him than on me. He is grayed at his temples, but otherwise has very little hair. His eyes are magnified behind round-rimmed glasses, and I see mine are a mix between his and Ma's eyes. But I struggle not to look at his scar. It's a deep crevice that connects his mouth directly to his ear. He sees that I've noticed.

"Old war wound," he tells me. "Got it in Vietnam."

"Oh," I say. "You were there too?"

"Yep, paving the way for my kid brother. I was there in sixty-seven, sixty-eight." He touches his face. "It doesn't hurt though. Just looks bad."

I hint at a smile and say, "I wish Ma was here to meet you."

"I'd like to meet your mama sometime," says Randy, in his Southern drawl. My uncle, Randy.

"Does your father know we're coming?" I ask as we walk

through the doors of the nursing home and turn left down the hall.

"Yep, I told him. You should have seen the look on his face when he found out he has a grandchild by Ernest. He cried. Doesn't do that much. Always been a tough old bird. He's just really gone downhill in the past couple weeks."

"Lisa?" Katherine Ann touches my arm. "I think Mama and I are going to wait out here. We don't want to overwhelm him. Why don't you and Daddy just go on in?"

"You sure?"

She nods and smiles at me, and they kiss John Porter, who appears completely out of his element. I take his arm in mine and say, "You ready?"

He gives a single nod, keeping his eyes on Uncle Randy who pushes the door open. We wait at the doorway and see a room that looks much like one you'd find in a hospital, except slightly warmer, fewer machines, more touches of home. The walls are gray with paintings of flowers and barns, and I can see the foot of a bed. There's someone in it though I can't see the face yet, feet covered by a rose-colored blanket.

"Daddy?" We hear Uncle Randy talking softly. "I brought some folks to see you." He pauses then says, "Come on in."

My grandfather is long and thin. His full head of gray hair is pressed down on one side. He has a thin layer of white whiskers above his mouth. I see a Norelco shaver on the table next to him. Looks like someone was trying to get him ready for company.

The wrinkles on his face must have melted away from lying in this bed so long. His lips are drawn, but his eyes are open, pale blue with black constricted pupils. He holds his eyes wide and looks at me. Then he turns to John.

"Mr. Marquette," John says, clearing his throat. "I'm John

Porter. I was your son's . . . I served with Ernest in Vietnam, sir. I—" He pauses, beginning to cry. He sniffles and says, "I'm so sorry about what hap—"

John pulls out a handkerchief and wipes his nose. My grandfather lifts his shaking hand toward him and John takes it. His head moves back and forth on his white pillow as if to tell John not to be sad. Then his lips move. Instinctively we lean closer to try and hear what he's saying, but it's hard to make out. We look to Randy to interpret his father's coarse whispers. Then we hear for ourselves.

"My . . . son. Thank you. Thank . . . you."

I am crying now too, seeing the effect this is having on Mr. Porter. His shoulders are trembling and I put my hand in the middle of his back for comfort.

"This . . . is your granddaughter," Mr. Porter explodes, then he moves away so I can take his place. He stands in the corner, head in hand crying silently.

I smile at my grandfather, old, helpless, dying. I take his hand in mine and feel its coolness, so grateful to have this opportunity to see him in person. It's as if my whole life has come down to this one moment and it all makes sense. My grandfather searches my face and the corners of his mouth attempt to lift into a smile, but it doesn't quite make it.

"I'm so happy to finally meet you, Grandfather. My mother loved your son very much. From what I hear, he was a wonderful man."

His lips are dry and his mouth open. He tries to communicate but no sound comes out.

"Daddy, you want some ice?" asks Randy.

His eyes dart to him and he nods. I wait while Randy uses a spoon to fish a piece of ice out of a glass of untouched iced tea.

He sets it gingerly in his father's mouth and the old man works on it, gratefully, slowly.

His hand moves, groping for the side table, and he touches a book.

"You want this book?" I ask. He shakes his head and motions again. I see them now. I push the book aside and pull out a small stack of black-and-white photographs. I lift them to my eyes and flip through silently as if I've slipped into a quiet cocoon. My mother is there before me, young, beautiful. She stands in the doorway of a thatched hut in Vietnam. Another one shows a young John Porter posing like a strong man for the camera. And yet another shows my father, Ernest, uniformed and smiling back at me with my own face. He is drinking out of a tin cup. He is happy. He is alive.

I press the photos to my heart and thin tears slip from my eyes. My family. My history. My heart.

"Those are from Ernest's camera from Vietnam. The film was still in there when they brought him home. Daddy wants you to have these."

"Oh, are you sure?" I look into my grandfather's eyes and he confirms it. "Thank you so much. You don't know how much this means to me." I take his hand in mine and squeeze gently.

Grandfather lifts his head a little and says, "Your daddy, my son . . . loves you."

"I know," I say. "I love him too."

He closes his eyes and shakes his head slightly. "Your daddy . . ." Grandfather turns to Randy and lifts his other hand, bone-thin, frail, trembling. He's trying urgently to convey something.

His hand drops back down, his eyes close from exhaustion, and he mouths, "Open it. Randy. Open it."

"Okay," says Uncle Randy. Then he moves to the other side

of the bed, and before I realize what's happening, a curtain I didn't even realize was there begins to pull back.

There is another bed in this room with my grandfather. There is another patient in the room with us.

CHAPTER FIFTY-NINE

The Waterfall

Lisa

John looks as if he's seen a ghost and he moans a frightening, guttural sound.

"Oh, God, no," he says.

He stumbles to the other bed where a figure lies twisted with curled limbs, sunken face, and mouth gaped open. John falls to his knees at his bedside.

I am stunned, looking from John to the figure to my grandfather and finally to Uncle Randy.

"Who is this?" I say.

Randy puts his arms around my shoulders and holds me tight.

"Miss Lisa, this . . . is your daddy. This is my baby brother, Ernest."

My legs go weak and Randy holds me upright. The photographs sift to the floor.

"What? How can it be?" I am covering my mouth, tears streaming down my cheeks, feeling as if this must be happening to someone else, not me.

"He's been in a coma."

"All these years? But I thought he was—"

"Daddy took care of him. He was his whole life. After Mama died and he sold the store, having Ernest was all that kept Daddy going."

"So many years though . . ."

"I know, I can't explain it," says Uncle Randy. "Thirty-eight years. I don't understand myself. Since Daddy fell sick, I've been taking care of both of them. Even been reading the Bible to Ernest. I don't imagine he's heard me, but just the same, it's helped me some."

I move around John's crumpled body and sit on the side of the bed. There is a frayed brown leather Bible on the corner of the side table. It says Ernest Marquette in gold foil letters. "Father? It's me," I say, my tears making little plopping noises on the bed sheets. "I'm your daughter."

My father's eyes are open, staring over my shoulder. He looks nothing like the young soldier in the photograph. I touch his cheek. "Can you hear me? My mother is Doan Vien. Remember her in Vietnam? She loved you so much. You had a child together. I'm your child." Seeing no response, I grab for a tissue and wipe my eyes. "I'm so sorry I never came to see you. I would have come. I would have been here. I just never knew you were alive. Oh, Father, it's so good to finally meet you."

I feel as if my soul is mending itself, needles sewing wildly.

"She looks a lot like you, Ernest," says Uncle Randy, rubbing my back. "You ought to be very proud. You have an amazing daughter. Her name is Lisa."

John seems to find his strength and stands up. He wipes his hands on his pants legs and moves to the other side of the bed. Then he does something I will always love him for. He leans down, kisses my father's cool forehead, and whispers close to his ear, "Oh, I'm so sorry, buddy. Can you ever forgive me? You don't have to hang on anymore, brother. You don't have to hang on . . ."

Ernest

Ernest hears voices ebbing in and out like waves rocking up to the shore.

". . . good to finally meet you . . ."

". . . have an amazing daughter . . ."

". . . you don't have to hang on . . ."

"Your time is now," says Eldest Fish.

"They're here for me," says Ernest. "They're finally here."

"Yes. You can go now, my son. Everything will be all right."

Ernest's body is weak from not eating for days. He doesn't know what time of day or night it is up on Marble Mountain. His vision is almost completely lost. But his hearing is amplified. He knows this is it. It is time.

"Would you like me to try first, child?"

"No," says Ernest. "I'm not afraid anymore."

Moving back slowly, Ernest says a quick prayer, ". . . Your will be done." Then he musters his strength. He swims faster than he knew possible past lotus leaves, past young, lost fish, past the comforting presence of Eldest fish. And in a flash, Ernest is soaring up the waterfall, droplets splashing, the coolness of fresh air caressing his skin, scales trailing behind him like broken chains. He is alive again. He feels Life in all its glory.

Suddenly, the light shifts, and Ernest knows he is far from Marble Mountain, far from the pond that held him captive so many years. His spirit has drifted away one last time. He sees a young woman crying and loves her. Somehow he knows she belongs to him. He sees Brother Chong, finally at peace. He sees his buddy, John Porter, wiping his nose, sees the gray walls turn to bright light and swims for it, just keeps swimming fervently. He is aware that he has no more fins but legs and arms instead, a human body, strong and intact. He is human again and has shed his skin, his blood growing warmer the closer he gets to the light.

A human hand reaches down and pulls him upward, embracing him. In an instant, a blissful, blinding second, it is all over—the pain, the anguish, the confusion, the waiting. The shackles are broken.

Ernest is in a new body—and free at last.

EPILOGUE

<hr>

The Mistress

Doan Vien

I have spent my lifetime loving two men. Mourning two men. Grieving for what was not to be.

In my country, there is a word for a woman like me. *Tinh tu*. It means shameful, unvirtuous. I was taught at an early age that a woman must live by the four virtues: *cong, dung, ngon,* and *hahn*— the last meaning chastity. An honorable Vietnamese woman remains pure before marriage and faithful only to one man.

But you must understand. In the charred remains of my life, I was no longer a daughter who knew her place; I was an animal, desperate to survive. No family or friends stood by my side. They were all dead. Only Brother was alive, a soldier off fighting with the Americans somewhere. At the time, I did not know his fate. He was gone and, in my mind, dead like the others. I cannot explain how it feels to be firmly rooted in the earth one day and floating like vapor the next.

In the beginning, the two American soldiers would come together to patch my roof with fresh reeds, or to raze the remains of the other huts, or to bury the bodies of my kin. They did not have to come. I had nothing to offer. I was a shell of a human, but my outward beauty remained. It did not yet show the scars of war.

I was greedy with the love of my American soldiers. I maintained my secret with each by sharing glimpses only when the other was not there. I was conflicted over this, of course, but I needed them both to love me. If I had had the love of the entire American army, it would not have brought my family back. It would not have returned my spirit to its former, vibrant self. I know this now. But I did not know it then. I knew so very little.

Weeks had gone by and the Americans found ways to come back to my burned-out hamlet and rebuild that which was not completely destroyed. I spoke little English and the soldiers little Vietnamese, but between us, it was enough. Most of the time, words were not necessary.

In those darkest of days after my people were killed and my village burned, I knew no difference between the hunger of my belly and the hunger of my heart. They were one in the same. My belly was empty so I filled it with the affections of my soldiers, but only glances or smiles. Never a touch. I wouldn't dare allow that. Wouldn't dare until—

The American soldier, Ernest, had come to visit me again. And he was alone.

On this day, he entered my hut and removed his cap, stooping to avoid hitting the thatched roof. I bowed and handed him a bowl of steaming *pho*. It was the first time I had cooked for him, and seeing the soldier's surprise, I nodded as if to say, "Eat."

He moved to the little table and sat cross-legged on the floor. My heart warmed with his every sip. It made me feel less worthless. I knelt a few feet away to ensure the soldier was pleased with my offering, and he indulged me by groaning with pleasure and slurping as loudly as possible. When the bowl was emptied, the soldier pulled his knees up, resting his arms on them and clutching his hands together. He was quiet, unsure what to say to me.

He had been so kind, and I was feeling something for him. I was glad to know there were feelings that existed inside of me that were not fear and sadness. The hairs on my arms pricked as I boldly looked him straight in the eyes for the first time. I had made myself as presentable as possible. I was clean and wearing a pink *ao dai*, and my hair was tied with sticks behind my head. I knew, to him, I was an exotic flower in a field of dung. He was clinging to me in an effort to keep his sanity and his soul intact, much as I was to him. He had done so many wonderful things for me. For my country. I was filled with gratitude and felt unworthy, sitting in his presence.

When he inched closer, I touched my fingers to the tops of his hands and began crying silently. The warmth of his skin brought back memories of family, of holding my nieces in my lap, of hugging my sweet mother. A few feet away, the floor was painted red with the fading stains of my parents' blood. The soldier reached up and pressed my tears away and gazed at me, another survivor in his hell. He could see into me and I, into him. Our souls moved closer with the sounds of the rain. It hit the roof with dull thuds and filled the air with hot steam. Our earthly bodies touched. Our spirits connected and soared.

In all honesty, my heart, in its diseased state, would have clung to either man who had walked through the door, for I truly loved them both. But it was he who had come to me that day, so it was he whom I lay with. You must understand, I was crazed with hopelessness. By connecting my body to his, I was able to escape my soul for a short while. I became someone other than the sad orphan the war had left me. In the moments lying in my soldier's arms, I was a woman in love.

When the rain had eased and my soldier was leaving, he stood in the doorway and beckoned for my hand. He bent down, took it gently, and kissed my open, shaking palm. Then he set a photograph where the kiss had been and promised me, his lover, that he would return.

He did not return.

Neither of my American soldiers came back for me. My grief was unbearable in the following weeks when I knew I was going to have a child. Alone. In the middle of a war.

In the greedy clutches of my ravaged heart, I'd not thought about the possibility of a child. Or that the child I would bear would be plunged into a pit of confusion. I did not think that far ahead. When the world is ending, there are no thoughts of future to be had. Only minute by minute, second by second. Am I alive? Am I surviving? I simply needed the love of my soldiers like a man needs bread to survive. Like a man needs water.

I was so young then. But it is no excuse. Youth is no excuse for carelessness that haunts. My greed, like my murdered ancestors, will haunt me and my family for generations to come.

ALL THESE YEARS, I knew John Porter was alive, living in Charleston. When Lisa was sixteen, his picture was in the newspaper for winning an award for architecture. I remember seeing his face and falling to my knees, not because the man I loved was alive, but because the other man I loved was *not* alive. Had John survived the war and not come back to say good-bye, he must have learned the truth about Ernest and me. All these years, I felt in my heart—John had killed Ernest. Over me.

It only made sense. They had gone to China Beach after I

had been with Ernest, and after John had asked me to marry him—and after I had rejected him. When neither man came back, I assumed they were both dead. I could grieve this properly, in a way. But seeing John's face again, remembering his temper, I knew it in my soul. John Porter had killed his friend. He'd killed my lover, my daughter's father. How could I ever forgive a man such as this? How could I ever forgive myself?

All these years I believed a lie.

With circumstances and half-truths the Universe often creates lies for us. More rarely, the Universe gives us glimpses into the truth. Many times it uses people to do its handiwork. My daughter, Lisa, she is such a person. She is a good girl. In her heart, she searched for her father and found him. In her journey, I learned that John is a good man after all. He is still the man I loved. No longer must I suffer the fury against him, no longer the guilt over Ernest's death. This truth has set me free.

I cannot tell Lisa I knew all along John Porter was alive. Had I opened my mouth, perhaps there is a chance she could have spent more time with her father before he died. Yes, I regret my silence. Yet another regret of my life.

My daughter will never know her father. But she has new family in Georgia, and I'm happy for this. Roots keep us from flying off the face of the earth. She feels a kinship with Katherine Ann, and this is good. I do not mind if she sees her, but I will not return to Charleston again. My peace with John Porter is complete. No need to tempt fates again. I can only dream of what might have been.

Lisa will work in our family restaurant for as long as needed to take care of us. She is a hard worker, an honorable girl. I hope that she, too, will love a man someday just as I still love my American soldiers.

I have rejoined my daughter in Le's Kitchen, preparing the

food. I sit in the corner and watch my child. I see the strong woman she has become. She is talking of adding Vietnamese dishes to the menu, but I don't know if it's a good idea. She assures me certain loyal customers will always be this way, loyal, but I suppose we will find out soon enough. I see how hard she tries to make up for the years she has forgotten, for the country she has forgotten. But *this* is her country now, and these are her people.

And this is our story. In the end, it is all that we have.

ACKNOWLEDGMENTS

I gratefully acknowledge my stepfather, Hollis C. Lucas, Jr., for teaching me the importance of love of country and of the sacrifices of men. I love you and thank you. To my mother, I'm having the most fun sharing our love for words! Having your nose in a book every morning inspired me to write, I've no doubt. Thank you for being my reader, among so many things. I am grateful every day for my husband, Brian, who continues to support my passion for writing even when the numbers don't add up. Hang in there, honey! To Olivia and Cole, my children, you are my world. I thank you for your love and your patience and for the fun you inject into our lives. May you each find your passion through Christ . . . preferably sooner than I did! I love you forever.

Thank you to my wonderful editors, Amanda Bostic at Thomas Nelson and Rachelle Gardner. I've grown as a writer under your guidance and encouragement! To Mark Gilroy, my agent, thanks so much for handling the business side of things. And to Allen Arnold and the entire fiction team at Thomas Nelson, especially

Jennifer Deshler, Katie Schroder, and Mark Ross, continued thanks for allowing me to keep writing!

Several people helped in the making of this book. Thank you, Jim at the Mount Pleasant Barnes and Noble, for spending time with me in the war section and opening up so frankly about your own experiences. You made quite an impression on me. I am so pleased to have spoken with Elizabeth Schwartz about her very own water-loving group of ladies, the Water Lilies. Your stories inspired some of my most favorite characters. Thank you for letting me use that wonderful name! Melinda Theiling Kornahrens took time out of her busy life to make sure this book was authentic in voice and honoring to the Vietnamese-American culture. I am indebted to you all.

To George Pope, many thanks for reading over my manuscript so speedily and giving me the a-ok. I hope to be reading your published book next. To Fred Robinson, Irene Lofton, Sheila Kesler, and everyone else in the Seacoast Christian Writers' Group, you are a terrific support. Your encouragement is priceless. And to Red Evans, our beloved author friend who's now in heaven keeping the angels in stitches, you are sorely missed. I will "always keep writing" just for you.

Many booksellers have gone out of their way to put my books in readers' hands: the Mount Pleasant and Charleston Barnes and Nobles; WaldenBooks in Charleston; Litchfield Books in Pawleys Island; The Bookstore, Inc., in Greenwood; Books on Main in Newberry; Bay Street Trading Company in Beaufort; Books-A-Million in Charlotte; and so many more!

To Congressional Medal of Honor Recipient Colonel Roger Donlon, I'm honored to have met you. You have inspired me and countless others with your integrity and heroic acts. Many blessings to you and your family. To my own family, David, Andrea, nieces, nephew, aunts, and uncles, thank you for being my sturdy roots. To my father, Gary, and family, I'm so glad you're in our lives. And to my dear friend, Jennie Harding, what a blessing to have you across the street. You will always be family to me.

Now to my Father in heaven who gives me the stories and the strength to write them, to Him be the glory.

NOTE FROM THE AUTHOR

One evening on my parents' anniversary, we were sitting at dinner when my stepfather opened up about war things. I learned for the first time about a buddy he'd had who'd died in the Vietnam War. I never knew about this man. Later he showed me a photograph of the two of them, young men, friends in a foreign land. It was this realization—that I'd never known about this man who'd been so close to my stepfather—that inspired me to write this book. Thank you for serving our country, Roger. May you rest in peace in heaven.

The research for this book was at times an obsession for me, at times disturbing, and at others a labor of love. One such day was May 23, 2007, when I attended the Congressional Medal of Honor Recipients Gala aboard the USS *Yorktown* in the Charleston Harbor. On this day, my stepfather was as-of-yet unaware that I was trying to learn all I could about the war. I was still in stealth mode, treading very lightly as this was new territory for me. I did, however, call him and ask if he wanted to go with me to the gala. He didn't think I was serious (probably due to the cost of the tickets or because I'd never taken an interest in military things before). It was a last-minute request, and he politely declined, as he was planning to be out of town.

The event was amazing and humbling as described in this book, but unlike Katherine Ann, I attended alone. At my table, I was placed fortuitously next to Medal of Honor recipient Col. Roger Donlon. In 1964, Donlon received the first MOH in Vietnam. I encourage my readers to look up Col. Donlon's official citation and those of other MOH recipients on the Congressional Medal of Honor Society's Web site: www.cmohs.org.

It was a pleasure meeting Col. Donlon and his wife, Norma, and before we parted company, Donlon gave me a business card to give to my stepfather. On the back, he wrote the words "Welcome home."

Early the next morning, my stepfather arrived at my door, eager to hear all about the event. He couldn't believe I had gone . . . and frankly, neither could I. I told him all about the evening and handed him Donlon's card. The look in his eyes when he read the words on the back was definitely worth the price of admission.

If you would like to learn more about the Congressional Medal of Honor Society visit www.cmohs.org, or to visit the Medal of Honor Museum aboard the USS *Yorktown* in the Charleston Harbor, SC, visit this Web site: www.patriotspoint. org. I assure you, you will not be disappointed. Bring your parents, your children, your war heroes. We're never too young or old to appreciate the heroism of our men and women serving in the armed forces and to support our troops.

God bless you, reader, and God bless America.

For more novels by NICOLE SEITZ,
look for *The Spirit of Sweetgrass* and *Trouble the Water*

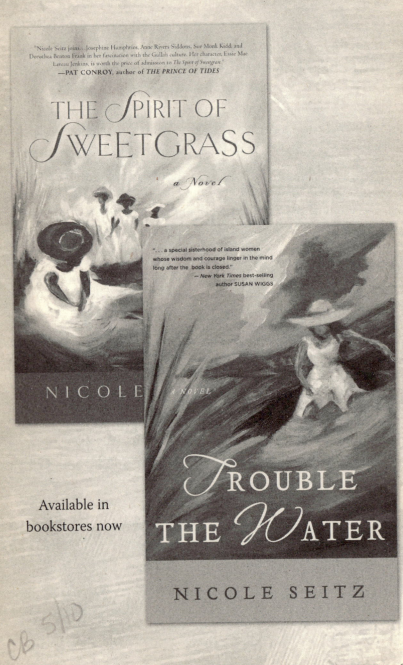

Available in
bookstores now

CB 5/10